Devil's Mountain

Devil's Mountain

an *O'Toole Novel*

by PATRICK FOX

iUniverse, Inc.
New York   Bloomington

Devil's Mountain

An O'Toole novel

iUniverse books may be ordered through booksellers or by contacting:

iUniverse
1663 Liberty Drive
Bloomington, IN 47403
www.iuniverse.com
1-800-Authors (1-800-288-4677)

ISBN: 978-1-4401-1268-3 (pbk)
ISBN: 978-1-4401-1269-0 (ebk)

Printed in the United States of America

iUniverse rev. date: 12/23/2008

"The sum of evil in the world would be greatly diminished if only men would learn to sit quietly in their rooms."

Pascal ("Penses")

September, 1972

The Aussie and one of the Brits came out first, both clad in the white suits, with the Brit cradling the vacuum bottle in his arms like you might do with a baby who had just wet himself, and the Aussie carrying their headgear. At a word from Jones-Stuyvesant, First Sergeant Rhys Williams stowed his rifle inside the tent, signaled the other jack of all trades, Peckham, and hurried over the gravelly beach to the boat. Maybe this would be the last trip, Williams thought, as he unshipped the oars and checked the tarpaulin that covered the gear amidships; and at least this time there would be no sheep aboard.

He did not like working in civilian clothes. Nor did he like the sea, or the bone-numbing cold and mist that went with it in northwestern Scotland at that time of the year. But most of all he did not like boats -- treacherous and unnatural little conveyances that only sometimes stayed afloat on that same sea. Williams was twenty-seven years old. First Brigade, Royal Wellington Fusiliers, nine years. It was high time somebody up there realized that he wasn't doing what he'd been trained to do, which was directing cannon fire at opposing infantry, not cockleshelling back and forth across five hundred yards of the choppy, fog-shrouded Banford Channel. But Sergeant Williams was not one to complain. The tall scientist with the lined face -- Fildes was his name -- wanted the job done. What he said went. There must have been a reason for Williams' presence, even if it hadn't yet become apparent to him. But a grocery clerk from Christchurch could have rowed the boat, for God's sake, and, with three or four minutes of indoctrination, connected the wires when the time came. Oh well, he could wait it out if they could.

He and Peckham nosed the dinghy into the slight chop, letting the stern rest on the beach to afford a dry embarkation for the two white-suited scientists and their cargo. One of them stumbled at the top of the eight foot decline above the boat. Two of the others caught him by the shoulders and pointed him in the right direction. He shrugged off their help and skittered down across the gravel, dunking one white-booted foot into the foam at the shoreline in the process.

They were a sorry lot, Williams thought. Not the marines who'd driven the lorry up from someplace called Porton Down, nor the two Welsh farmers who had been in charge of the animals. It was the others. The scientists. And the observers; with their tweed jackets, thick, woolen trousers and yellow rain slickers. All right, they had all been hand-picked, no doubt, and each had his function. Need-to-know and all that. But had the fat one --Jones Stuyvesant--really needed to rig up his wind speed contraption eighteen or twenty times a day? And had the young American lieutenant--Claycombe, if you could believe the legend on his cellophane and rubber band-wrapped identity badge--had to daub the heavy white fire suits with the red penetrant, morning, noon and night? Young. Hell, they were all young. Except for Fildes, who must have been in his mid thirties. Claycombe? Twenty-four, tops. A shavetail. Twenty years of school and zero of war. What were they trying to prove? If his training back in Auckland had taught Williams anything at all, it was that a vacuum bottle-sized bomb – if it was a bomb – like the one the Aussie was loading into the boat wasn't big enough to change the outcome of any war no matter how powerful the explosive or how deadly the gas it might contain. What were they all so afraid of? He'd hate to have had any of these haggard, red-eyed, ivory-towered, think-a-lot-but-do-little physical rejects on a howitzer crew on a front line somewhere. Firefights didn't allow much time for thought.

Jones-Stuyvesant had finally measured a wind that he found suitable--high time, Williams thought, after bloody six days and seven nights on that lifeless, godforsaken crag of a coast on the slate-gray Irish Sea, with no laughs, and forget about wine, women and song. Five, maybe seven or eight knots, blowing from the east, out to sea, toward the island. Jones-Stuyvesant had walked over to the ops tent, nodding at Williams as he passed. The sergeant had taken his sentry position outside the entrance flaps, holding the American M-1 rifle at ready arms, feeling a bit silly in mufti. Claycombe and three others had joined Jones-Stuyvesant in the tent and someone had secured the drawstrings at the entrance.

"All right, Williams."

Jones-Stuyvesant's voice. Williams, still holding the M-1, had done his best to kick the sandbags into position along the bottom perimeter of the closed entryway.

"Done, sir."

"Very well," came the answer from inside.

All right, he had to admit that they were taking proper care. At least as much care as the Brits ever did. But if it was a powerful, new secret weapon, why not have the little spit of land flanked by a company of infantry? Everyone knew how to keep his mouth shut, if that was the problem. And why not have a bigger lorry to bring the glass container with its molasses-like brown sludge up from the South? Or at least a guard truck with a few Royal Marines.

He had heard Claycombe inside the tent. Something about not being the time or the place. Claycombe's flat vowels were unmistakable. An answering grumble from one of the others. Williams couldn't make it out. That seemed to be the way of things. Claycombe in opposition, the others pushing ahead, Fildes calm and insistent. Not that Claycombe hadn't worked long and hard on the protective firesuits, or whatever they were. Maybe he was able to separate things in his mind.

Well anyway, the big mixing operation or whatever it was inside the tent hadn't taken more the eight or ten minutes. And now, here they were, bouncing across the channel, for the second-to-last time. It was to be hoped. To Williams, who was not overly fond of horses, the ride over the quirky, two-foot chop was a lot like trotting, but with the added discomfort of the forty degree salt spray whipping across your face and caking up in the corners of your eyes. Two hundred yards to go.

Ten minutes later, they pulled the boat onto the gray sand of the island's eastern shore. Williams and Peckham wrestled off the tarp, and offloaded the bicycle-wheeled gardener's wagon and the explosive, detonator and back-up fuse. Tenderly, the two scientists laid the thirty inch long canister into its fitted resting place in the wagon. They donned their helmets, and Williams sealed the zippered seams with adhesive tape. He went through the connection routine one final time. The bayonet fitting mechanism at the bottom of the canister, the female receptacle in the explosive device, the red and green connect points for the detonator, and the ratchet release for the reel of twenty-gauge wire welded onto the rear of the wagon. Williams could hear the muffled "right" and "All right" from behind the amber face plates.

The bulkily-clad men in front of him appeared to be making the prescribed visual checks of the fifty Highland sheep, tethered, concentrically, and at different distances from the high point that was the destination. Every few steps, a rustling in the unmowed heather to the side of the pathway would remind Williams of the island's large population of small but hardy gray rabbits. Cute little buggers. Ahead, he saw the scientists stop, slip the ratchet lock on the wire reel, fix the wires to the staff of the orange flag marking a point two hundred feet from the top of the hill, and proceed.

At the top, they gingerly unloaded the canister, mounted it to its explosive base, and attached the two wires. After a last look at the checklist and a wave to Williams, they started back down the path, breaking into a top-heavy, lumbering trot and abandoning the gardener's wagon about fifty feet before they got to Williams' station at the orange flag. They clumped on past him. He waited until they had reached the boat, and with Peckham's help, nosed it back into the channel.

He attached the wires to the detonator, pushed the timer test button, saw the red pin light, and hit the switch. He had eight minutes. They'd timed it bloody close, he thought. All well and good for the men in the white suits. Something to do with the wind. He made his retreat down the path, trying not to hurry. He was a pro, and he wasn't about to let them know that he might doubt the accuracy of the timer.

They were two minutes into the return voyage across the channel when the bomb went off. Williams, rowing and facing aft, saw the smoky cloud and heard the sharp report of the plastic explosive a couple of seconds later. He stopped rowing, and with the others, watched the cloud rise up to merge with the foggy, hundred-foot ceiling, and drift slowly away from them and the mainland, over the western end of Banford Island, toward the open sea. Williams had set off larger explosions and seen bigger, more colorful clouds, but the scientists seemed pleased. Except for the American, Claycombe; he was the only one to refuse when Fildes himself poured the paper cups of champagne.

It wasn't until the third morning after the explosion, when he panned the binoculars across the misty little island and witnessed for himself the agony of the asphyxiating sheep, bloated and dying at their tethers, and the last, spasmodic throes of a thousand pestilence-ravaged gray rabbits, festering and putrescent at the shoreline, that Williams began to understand just what it was they had been celebrating.

I

The first thing I heard was the metallic pop as something smashed through the chain across the access road, fifty yards from the house. There was a tinkling noise, as what was left of the halogen headlights sifted down through the aluminum grillwork and the steel bumper supports of what turned out to be a black Yukon SUV. There was a second one, but things were happening too fast to be sure about what it was. Maybe an older Izuzu Trooper; '98, say, and muddy up to the fender wells. Yeah, that's what it was, and maybe not that old after all. They slewed into the yard in line abreast, and I have to admit being a little slow on the uptake.

The problem was one of perspective. The farmhouse had been built to a different scale than the two oversized gas-guzzlers, and I was briefly sidetracked, thinking about smaller people and larger families and time. The immensity of the unfenced and newly-seeded front lawn, the length of the shadows and the depth of the autumn colors in the late-afternoon Adirondack sun, and the time-warped incongruity of our vantage point— behind the phalanx of state-of-the-art, double-insulated window panes, but recently installed in the south-facing outer wall of the eighty-year-old structure—even further diffused my sense of place and proportion.

The Yukon led the way, fishtailing toward the house, skewing its rear end around, and sliding to a stop about ten feet from the front stoop. The second driver geared down the Trooper and powered his way to the side of the house and toward the barn around back, spraying dead leaves and muddy gravel on Pierre, Molly's old black Labrador, who by then had had just enough time to struggle to his feet. The barking was a little tentative at first, but as the four business-suited Secret Service types tumbled out of the far side of the Yukon and rolled to their respective feet, the dog regained his breath. The recoil from the ensuing barking was violent enough to actually force him backwards for three or four inches on each five or seven-yip salvo.

All of this had taken maybe ten seconds. I had moved to the front door to watch the advance of what I assumed by now to be the enemy. I saw over my shoulder that Molly had jumped to her feet. She crammed the papers and the manila envelope into the front of her corduroy jodhpurs, and looked over at me as if to see if I thought that that had been a good idea. Before I'd had time to shrug, she'd grabbed the old 30/06 from the rack by the Franklin stove, and approached the broad, thirty-two-paned window to the right of the front door. She used the wall between the window and the door for cover. She broke a small, shoulder-height window panel, thrust the rifle through the jagged aperture, and fired two warning rounds into the cool mountain air. The blast cracked a neighboring pane. I headed for the back of the house, armed with the poker from the Franklin and thinking about the Browning in the trunk of the BMW. The barking had stopped when her shots were fired. The following two seconds of total silence made me stop at the dining room door and look back toward her. She was wiping her brow and leaning against the wall for support.

The two seconds were all they gave us. There were no shouted and bull-horned negotiations or explanations of purpose. Nobody said anything. The thirty-one remaining panes in the beautiful old restored front window imploded on the front room, a millisecond before I heard the nearly simultaneous blasts of four sawed-off shotguns. Shards of glass and splinters of puttied and white-painted wood were sandstormed into the room, and I felt a hot, stinging sensation on my raised arm and the parts of my face not covered by it as I dived to the littered floor. Molly was down, near the window, trying to shake off the concussive effects of the blasts. She didn't look to be otherwise injured. I slid across the room on my elbows and knees, and gathered up the rifle. She rolled to her feet and high-tailed it toward the other end of the room, making a pretty nice low hurdle over the two-foot-high balustrade that separated her doctor's office from the rest of the room. Maybe she had some more fire power stashed in the back. I cranked another shell in from the magazine, and waited.

These guys were pros. They knew how to get in and what to do when they got there. There was a loud crunch as the back door was bashed in by some sort of battering ram that was most likely the shoulder of a large man. I remembered having left the door unlocked. They seemed to prefer the shock value of the unnecessarily rude and noisy, and I had to admit that their tactics got the adrenaline going.

All right. I didn't know exactly who they were. But they obviously were not in the mood to explain their presence, and they were not all that worried about who I was or whether or not I got hurt; so, what the hey. I let go a couple of rounds through the dining room door, sighting on the label of a quart can of Sear's Eggshell Latex next to the step ladder. Left, by about an inch and a half. I rolled over toward what was left of the window, and took a fast look outside from the lower left corner of the six-by-eighteen hole in the living room wall. I fell back to the floor. Pierre had been lying on the front lawn, barking feebly and trying to get up to help out. Somebody had conked him pretty good, probably with a rifle butt. Smell of cordite. No one else around. That was bad.

I didn't hear any bells, owl-hoots or phony bird calls, but somehow these guys had the synchronicity of the whole thing down to an art. Bang-zoom. Two more shotguns blasted out the thirty-two panes on the other side of the door, two Uzi-laden commandos vaulted into the room over the sill of the first thirty-two, three guys in white spacesuits and glass-faced helmets not made for motorcycling dived through the dining room door, and a fourth man in another business suit Nureyeved into a crouch behind the space guys and started spritzing the room with bursts from his Uzi, none aimed at any point lower than twenty-four inches or so above the floor; just to keep everybody honest kind of thing.

I'm not sure they had known about my being there. But Jesus, it seemed like an awful lot of firepower for just the one woman, even if she was five-ten and a pretty good shot at that. I'd made up my mind, though. I shot the dining room door barrage-and-enfilade man in the left knee just after he'd rammed home his second clip; he did a finger-on-the-trigger back flip toward the kitchen, leaving a neat line of nine millimeter holes in one of his front-window friend's pants and leg, across the ceiling and probably back into the kitchen. There were no more shells in the 30/06. I jumped up and approached the other front-window man. I must have brandished the rifle with convincing menace, because the damned guy jumped up and backed away from me, Uzi and all, making admonitory but defensive let's-just-wait-a-goddam-minute-bub gestures with his free left hand. Then four arms, clad in a clammy, white, snakeskin-like fabric with the smell of antiseptic, quadruple-Nelsoned me and forced me to the floor, face down. The third spaceman had retrieved Molly from the small room at the rear of her office. He must have tapped her a couple of times. She wasn't resisting, as he dragged her back across the floor and dumped her next to me. He put his knee in her back, expertly broke open a disposable syringe, and unceremoniously jabbed it into her left buttock, right through the cords and the yellow underpants I had watched her put on a half-hour earlier. Her eyes were still open, and I imagined I could see in them the reflection of the two white guys on my back preparing the same sort of treatment for me. It wasn't my imagination after all. It was a muscle relaxant and it worked fast. I guess I was losing my sense of perspective. I seemed to remember a similar beginning in another incident somewhere in the Far West, with a girl named Jenny in the right front seat and then some help from a big guy named Elmer. Funny how the mind works. Or doesn't. Molly mouthed a word to me just before our eyes closed in unison and the roaring in my ears got as loud as it did two or three seconds later. It was the first attempt at communication by either of us since the driveway chain had been popped by the grill of the black Yukon. I didn't know what she was trying to say. It's hard to concentrate on lip-reading when you feel like you're dissolving.

Forty-eight hours earlier.

II

The traffic on 95 had been light, there were no new mechanical glitches in the BMW, and what was to have been the beginning of a three day weekend with Bill and Dolores Chase at their apartment on Perry Street in the west Village had started off on schedule. I say their apartment. Actually, I've paid part of the rent and kept some stuff there ever since they got together and I was transferred from ONI New York into our little non-military outfit in Washington. It's a nice place to come back to, and Bill and Dolores don't ever make me feel like the man who came to dinner and stayed that I sometimes imagine myself to be. I'd been on the move a lot in the previous week, and a quiet evening with a couple of fiends and a couple Beck's would have been just what the doctor ordered. But then this girl Kelly, who was the younger sister of one of Dolores's flight attendant buddies, got a last minute invitation to replace somebody at the Bitter End, and, good intentions notwithstanding, I agreed to go along with Bill and Dolores to catch her set. Rumor had it that the Bitter End wasn't going to be around much longer, and we'd seen some good music there in other times. The set was scheduled for midnight, and Dolores assured me that this Kelly would only be on for twenty minutes or so.

Of course, the set didn't light off until a quarter after one, and the late start made it difficult to like the opening act. Would-be rockabilly millionaire achievers without musical instinct. They might have spent a couple of years in the boondocks with an idea and maybe even have stuck with it. But not them. No. They'd obviously hired or been sold a choreographer, and they had their rockabilly steps and exquisitely timed extemporaneous hee-haws down to a tee. The audience seemed to buy the act, though, and a few valiant shills even managed to inspire a half-house standing ovation after a particularly tumultuous and patriotic encore, emptily dedicated to our armed forces everywhere. Not that they had a chance with me, any-way. They blew it when they showed up with a drummer. Nothing against drummers. I just like my guitars and banjos neat, and my grass-roots au-thentic. I'm a helluva guy.

As it happened, in spite of the lateness of the hour, Kelly Santinio turned out to be a pleasant surprise. She was from Florida, and Dolo-res told me that her family was originally from Cuba. She sang good old South-of-the-border folk songs like Melancholy Baby, Always, Remem-ber, Sunny Side of the Street and What'll I Do. She had a good piano guy with her, named Doctor Howie, and a chubby teenage girl genius patted out a perfectly appropriate isst-sss-sss isst-sss-sss on a pedaled top-hat cymbal and a single little snare next to Dr. Howie's upright Yamaha. It was timeless, but out of synch with the sprinkling of moguls in the audience of forty or fifty. They didn't seem to relate to someone who did it so simply, who ended each song only once, who let Dr. Howie do his thing every so often, and whose every effort was not an attempt at showing them the hit single of the new century. There were some shared winks and chortles, checks were paid or signed, and we got to see the rest of her half-hour almost alone, without the arguing the buying and selling. That's when I started getting a little grumpy, I guess. The Bitter End was having a Talent Night, but you had the feeling that it was just another floundering search for what might turn out to be a rewarding direction, and not something that anyone was committed to. There was no particular person to blame. Not the customers. They're just listening kids, searching for something that can't be found, especially when they have to take out the folks' American Express Card and pay a thirty dollar music charge before they even start buying the macadamia nuts or whatever. Anyway, Kelly was wonderful, but it was a long night at the Bitter End.

And then of course we had to cab it over to Tenth Avenue to have a nightcap breakfast with the cops and the cab drivers and everybody else at the Market Diner. Kelly and Doctor Howie had had to catch their ride back to his apartment in Hoboken, so it was just the three of us, the regu-lars, and twenty or thirty disconsolate, purple-haired, tongue-ringed rejects from an SRO'd late concert at some place called Son of Sam's, who all used the High School of the Performing Arts speech style that has mysteriously taken over for anyone in the United States under thirty-five for the last ten years, which I am sooo not into. Nor capable of, come to think about it.

Dolores tells me that Bill isn't always this way, but something about my arrivals brings out more contemplation and philosophy than usual in him. Well, when that happens, when he's your old wing man from more than a few years ago, and when you're at the Market Diner at three A.M. on a Friday morning in a hot September, you just have at the good scrambled eggs and toasted bialys and let Bill go on his sardonic but still good-humored way.

"These people at the Bitter End aren't any different from anyone else, O'Toole. We all want something, but we don't really have time to figure out just what it is. We're becoming a nation of amoral consumers. We don't even have enough time to stop in for five minutes at the bedrock fast food infrastructure of our economy any longer. We're voracious. Look at the people coming out of the K-Marts, arms loaded with huge, second-rate paper bags, stapled at the top to show that the third-rate goods have been paid for, looking for another place to buy some chocolate chip cookies or have their films developed, with the kids coming along behind like yapping baby wolves, hungry for anything at all times, with the same vapid, questing-for-the-unattainable faces as their parents. I'll tell you--"

"Bill! Give O'Toole a break. We've been hanging around all night, and I myself feel like I've been shot out of a cannon. Remember dear, he's the one who was thinking about a quiet evening around the house."

"Oh hell, sorry. It's just that place tonight. Kelly was what it should be about, and nobody's interested. It's not encouraging. It makes me dumb."

"Why dumb!" I asked, knowing. Sort of.

"Just dumb. It makes me think that everyone else was right all along; that maybe I should be practicing law, and have medical insurance, and profit-sharing, and nest-eggs, and four kids to tell what to do to, and--well, you know what I mean. It's all some kind of confirmation that I--that we all need, but don't always get. And seeing Kelly at the Bottom Line reminded me."

"Honey, don't forget about me. And O'Toole. You've got us and we're not forgetting. We can be your record, can't we, O'Toole?"

"For sure. And I like to believe it works both ways."

"Hey, both of you, I know that and it makes it better, believe me. But sometimes I don't feel like I've been coming up with my share of winning combinations, and it gets harder and harder to reaffirm my faith in the future."

"Yeah, and the future keeps getting compressed," I added.

"Oh my God, T-R-U-T-H. The older we get, the more time we need and the less--well, anyway, it makes it hard. More people die, or go away, or get mad at you or crazed--we don't have enough people or enough years to go around, and--"

"Honey, you're not even forty years old! And I'm twenty-eight. We can have kids and stuff. And you write, and you produce, and you work hard. And you live simply. And I love you, big payoff or not."

"And I love you, kid. I'm probably just trying to make myself interesting. Let's the three of us go home and have a beer and get some sleep and promise not to let me talk any more."

That wasn't the end of the conversation, of course, but it got less one-sided from then on. We finally got home, and had a couple of beers and a few laughs at a Bob and Ray album. Dolores is thinking about family and maybe not working full-time for a while, and Bill's still waiting tables at a place called Cafe Fred on Bleecker, banging away on his Silver Reed and getting good-but-no-cigar rejection letters from all comers in what seems to be a tight market. I filled them in on what had happened since I'd been in New York four months earlier, leaving out the stuff that was classified or boring, two categories that often coincide. We finally knocked it off and got to bed about five A.M. I went to sleep and probably dreamt about friends and uncomplicated girl singers from Florida and Cuba.

III

Late nights are nothing new on my weekends in New York. But early mornings are. I didn't even speak to Dolores after she woke me to tell me I was wanted on the phone; I didn't want to disturb her as she sleepwalked back down the hall to their bedroom. The caller was Dave Perkins, the weekend duty officer at Fish and Wildlife in Washington. It's a tough shift: six P.M. Thursday through six P.M. Sunday, no time-outs, not stacking cement, maybe, but long. There was a problem. A guy was in the hospital in Lake Placid, New York. A doctor. He worked for some humanitarian research outfit outside of Lake Placid. He and his wife had a private practice on the side. He'd been out in the woods for some reason and had gotten very sick very fast. Dave didn't have all the details, but he did know the guy had been admitted to the hospital twenty-four hours earlier.

"He was found by a couple of local kids on a small lake up in the high peaks area. Near a town called Keene. I guess he was unconscious. They got a ranger on a backpacker's cell after they'd dragged him down to the nearest trail, and the ranger jeeped him on into the hospital in Lake Placid. Memorial, I think it's called. The hospital had to report it to the local police and they called us."

Perkins wanted me to drive up there, pick up a Gatson field test kit in Glens Falls on the way, and to look into the thing. It was better to have someone from the Washington office. To cover us on the seriousness of our response. Overdoing it was the best insurance, O'Toole, and I happened to be the closest, and I liked that mountain greenery anyway, as he remembered. Check for sulfur dioxide, nitrogen oxide, dry deposition, dead fish, anything I could think of. Then maybe I could help the hospital on the diagnosis, Perkins suggested, and possibly provide another page for the departmental report to the United States-Canada Commission on the effects of coal burning in Ontario and the Ohio Valley, and on why it was that eastern New York rain is forty times as acidic as it is upwind and twenty miles to the west of the high stacks in that valley. If it would make me feel any better. Anyway, I gave Dave a probable, call you right back, and made the call to Miss Quantrell's scrambler in Washington.

Now, early morning notwithstanding, I'll admit that it isn't a bad idea to do a legit assignment for Fish and Wildlife once in a while, if only to keep the lie of my cover alive. Not that the cover was all that effective, considering that the staffing of Fish and Wildlife Services the world over by undercover operatives is widely known and expected. Knowing Gregory's mind, that's probably exactly why he'd picked it for me.

Our outfit is called Structure. It's supposed to be very small and very special in its mission. It does things the bigger guys can't afford to get involved in; too small, or sometimes too big. It's run by this guy Gregory, who's a stickler for paper work, economy, the chain of command, and above all, respect for the rule that there can be no responsibility without a commensurate authority, whatever the hell that means. He's not all that bad. He is not known for his sense of humor. He didn't laugh at all when I suggested that we could really insure and guarantee the continued obscurity of our organization by simply locating our office in the Pentagon. He prefers our brownstone on K Street, anyway. And even that is something new. Until a few months ago, there was no office at all; just a phone number, with an always-present and efficient and equable Miss Quantrell or her voice mail on the other end to act as go-between for Gregory and our few operatives. Now she's been joined by a twenty-four-hour, three-person staff and some serious electronic gear.

Gregory hadn't been in great spirits of late, and I'm not so sure that the dubious results of my recent working vacation out West might have been partly responsible. There was a beautiful, five-foot-seven, blond girl named Becky, who had gotten out of a hospital in Billings, Montana. She was back home, but still not herself, according to my big friend, Elmer Linthacum. He and I have been on the phone a couple of times. Elmer had dropped by the hospital twice a week, driving the three-hundred-mile round trip from Ringling in his '64 Chrysler and thinking nothing of it.

"You know how it is, O'Toole," he opined into the phone in his inimitable Stubby Kaye tenor. "Dammitall, it's sad. That pretty little thing, smilin' one minute, and cryin' the next, and ya' never can tell when it's gonna start off again. She got your letters, I guess. But she didn't want to talk much. Can't push it, though."

Yeah, Elmer was right. You can't push it. If I hadn't shown up, maybe her father would still be alive. Sure, and maybe a chubby little Frenchman with a bad knee wouldn't be still limping around wiping his brow with a silk handkerchief, and some well-financed clout-wielder in higher circles who had dissuaded whomever Gregory's superior was from further pursuit of the Frenchman and his friends might at least have had to cool it for a while. And maybe I wouldn't have seen the faces on a couple of nice people when I told them just why it was that their daughter Jenny wouldn't be coming back to Big Piney, Wyoming. Ever.

I suppose Gregory figured that I was the only one to pin it on, and I can't say I totally disagreed with him. It's a long story, and the upshot is that it wasn't a very successful operation. Hell, it wasn't even an operation, officially, and that's probably why Gregory was content to let me cool my heels for a while in my cover job at Fish and Wildlife and willing to give Miss Quantrell the okay for me to head up north to the Adirondacks; or maybe it was because it was already about ninety in the shade in D.C., I don't know.

I promised Miss Q that I'd check in with her on Monday, and probably be back in Washington by Tuesday. I checked Bill's road atlas, called Perkins back, and told him I'd get to Glens Falls before lunch and to Keene by two or three that afternoon. My only consolation was that Miss Quantrell had sounded a little bit like she might have had a late night herself.

IV

There were seventeen front suspension-imperiling holes in the center lane of the New York Thruway on the measured mile sign-posted between Exits Fifteen and Sixteen Northbound; holes that dangerously disturbed the usual sure-footedness of my poor old 325i. I multiplied the seventeen holes by an index finger-estimated three hundred miles and then by an arbitrary five-point-five for the average number of lanes, and concluded that there were exactly 28,050 potholes on the New York Thruway. Some of them had been given a lick and a promise, but they didn't seem much less jarring than those that hadn't been touched. So the tax money had probably gone to waste. I mean the money used to pay the four-man crews their twenty or thirty dollars-per-man-per-hour, the truck expenses, and the brother in law of the state Procurement Official who probably had had to make his profit on the purchase and turnover of the five or six thousand hundred-pound bags of hot asphalt at $47 a pop that he no doubt had gotten cut-rate from a New Jersey subsidiary of Waste Management, Inc., when they had had an unforeseen overage and a consequent need for a bail-out on a subcontract to the feds for an Interstate job somewhere in New Hampshire.

And it was one of those triple-H September days, when the jet stream had made an unseasonable northward retreat to Hudson's Bay, and left the entire eastern half of the United States under a stagnating mass of sulfurous, carbon monoxided "air", ninety-eight degrees Fahrenheit on the surface, and probably the same temperature, with five knots of moisture-laden wind and haze out of the southwest, at twelve thousand feet. It would have been a typical morning if you happened to have been becalmed in mid-summer in the Horse Latitudes. I cursed one more time at the absence of the vent-wing window in modern automotive design, reconsidered yet again my long-ago decision against splitting for the Bavarian air conditioning, and decided to get off the teeth-rattling, face-wrinkling Interstate and to try to cheer myself up on the local roads for a while.

It was at Exit Sixteen, at a place called New Paltz. I banged a right onto a wide two-lane road called U.S. 9-W, and followed the signs for Kingston and Saugerties. It might make my make-work trip to the Adirondacks take an hour longer, I told myself, but I like small towns. And post offices, and car dealerships, and diners; better than I like warmed-over hotdogs on the Thruway at Howard Johnson's, or Savarins, or whatever they're currently calling those restaurant-high-priced gas mart-state governmental-hanky-panky centers from which some nonresident non-chef non-oilman rakes in the chips every twenty-seven miles once a week. You know, little kids coming in, expecting something, and the parents trying to relive some trip that they'd made twenty years ago, which was itself perhaps twenty years or so after the last good food had been served. By a human being. Not by a machine. And without having someone beep—beep your three-inch-square prefabricated grilled-cheese over the top of some check-out device for $6.75. Hell, I suppose they were just lucky to get out alive. You never can tell when some marauding band of surly-looking, spiked leather-festooned, Kawasaki-jockeying latter-day Hell's Angels might decide that your time has come, either.

I blitzed along at about forty-two miles an hour, which was about what I could get to before I'd run into a stop sign, or a school zone, or another defunct miniature golf range, or another boarded-up service station, or one more biodegraded pre-war pre-motel twelve-by-twelve-cabins-for-rent-area whose broken dream dilapidation seemed to call for moderation in speed, if only for respect and reflection.

This search for small-town, decent-valued basic wonderfulness was all well and good; but after about thirty-five or so miles and three or four hundred permanent-floating-yard sales, foisting onto the public the kinds of things I don't have to go into they've become so predictable, I said the hell with it and got back onto U.S. 87 at Exit Twenty. Going north again. A red Kenworth with an iced-up refrigeration unit, towing one of those newly-authorized, double-width and double-length rigs that had to be at least a hundred ninety feet long, and sporting somewhere in the neighborhood of four hundred pounds of macho chrome gewgawry on the roof of the cab, gave me a prolonged blast from a brace of trombone-length air horns mounted next to some kind of antenna above the driver's seat, and let me know I was back with the big boys. I edged my way into the outside lane, let the speed of my personal little four-wheeled blast furnace build on up to about 78 miles-an-hour to keep my place in the madcap race to the north, and, between potholes and the careening, catastrophic sideswipes that threatened always to ensue, I scanned the heat-seared crops, junk-yards and PCB'd streams alongside, thought back on the night before, and wished that the phone call could have come a couple of hours later. I might have been in better humor with four instead of two hours of sleep.

From eleven-thirty to eleven thirty-two A.M. I got bums-rushed through Albany by a phalanx of overheated Whites, Diamond-Ts, Peter-bilts and Kenways, which forced me to keep my eyes riveted to the eight-foot-wide fast lane that they'd locked me into. As far as I could see in the fleeting glimpses of the passing countryside that my belching eighteen-wheel ushers allowed me, the only thing that had changed was the name of the highway. It was now called the Northway. As for the rest—the patch-on-patch six lanes of melting macadam, the shoulder-to-shoulder traffic, the billboards, the inaccessible, speeding truck-blocked rest stops, and the flat, brown, fenced-up-but-unmanicured truck farms on either side of the road, all interspersed by green signs announcing the exits for places like Malta, Galway, Rock City and Mechanicsville – well, the names might have been different, but there was little else to distinguish this eighty or ninety mile leg from the previous one. I mused disinterestedly on the pos-sibility of someday retiring in a place like Mechanicsville. Especially if I held on to the BMW.

So, here I went again. I had it all figured out. The doctor was a real Ar-rowsmith, and she, his wife, was a researcher who worked with him. They were looking into a cure for something exotic, no doubt. There was only one problem. Here we had a young, dedicated, altruistic couple of nice folks. They'd forgone the automatic $200,000 a year guaranteed to any young M.D. going into practice anywhere, once the office mortgage, the used autoclave, the stethoscopes and the leather furniture -- plus all the de ri-gueur purchases from Best Buy and the MedPro software -- had been paid for, and assuming of course that the low-interest government loan would have been allowed to languish for a while. And this particular doctor, who surely hadn't lived up to the expectations of his man at Smith-Barney, had made the further mistake of eating a lake trout from the wrong lake on his day off. So instead of preparing cultures, isolating toxins, bumping off white rats, or whatever the hell these kinds of guys normally do while they walk around the quiet laboratories in their white coats mixing up the Petri dishes, or say straightening the broken ankle of the occasional down-state Brooklyn snow-bunny from the Whiteface Mountain Ski Resort when the clinic was chock-a-block, this doctor – Wager was his name – was himself in Intensive Care in the Lake Placid Hospital, flat on his back, red in the face, and probably hooked up to all kinds of strange machines to keep him going until somebody figured out just what it was that he'd gotten himself into. Well, I'd give them a hand, spend a few hours in some nice mountain country, and get back to New York on Sunday at the latest. Acid rain is serious, sure, but people didn't die from it, as far as I knew. Not quickly, anyway. Lakes maybe, but not people. Not overnight. I'd get some good dope for the F and W report, the bad acid rain would finally go away, and the good doctor would be good to go. Simple.

V

About six or seven miles north of the town of Lake George, I felt my crenellated brow begin to soften, and I realized that I had probably been maintaining a deepening squint and a furrowed grimace for the last four or five hours. I was still on U.S. 87, The Northway, but the cleaner air, the quickly rising foothills of the Adirondacks, the occasional receding glimpses of Lake George off to my right, and the fact that the traffic had thinned enough to afford me an eighth or even a quarter of a mile of highway to myself every so often must have done the job. Except for a brief lapse, when I stopped for a Texas Chile Dog and a coke in Schroon Lake, across from the headquarters of the billboarded Universal Church of the Divine Revealer, a sprawling complex of two-story, New Orleans-motel-style dormitories, some admin and money-counting buildings, an Olympic swimming pool and a large, utility-bill-defraying rent-a-boat concession by the lakeside, the scenery was coming around, no longer hidden by so many signs of the frenzied quest for the quick buck. Things were looking up.

    I left 87 at Interchange Thirty at Underwood, and began climbing northwest on route 73 for the last fifteen or so uphill miles into Keene. Some of the hardwoods dotting the deep evergreen forests on either side of the road had begun to yellow, and if I really wanted to get a jump on time – for once – I had only to lift my eyes. From the black, mountain-shaded forests to my left, to the deep sunlit green of the pine and spruce shag carpet to my right, over the sprinkling of yellowing-then-reddening hardwoods higher up, and finally to the treeless brown and snow-sprinkled top of what a road sign announced to be Mount Marcy ("Highest Point in

New York"), a few miles distant on my port bow, I had my own live change of seasons, complete with instant replay.

I saw more signs for the High Peaks Area now, and every mile or so there would be a Vien Lignes double-decker bus disgorging a load of French-Canadian hikers, who stood in groups of three or four on the shoulders of the road comparing maps, trail markers and lederhosen. The road followed the quick meanderings of a cascading stream running back toward Underwood, and, occasionally, I passed deep pools of what looked like very cold water, momentarily captured by unevenly weathered notches in the billion-year-old mountainside.

I passed through Saint Hubert's and Keene Valley, noted a quarter-mile-long mowed clearing to my left with the sanguine name of Marcy Airfield, and, two miles farther on, found myself entering Keene. I could immediately see that it was short on modern conveniences: no motels, no McDonalds, only one gas station, no miniature golf, no salt water taffy emporiums, no Starbucks – a wasteland. I pulled into the battered gas station, next to two shiny new Amoco pumps on a fifty-year-old island of decayed concrete, shut off the ignition, and got out to stretch my legs and restore the circulation to my lower back.

After three or four minutes, an old geezer in freshly-laundered iron-gray Sears work clothes walked over toward the car from a lean-toed apple and cider stand, flimsily attached to the side of the sagging station. He was clean shaven, but something told me he might have been know to have put away something stronger than apple cider from time to time.

"How's it goin'?" I volunteered.

"Barely. What'll it be?"

"Fill it, I guess. Half regular, half premium. You mind?"

"Oh hell no. Lotta people into half and half these days. Ya got a knock or something?" He rang the unleaded regular pump back to zero and stuck the nozzle into the filler pipe.

"No. Just like to clean it out every so often with that ninety-three octane. Stop when you get to six gallons, if you would; then top it off with the premium."

"Okay. Our Nation's Capital, huh? Long drive."

"Yeah. Cooler up here."

"Well, we try to keep it that way, to keep the mosquitoes and black-flies and no-see-ums happy."

He topped it off with the unleaded premium.

"That's all she'll take, I guess. Right at twelve gallons."

"It's about what I figured on."

"Well, you can save yourself another big forty-eight cents if you wanta pay cash."

"Fine. Nice pumps."

"Yeah. Well, Amoco's treated us okay. Never can tell, though. Gulf moved out, so we changed to Shell, then Mobil for a while – who knows? Sittin' in the chair one day, shinin' shoes the next. Is nice to have those electronic pumps though."

"You get a little more for a gallon up here than they do down where I come from."

"Don't you think I know it. But it don't make no never mind, really, 'cause we only mark it up about six cents a gallon no matter what the price we sell it at."

"Doesn't sound like much of a markup."

"You better believe it isn't much. And don't forget we pay on what's delivered, not what's pumped off the island, so we have to eat the spillage, leakage, delivery cheatings and truck pump errors ourselves."

"You own those cabins back there?"

"Yep."

"Any vacancies?"

"Vacancies? Hell, mister, they're all vacant. I just keep 'em tuned up to keep the wife happy and myself from gettin' down in the mouth."

"Why do you suppose they don't rent? Seems like a lot of tourists around."

"Oh yeah, but, you know, people don't wanta stay in this kind of a place anymore. They don't, whadyacallit, identify with it; probably cause they can't picture anybody on the TV stayin' in this kind of a setup. They want a – well, a name brand. I can understand that. Lately, we been thinkin' about a Cumberland, 7-11 type a' deal, maybe even a laundromat. But, I dunno."

"What do you get per night for the cabins?"

"Well, for that nicest one, the green one with the good screen door, it's twenty-four single, thirty double, third night free."

"If it's available, take two nights out of this, and this is toward the gas, okay?"

"Just yourself?"

""Yeah, I guess so."

"You got a deal, Mister. Don't forget about that third night free. And if you want to have a drink and somethin' to eat, why, I guess I'd have to tell you to go over to the Elm Tree. It's right down the road about a hundred and fifty yards, just before you get to the bridge over the Ausable. Guy named Purdy runs it; he and I don't get along all the time, but I'd have to admit I never been poisoned over there. Tell him Pete over at the Amoco told you about him."

The cabin was from another time, all right. It was about sixteen by sixteen, and the gloomy light from a couple of forty watt bulbs revealed a peeling U.S. Navy standard pea-green paint on the sagging walls. There was a joke bathroom, a pretty good double bed, a yellowed 1989 Mobil calendar, and new screens on the door and the two windows. I washed up, changed shirts, left my bag, and locked the door behind me with the old Woolworth's skeleton key.

* * * * * * * * * * * *

Every so often they would open the sliding door to the two-foot-long, eight-inch-high aperture above my head. The barely perceptible glow through the one-way glass was all the illumination we got. Sometimes there was no light at all when they opened it, and that was how I knew when it was night. The ride was smooth, and it took me the better part of an hour after regaining a semblance of consciousness to determine which way was up. The aperture was above and forward of my head. That meant that I was to starboard, lying on my back on a hard bunk. She was a couple feet to my right, lying in what I assumed to be another bunk to port, and her breathing was rattling, wet, intermittent, and interrupted occasionally by an incongruously rasping cough.

After a while I got pretty good with the varying configuration of transmission, engine speed and road condition. I had to rely on the inertial navigation system built into the body – circulation, the ear canals, and the minute alterations in pressure on my back. It would have been easier if they hadn't had me tied down so firmly, and if the swathe of tape over my mouth hadn't begun to bother me. At first it was the sniffles, and after a while I had to move my head ever so slightly to one side just to keep one nostril relatively clear of congestion.

We crossed some water after a time; maybe two hours after I had awakened. The combination of whatever we were in and what was carrying it was apparently not so large that it couldn't be put on something that floated and moved pretty well over what I assumed must have been the surface of a large lake – Champlain, maybe. I could feel a steady vibration against my back. The rhythms of the turbine engines and the cavitations of the twin screws were punctuated by an intermittent chop and the occasional slap of a good-sized wave. The cold front must have slowed down on its passage to the east.

We disembarked – on the other side, I assumed – about forty-five minutes later. It took a good deal of arm work for our driver to jockey us off the barge. Or ferry. There was some intricate backing and turning. We were a semi rig. A tractor, pulling a trailer..

When we finally got back to a highway, the guy in the aperture started using a strong light to check out Molly. I got a glimpse of her and just a quick impression of the space around her before he swung the light over to my face. For some reason, I played possum, which, in my trussed-up condition, amounted to closing my eyes.

Molly had looked awful. Her face was swollen and there was an oily, brown mucus issuing from her nose and mouth. They hadn't bothered to tie her down. On the port wall was a rectangular cover, with a circular dogging device in its center. It had been a recent addition to our chamber, if the professional braising around its perimeter was any indication. That was all I could see before the light man turned his attention to me. Shortly after that, the aperture door slammed shut, and our dark ride proceeded to get a bit rougher. He was a good driver – but he was pushing it. I inferred that they were worried about Molly's condition. I was too. Also, it was getting harder and harder to keep a nostril open, and I was having a hard time working the foul-smelling tape back toward my front teeth.

VI

The drive from Keene to Lake Placid would have made a great mille miglia; the BMW handled well, and it almost made the whole trip worth the price of admission. It was fourteen up and then down miles over the high peaks and by Cascade Lake and some more, clear-watered mountain streams, and they'd left everything pretty much the way it probably was before we got here.

Lake Placid had been stuffed with everything that a self-respecting mountain-lake-resort haven-twenty-first century tourist trap should have been: three dollar ice cream cones, a Bert 'n Ernie's Real N.Y. Deli, at least five fancy food places that sold stuff like fresh scungilli salad at fourteen and change for a quarter pound, the obligatory Rouse Corporation-style restored paper mill-now multi-floored-boutique called the Alpine Mall, and, this particular day, a probably not unrepresentative convention of three or four thousand Northern New York Volunteer Firemen, loaded down with cases of Moosehead and fifteen-foot-long tasseled yellow banners proclaiming the origins of their overweight bearers to be Deauxville, Saranac Lake, Chateaugay, or whatever. A lot of short, chubby women and hundreds of desperate-eyed pre-teens followed the as yet unregimented passing parade; they all looked somewhat flabbergasted, as they were forced, by speedily encroaching facts and slimming bankrolls, to acknowledge that this year's convention might be just another slow and boozy reenactment of the predictable. I retreated, got directions from a beefy cop in mirrored sunglasses at the east end of town, and followed the blue signs past the dozens of motels toward the hospital. It was just before four in the afternoon.

Lake Placid Memorial had passed its heyday some years earlier. It was one of those granite and limestone, state of the art-circa 1922, cloned institutions that looked a little smaller each time you came home.

As with most of the medical facilities in our country today, there was a profusion of check-in, registration, scheduling, appointment, billing and insurance desks, but with absolutely no evidence whatsoever of anybody actually taking care of anybody. I waited about twenty minutes at the information desk while eight or nine staff people tried to convince an old black man that he had not been there since eight-thirty A.M., that if he had then what had he done with his blue card, and if he never got one, then where was his yellow appointment slip, and if you say you gave it to us, then what was the name of the person who took it? The aspect least important to the hospital personnel I saw was the man's need to have the stitches taken out of his good eye, which was fast becoming his bad one. Well, it was his own fault, he was told. He should have told someone before twelve-thirty, when the clinic hours were over. All that was still going on when a harried nurse spared me a what's-your-problem-and-make-it-quick glance; I got in Wager's name, and was told he was on Four, New Wing – take the elevators in the back.

They had Doc Wager in Intensive Care. Precautionary, the doctor told me. He was an Indian internal medicine man named Rashid, whose serene composure made it difficult to tell whether he was twenty-three, forty-three or sixty-three.

"No, Mr. O'Toole, the symptoms are not inconsistent with a poison of some kind. But they were not inconsistent with an infection, either. We took a culture. Positive. Unidentified as yet. Let me see. He examined a metal-bound sheaf of papers that a candy-striper had handed to him. "Yes. Patient is responding to cephalosporin – Keflin – and a full gram of metronidazole IV – for the anaerobic component, if it's a mixed infection, I suppose. Yes. Fever down, breathing somewhat easier, abdominal cramps and intermittent muscular contractions subsiding. No diarrhea."

"That's some infection. Has he been conscious, then?"

"He has had moments, and they seem to be coming more often, and lasting a few minutes longer each time."

"So I gather you wouldn't buy the acid rain idea?"

"It's possible, of course. But give us another twenty-four hours, Mr. O'Toole; we'll save ourselves from wasting effort on conjecture, and perhaps Doctor Wager can tell us himself how it is that he is here." He spoke with a slight and unplaceable sing-songy upper-class lilt, sort of like Peter Sellers doing a Calcutta-born, Eton-educated, long-time resident of Jamaica.

"Would it be possible to see him now, Doctor?"

"I would think not, Mr. O'Toole. Not until he is a bit better, and until we have a report from Albany on the culture. We did allow young Mrs. Wager to visit him for a moment last evening; it was, as they say, touch and go for a while, and we relaxed the rules in that case. His employers – the Beckman Institute – have been very solicitous, but we have refused to let their representatives see him, either. Maybe tomorrow will be different."

"What is the Beckman Institute?"

"I do not know all that much. I have been here somewhat less than a year myself. It is a privately-funded research facility, west of Keene, in the mountains. Molecular immunogenetics, I am told. Eukaryotic regulation and genetic recombination would be natural areas of investigation, I suppose. I was told by the Beckmann people that Doctor Wager had experience in prokaryotic expression vectors and animal virology, but that there was no chance at all that he could have contacted anything at the Institute."

"Is it enough that they say no chance at all?"

"We'll know tomorrow, Mr. O'Toole. If Doctor Wager continues his improvement, we'll no doubt be able to determine the source of his infection at a leisurely pace, I would think. Contagion may not even be a problem. The Beckmann Institute seems to have a very good reputation, and although the educational requirements for employment there rule out any direct impact on the chronic unemployment problem in the county, its presence does benefit the local economy in other ways. So. We are asked not to jump to conclusions."

"I see."

"Come back tomorrow, Mr. O'Toole. We will have some answers. I am sorry, but my no doubt premature assessment is that your trip will have been unnecessary. Acid rain will prove not to have been the cause of Doctor Wager's troubles. But we shall see."

I stopped by the police station, a wood, stone and black glass-custom-contemporary a block away and next to the town library, a Carnegie classic, where a team of masons appeared to be repointing the brick on the north side. The sergeant at the station gave me the names of the two kids and the ranger who had brought Wager back to civilization. He seemed glad to turn it over to me.

The kids, Joey and Donny LeCourier, lived with their mother, May LeCourier, in a trailer court in what the sergeant said was a wide spot in the road called North Elba, eight miles east of Lake Placid on 73. I must have passed it on my way over from Keene. She was a waitress at the Cascade Motor Lodge, also in North Elba. The ranger was a guy named

John Landborg. I called him from a pay phone across the street from the Alpine Motel, which was overrun at that moment by at least seventy-five eight-year-old hooliganish daughters and sons-a-firemen from Lowville, doing their level best to destroy the twenty foot in diameter, above-ground aluminum pool and what was proving to be the collapsible swings and slides alongside. I called him from a payphone because I kept getting a "no signal" on my cell. Come to think of it, I couldn't remember seeing any cell phones since I left the Northway, down in the foothills, where every truck driver seemed to be gabbing away on either a hand-held or a headset, barreling down the road at seventy-five or so, oblivious to traffic nuance, but no doubt taking care of important business. Back at the Alpine, I had to admit that the kids were having a hell of a good time, though, and I even started chuckling myself when one little skinny kid with an infectious laugh got particularly amused at something or other.

I got the ranger at the Nichols Brook Ranger Station on the fourteenth ring, and it sounded like he was a thousand miles away and underwater. He had to use a push-to-talk switch on his end, so the conversation, without the little grunts and uh-huhs and you-don't-says, seemed a bit disjointed.

"Sorry about that. We been sort of busy up here for September. One thing and another. Yeah, well, all I did was throw him in the back of my Laredo and get him on into Memorial. Those kids musta dragged him a mile and a half down to the road by that little wooden bridge where they called me on the emergency phone. They made a travois and everything."

"What did they say when they called? I mean, did they tell you where it was – "

"No. No, they didn't. I've been meanin' to go up there myself, but one, they said somebody from Fish and Wildlife was comin' in, and two, we had a lot to do around here with all this heat; you know, brush fires, spontaneous combustion, that kind of thing. But they just said where they were right then, that they had this doctor in tow, and how he was pretty sick and all. So, I drove on up there and fetched 'em out. If he pulls through, the kids'r the ones saved his life, I'd have to say. And they know their way around. You get holda them and they'll show you where they found him, all right. Not that far; up the East Ausable outa Keene, maybe a mile and a half, then due west on the logging road along Nichols Brook another couple miles, that's where they called me from."

"West, huh? Is that anywhere near that – ah – Beckmann Institute?"

"Well, yeah, it is. Course, Devil's Mountain Camp, that's all Beckmann family property, is about twenty-five hundred acres, and the Institute is up on fifty, sixty acres on the north end. I never been there, but that's what it shows like on the detail maps I got here."

30

"They seem to keep a pretty low profile up there."

"Yeah, you'd be right on that. They even got guards; and, tell you the truth, I can't say as I blame them. That research is valuable stuff nowadays, since nine/eleven and all, from what I can see. You know, they do it all up there. Like bacteria that eat up oil spills, and maybe someday stop Dutch Elm, or turn the Gypsy Moth thing around. I'm all for it, and I don't care if Beckmann makes his money on it, either. Patents, whatever. They mind their own business, I'll mind mine sorta thing."

"You ever meet any employees from up there?"

"Well, meet, no. I mean they most all of them drive by here when they go into town, but that isn't often, and nobody ever talks all that much. Hey, these guys, most of 'em, been to school for the first twenty, thirty years 'a their lives; they don't need to talk to me and lose their train 'a thought. They're all nice, quiet, thirty-, forty-year-old doctoral guys. I've never exactly been overloaded with complaints about all the laughter and partying goin' on up there, if you hear what I'm sayin'."

"I gotcha."

"Course, when all the bigwigs come up for the Devil's Mountain Rendezvous, why then all bets 'r off."

"What's this rendezvous?"

"Well, I'll tell ya. Startin' next Monday, Tuesday, you'll see all kinds 'a G5's and whatever droppin' into the airports over there at Saranac Lake and Lake Placid. Then all these guys in two thousand dollar suits and hand-made shoes start stumblin' off the airplanes, lookin' like they just put away a pint and a half of martinis and fired somebody, carryin' these fancy duffle bags. Well, they go on up to Devil's Mountain there for a for four, five days once a year and rough it. Well, not really rough it, from what I hear. I mean these birds are heads of some of the biggest companies in the world, and politicians, and what all. Foreigners and everything. Call 'em the Mountaineers. They have these different sorta clubs they belong to, and each club has its own area and each area has its own bighouse, with sleepin' cabins and whatever; oh, it's quite a thing. Then, course, all the prices start goin' up, and these call girls and whatever from Albany and even New York City start showin' up at the motels and all, and oh, they all have a hell of a time. Most of the locals just grin and bear it for a week or so til things get back to normal."

"Where exactly is this Devil's Mountain Camp, Mr. Landborg?"

"Call me John. You drive up 98 outa Keene there, and make a left at the cemetery turnoff. There's a sign there for the cemetery. Then you cross this little bridge over Nichols Brook about thirty, forty yards farther, then you stop right there. Look up. You'll see mountains, and there are three peaks that stand out, sort of. Ya got Pitchoff, Devil's and Sentinel. Devil's Mountain is the one in the middle and it'd be about four, maybe five miles from where you'd be standin'. And that Devil's Mountain is smack dab in the center of the Beckmann property. That's why they call it Devil's Mountain Camp, I guess. Camps is what they call them up here. Course, some of these camps are more like palaces, really. Listen, Mr. O'Toole, I gotta get back to work, to tell you the truth. You need any more help on this deal, feel free to call, or even drop by. And good luck to you."

"Right, John, and thanks for your help."

It looked like a wild goose chase, but I had pretty much decided to go through the motions and run the Gatson test on the lake where Wager had been found. I was going to have to get in touch with Mrs. LeCourier's two sons. The police had given me a telephone number, and I donated yet another $2.85 to Verizon to find out from the operator of Dan's Trailer Park in North Elba that there wouldn't be no need for him to run on down to her trailer because he was sure she was working at the Cascade tonight. I retrieved the BMW from the parking area behind the hospital, and headed east out of town, past the Adirondack Airport and two ski-jump towers, standing tall and forlorn over the snowless, four-thousand-space Olympic Games parking lots.

VII

The Cascade Motor Lodge was a 1940's vintage roadhouse that had been haphazardly pieced together and added onto over the years. There was a recently constructed, twelve-unit, off-season, thirty-six-a-night motel crammed onto the back of what must have been a two-acre lot. It was four or five miles past the airport, just beyond a Burma Shave-sized green sign with the legend "Welcome to North Elba" printed on both sides. There must have been forty or fifty cars and pickups parked in front of and around the ramshackle office-restaurant-bar building next to the road, and I smelled burning charcoal and broiling steak as I got out of the car. Slapping futilely at a swarm of Alaskan-sized mosquitoes that had suddenly materialized in the waning daylight, I hurried over to the entrance.

May LeCourier was one of those professional waitresses who made you think how nice it would be to have a restaurant if you just had her to run the place. She wore a blue and white, candy-striped cotton all-purpose serving uniform, a starched white cap to keep her curly brown hair in place, and her white shoes had ripples on the rubber soles. She was a bit on the chubby side, but she looked firm and moved like the wind. Gracefully. She had roundish face, and gray eyes that let you know that she'd had a few laughs to go along with what had to have been a few rough times in her twenty-eight or thirty years on the planet. She stopped alongside my holding position at the bar, balancing like a shotput a tray loaded down with steaks, French fries, salads, and a couple of baskets of hot bread wrapped in red napkins. There was a tiny wooden signpost jabbed into each steak to separate the rares from the medium-rares, and I made a mental note to have dinner there if I ever had the time.

"Mr. O'Toole?" Her face was a little flushed, and she brushed away a little perspiration from her forehead with the back of her free hand.

"Yes. Mrs. LeCourier?"

"Call me May. Veronica at the register said you might want to talk to me. Is it about the boys?"

"Well, yes, as a matter of fact – "

"Jeez, I'm going to have to hire a social secretary for those guys. Either that or tell 'em to stop goin' for hikes up in those mountains. First the newspaper, then the Lieutenant Governor's secretary calling, then the Boy Scouts, 'a course, and I don't know if it's ever gonna stop."

"Well, I'm with the United States Fish and Wildlife, and I was hoping the boys might be able to show me exactly where it was that they found Doctor Wager yesterday. It's just a routine thing."

"Okay, Randy, I'm coming!" She reassured a nearby group of uniformed Cadyville Volunteer firemen and their consorts with a wave and gestured helplessly at me. "I gotta run, Mr. O'Toole. Maybe later."

"Sorry, May, I can see you're busy."

"Yeah, it slows down about eight-thirty, nine o'clock. Oh, but some of us are going over to the Elm Tree in Keene after that. Jeez, I don't know, maybe tomorrow morning."

"I'm staying in Keene. Could I buy you a drink or something tonight, and maybe set it up for tomorrow? If it wouldn't get in the way of anything."

"No, no, that'd be fine. You know the Elm Tree? It's – "

"Yeah, I saw it today."

"Okay. Nine-thirty, ten o'clock all right?"

"Fine."

When she smiled, she looked at your eyes. She was one of those who listened, and who didn't forget people, times, and what it was that happened. Then she was on her way, deftly dodging the impromptu toasts, the slaps on the back, the leaned-back captains' chairs and the excited twosomes popping up to go stand in line at the ladies' restroom.

* * * * * * * * * *

For a guy whose main purpose in life for this particular couple of days was to get a half-a-liter of water from a dinky lake, acidic or not, it seemed to me that I was doing an awful lot of bar-hopping. Monty's Elm Tree Inn was definitely the hot spot in Keene, though, and they charged only five-fifty for a pretty heftily- poured Johnny Walker Red on the rocks; the soda on the side was free. Although the building had been imposing as I walked up the sagging wooden steps to the wrap-around porch, the bar was not much bigger than, say, an IRT subway car. And just at that time it was a bit noisier and almost as crowded. I got lucky, though, found a seat at the bar, and ordered my drink.

Most of the noise was from the other end of the room, where eighteen or twenty men and women alternately cheered or groaned at the faded picture and crackly sound on an old Zenith twenty-five inch color, guy-wired into a precarious perch on a crumbly two-by-four nailed to the wall about eight feet above the floor. It was the New England Patriots versus the Dolphins, and it looked like a real barn burner.

I sipped my Scotch, and tried to read the small print on a Monty's Elm Tree Inn business card that I retrieved from a candy dish next to the cash register off to my right. It advertised: "Monty's Elm Tree Inn. Downtown Keene, N.Y. 12945. Ron Purdy, Prop. Used Cars – Whiskey – Peat Moss – Nails – Land –Fly Swatters – Racing Forms – Bongo Drums – Wars Fought – Governments Run – Bridges Destroyed – Uprisings Quelled – Revolutions Started –Tigers Tamed – Salons Emptied –" There were a few more testaments to what a wag old Ron was, but the smoke, the noise, and in particular, the arrival of a particularly large, flannel-shirted, lumberjack-murderer who had just smothered the toy bar stool to my left made me think about greener pastures. I left a couple of dollars on the bar, grabbed my drink, and made my way through the three-deep crowd back toward the porch. A nice waitress near the door told me it'd be all right, and that she wouldn't even mind bringing a Purdyburger DeLuxe and a cup of coffee to me outside.

About a half-an-hour later, having inhaled a pretty good half-pound burger, I relaxed on an old white-painted wicker couch on the porch and mused on the uncertainties of life, as I breathed in the vaguely sweet but off-putting scent of several citronella candles waxed on the porch railings and watched the incineration of one flying denizen of the Adirondacks after another as they maniacally kamakazied into the zapping purple neon Korean vegetable stand electrocution device mounted above the door. May LeCourier and two other women wearing cardigan sweaters over their waitress uniforms showed up about a quarter after ten. She noticed me and told her friends she'd be on in in a few minutes.

"Hi."

"Hi, May. Sit down?"

"Sure. Sorry. The firemen kept showing up and it turned into a busy night."

"Drink?"

"Uh – well, why not. Just a Moosehead, I guess."

I walked over to the door, caught the eye of my waitress, and ordered May's beer and another Scotch for myself.

"Well, I called home and got the boys all set for tomorrow morning, Mr. O'Toole, if that's all right with you."

"That'd be fine. What time?"

"I told 'em you'd be by around seven-thirty. See, Joey, he's the oldest, he has to work cleanin' up at the Ford garage startin' at one, and I figured you'd need that much time, anyway. Hope that's not too early."

"No, the earlier the better for me."

"Joey says you'd need to either walk or have a four-wheel-drive to get up to the lake, and I thought you could use our Jeep, if you'd be willing to go for the gas and all. I don't think there's anyplace you could rent one. Not around here."

"That'd be a big favor. But I'd have to pay more than just for the gas. Could we work out a rental kind of thing?"

"Well, that'd be real nice. Maybe, say, ten dollars for the day, plus the gas. Would that be okay?

"May, I couldn't do it and feel right about it for anything less than fifty. Don't forget, the government reimburses me for it."

"Well, uh, okay, that'd come in real handy. It – it's not really mine, the Jeep. It belongs to my husband, Wendell. But he – well he hasn't been around too much lately."

"Sorry. Fifty it is, then. I'll be there a little after seven."

The waitress brought the drinks, including my soda on the side and a frozen mug for the Moosehead. We watched as she poured half of the beer into a mug.

"Anything else, sir?"

"Well, I guess not right now. Did you eat?"

"Oh sure, I'm fine, thanks," May answered. The waitress left us alone. Neither of us said anything for a minute or two.

"I dunno. After serving food for four or five hours, good as it is at the Cascade, well, you sort of lose interest," May explained. "Oh. You know where the Cascade is? Well, right across the road there's a little paved lane angling down behind the Twin Peaks Motel. You go down there about a quarter of a mile, you'll see some trailers; mine's the third one on the fenced side of the road. It's an Airstream; you know, aluminum. It's the only one."

She poured the rest of her beer into the mug, and prepared to go inside.

"Hey, May, you don't have to go. It's awful noisy in there, and I'd love to have another with you if you have the time."

"Well, I guess there's no hurry. It's just me and the girls out to break the monotony on a Friday night." She sat back down. "I don't know why, but Fridays are just the worst for me. It's the beginning of the weekend, and I've usually got plenty to do, but there's something about Fridays that makes me nervous. Didn't used to be that way. We – my husband and I – didn't mind just sitting around on a Friday. Well, on any night. We had the kids, and a little house up outside 'a Saranac Lake. He was working then, and it was before he started – well, he's so unhappy and all, he just started to drink more than he could handle. That's where the troubles started. And that's where I'm going to stop talking for a while. How do you like it up here?"

"I like the mountains, and I like some of the people, you, for instance, May. That drinking can be a slippery thing to get hold of, I know. Is he still around?"

"Oh yeah, but you know, now he's feeling bad when he's sober cause he can't do what he wants to do for the kids, and, well, I guess for me, either. So that makes him want to get off to some place and have somethin' to drink, and it all starts over. And that was okay, really. Nobody around here has more that a dollar-thirty-five in their pocket at any given time, believe me. So I can understand that part of it. For better or for worse and all. But, I don't know, after a while, it seemed like he didn't do anything. I mean anything. No walks, no hobbies, no fishing, no reading, no nothing. Then he just started living on the past – I mean, like he had thirty maybe forty things in his mind – people, times, regrets, successes, whatever – and the drinking just would stir these same things up into a different concoction on any given night, and he'd seem to somebody he didn't know too well or who didn't know him too well like the funniest and nicest guy around. But, if you knew all these things, why, after a while you could see that whatever he said was just a shotgun kind of a rehash of the same old ingredients, with nothing new, ever. And it keeps taking him longer and longer to get through with it. Like he has to make it – to stretch it out and make it through his turn to talk. Course, he knows it well as anybody, so he tends to move on to different people from time to time. But I think everything would be okay if he'd get a job. I mean okay for him; I'm not sure about us. A lotta things have been said, and some of them can't ever be taken back. Things that hurt more than you can forget."

May LeCourier and I and the bugs that never seemed to learn ended up sitting out on that porch for quite a while. She'd lived in and around Lake Placid or Saranac Lake for her whole life and until the last two years or so she never would have wanted it any other way. 'Course, it had been hard at times. She'd been the middle child of seven. Her dad had been a lay teacher at the Roman Catholic high school in Saranac Lake, but he hadn't been able to work since May's mother had finally died of cancer in February of '92. He just never could get used to the fact that she wouldn't be coming back. The officials at the archdiocese had been sympathetic, but when Mr. Sinclair hadn't shaped up by two months into the next school year, they'd asked him to take a sabbatical. They'd paid him full wages for another year, then half for a year after that, then nothing. Mr. Sinclair hardly noticed. He was still back in the late eighties, praying that May's mother wouldn't have to have yet another delaying-game operation, knowing that that's not the way things had been going, and wallowing in remorse for not having felt that could afford sending her to the Mayo Clinic, or maybe New York City back in 1985, when she'd first found the little lump. At least to some place that wouldn't have messed up on recording the exact locations of the radiation treatments on her chest, neck and what was left of her shoulder for that fateful six weeks after the mastectomy.

The September before her mom had gotten sick, May had gone on down to Albany to enroll at the State University, a year later than most of her friends. The delay hadn't been because of the tuition; she'd been salutatorian at Saranac Lake Public, out of a hundred eighty-seven in the graduating class, so the automatic State scholarship took care of that. But the living expenses, the books, the clothes, and the loss to the family of what May might make if she went to work and continued living at home, well, anyway, these were the things that made her hold off for a year.

She worked summerizing, winterizing, cleaning, and generally care-taking six summer houses around the south shore of Saranac Lake, and that could turn into a full-time job if you put your mind to it. With a few waitressing jobs on the side, why she'd put away almost eight hundred dollars over and above what she put into the family coffers by the time she caught the Trailways down to Albany.

She'd loved those months at SUNY. Back in Saranac and Lake Placid, why all anybody ever asked anybody when they came home was "How much does a thing like that pay a guy?" or, "I s'pose a job like that must set you up pretty good, huh?" Not that that was so awful. She could under-stand it. In Essex County, as they said, there wasn't hardly enough bread and butter to go around, so you could sure as hell forget about any gravy. Or the other famous line, you want to make a million dollars up here, simple, just work a million hours. But at SUNY, they didn't seem to think that way. The payoff wasn't the only thing. May started liking history and government and politics and even thought about law school, although she knew that that was a long shot and a long way off.

Anyway, like she said, that was when her mom had gotten the cancer. All bets were off. No one protested when May just up and left Albany in

March of 1988 and she didn't even write to SUNY or anybody to get a refund on the dorm and food service prepayment. She'd been working ever since, and she really hadn't had that much time to worry about what she'd given up.

She had known Wendell in high school, even though he was three years ahead of her; he'd been famous for having set a record for passes completed in one game against Lake Placid. They started seeing each other when he was home from his job for St. Regis up in Maine, then he'd been laid off and come back to work at the Dodge-Plymouth place in Saranac Lake, then one thing had led to another and she'd said yes. They'd been busy and young, and when Joey was born in late '92, well, May and Wendell figured that was about as happy as you could get. Then Wendell had got his back hurt workin' tow truck. He couldn't drive or lift anything for a while, the drinking had started, gotten worse, and here she was, "talkin' too much but buyin' the next round and blame it all on Friday nights," as May put it.

Yes, she'd even worked out at Devil's Mountain Camp during the Mountaineer retreats in '93 and '94, before the board had been forced to opt for males only on the waiting staff. It had been a tough thing to get hired on, because it was a plum of a job. Back then they'd had three sessions a year at Devil's Mountain, and that had usually meant about six weeks guaranteed work, close to home and real nice on the tips at the end. Oh sure, there'd been a lot of silliness up there from time to time, but you take four or five-hundred men, most of 'em over forty, some up to seventy-five and eighty, no wives and kids, and lots of liquor, why, you've got to expect a little flirting and maybe some occasional off-color remarks.

In fact, the only things that May hadn't particularly liked at all were the campfire theatricals that they'd put together once a week. They'd always start off and end with about forty-five minutes of incantations and exhortations involving this God of Duty and Light. Apollo, she'd remembered. They'd intone this thing about the founding of the Mountaineers, about how there had been this one guy who was a traitor and had actually divulged the secret recognition signal, and about what finally happened to him, and how this Green Knight came and saved the day for the two founders who lay wounded because of the traitor's misdeeds. Oh, it was quite a story they'd go through, with their in hocs, and their signos, and all. And they all had the whole thing memorized, said May, like the Shriners. I began to get the picture.

There was this big amphitheater, down by the lake below the main camp; there was a giant stage at the shoreline, with a battery of lights that would have given the Olympic Auditorium a run for its money. These old guys would get into costume, and, drunk or not, they'd get up on that stage and act the parts of men, trees, horses, devils, all that kind of stuff, even women once in a while. She'd seen two or three of them – the musicales – when she'd worked on after-dinner dessert, coffee and cocktails at the Blue Spruce Amphitheater – oh yeah, right, that was the name – instead of the back-breaking dinner shift back at Main Camp.

They had been like operas, with fifteen or twenty professional musicians up from Albany, a conductor, and some professional guest stars from New York playing the lead roles and doing most of the heavy singing. The themes of the performances she'd seen had usually involved a threat to the natural order of the primeval forest posed by some banished Angel of Darkness and Irresponsibility, brought to task by an enlightened, conservative Angel of Rationality who would fight through all kinds of pitfalls, threats, betrayals and the oversights of slipshod wastrels, and eventually triumph in his quest to preserve and more firmly ensconce the steady-Eddy establishment and the rightful status quo. Despite persistent two-hour-long efforts to hamstring him – by self-interested politicians, pandering to an uninformed and wishy-washy forest public, or by well-intentioned but short-sighted do-gooders, who obviously couldn't be counted on to be around for the long haul – the Good Angel would come through, just like the Green Knight had.

The finales invariably involved fifty or sixty paunchy and red-faced moons, rocks, ghost, elves and what-all, singing tearful paeans and lump-in-the-throat hosannas to sticktoitiveness, according to May, to the accompaniment of fireworks and Stars and Stripes Forever-type orchestral curtain calls. May's objection was that all these rich and powerful fifty-five-year-olds would then sit around until two or three in the morning, asking for more ice and occasionally just a little tonic water to go with their thermos-bagged half-gallons of Grey Goose pepper vodka. It had meant late nights, and less time with Wendell, Joey, and by then, two-year-old Donny Sinclair.

But late nights and troubled husbands notwithstanding, you didn't turn down work like that back in '94. Especially since May was pretty sure that Steve Beckmann, Jr. had probably put in a good word for her after she'd first applied, the winter before. Oh yeah, everyone around here knew about the Beckmanns. She'd baby sat for Steve the Third, Junior's son, and she'd seen old man Steve himself a few times during the Mountaineer retreats, and once driving his old car in the Fourth of July parade in Lake P. The Beckmanns, they'd given most of their original twenty-five hundred acres up outa Keene there to the Mountaineers. Some people said it was just a big tax angle, but May didn't know about that. They'd kept the original Sears family cottage on the north end of the lake and of course they had the Institute of Biology or whatever they called it up at the same end of the original property. It was awfully complicated. Where that family had made all its money, that is. Construction, she thought, but she wasn't sure just what it was they constructed. They weren't real close to anybody she knew, of course, but they helped the county out a lot, they paid their taxes, and didn't bother anybody. In fact, May knew the guy who sold them thirty, forty cords of hardwood a year, and the son of the grocery-general store owner down in Keene Valley who helped their camp handyman out every spring; they'd always had nothing but good to say for the Beckmann family, same as May.

She might have had a tough ten years, but May didn't look beaten down. Whatever she'd been through, why, she was also aware that an awful lot of people had had it a lot worse. But God knows she wasn't averse to talking about it. I don't think it had anything to do with the four Mooseheads she had put away by a few minutes after midnight, when her waitress friends finally emerged from the bar, and who cared if it had. The Pats had won, Purdy had bought the last round, and another Friday night had gone by the boards. I pooh-poohed May's apology for monopolizing the conversation, forced her to take the fifty for the use of her jeep the next morning, and after another disturbing look into those clear, gray understanding eyes, I told her I'd see her a little after seven A.M. She shook my hand with a firm grip, and she and her friends headed off to their car. May announced that she'd be doing the driving, and there didn't seem to be any argument about it. The bill came to twenty-seven and change, and the waitress hadn't forgotten the Purdyburger. I paid up, left a five for the tip, and walked fairly steadily back up the lonely road toward the cabin behind Pete's Amoco.

* * * * * * * *

It's amazing how selfish you can get when you're really sick. I mean physically, painfully, weakeningly, no-help-in-sight kind of sick; with no assurance that it's not mortal, and with no way to make the hole in the tape over your mouth any bigger so you might breathe in and cough out without the pressure buildup both ways that made the headache even more explosive than it would have been. I didn't care about what it was that I was in. I didn't care about where we were going, and I'd forgotten just exactly who it was we were. I didn't think about Beckmann, about Molly, about Lake Placid, and certainly didn't ever even consider Gregory, or the future of our country, May LeCourier or the Olympic Games. The only thing I cared about was making the headache stop, the spinning abate, the heat go away and the shivering slow down. My throat had been sore even before I'd started swallowing the blood, but by now, maybe four to six hours after crossing the lake, the tissues were raw and swollen enough to make me think the throat might close off entirely. Not that I cared.

I felt someone lay a cold, twelve-pound sledgehammer on my left temple, as if sighting for the bonk that would finish me off, and I was rooting for them. Then the hammer rubbed my brow and then my cheek with something wet and even comfortable. It was a hand with a cool, moist cloth of some kind. It didn't really matter that much, I thought, until she ripped the tape from my mouth. Then I was mad. There was no question but that eight or ten square inches of pretty good skin and facial tissue had gone with it; sure, I could breathe a little better, but – then I realized that I could breathe a lot better, and it made the difference.

The aperture man picked that moment to make his move, and the light caught Molly sitting up on her bunk and leaning over to me. She was weaving, and her face didn't look much improved when she turned it directly toward the light. It had been an effort for me to open my eyes, and the damned light had almost blinded me. Molly slipped to the floor, instinctively grabbing the side of her bunk as she went down. There was what sounded like a bone-crunching impact with a steel floor, and she was unable to stifle a cry of pain. Then she pulled her way back up to her bunk and slumped, exhausted by sickness and extraordinary effort. The light played on the two of us for another thirty seconds, then the door slid home. A minute later, she squeezed my arm twice, in quick succession. It wasn't the squeeze of someone on the way out. It was urgent and commanding. The next think I knew, she'd raised my head, and was actually holding a goddamn plastic container to my lips. It was water and it came at a very important time. Then, all of a sudden, she was whispering in my ear.

"You've got to take these now. You've got to."

One by one, she forced three horse pills down my throat. On the first she had to hold her hand over my mouth to force me to swallow. Then I took my medicine like a good boy. She gave me a short water and breathing break between each ordeal. The last one was bigger than the first two.

For the first time, the guy changed his schedule on the aperture move. The light caught her bending over me. I'd taken the third pill by then, and she started her weaving, on the way out act. I still didn't feel all that well – I felt awful, actually, but the removal of the tape had given me some hope. It wasn't hard to convince anybody interested that I was in a bad way. I could taste the blood in my throat again, and there had to be some on my face and the area around my head from all the coughing. He looked at me for quite a while. Through the slits of my swollen eyes, I could just see Molly's face in the penumbra of the light that shone into my eyes from forward and above. She put her left hand up to her head, and I'll be goddamned if she didn't manage an ever-so-slow wink through her reddened right eye. There was no mistaking it. Then she went clumsily back to her bunk. The aperture door slammed shut, leaving us in the dark. The headache came back strong, and I got selfish again for a while.

VIII

At six-thirty the morning after my talk with May LeCourier at Purdy's, it was already eighty in the shade. A bunch of bleary-eyed locals were trying to focus on Wolf Blitzer or someone at a truck stop outside Lake Placid, and I was the bleary-eyed-no-cell-signal stranger at the pay phone, waiting for breakfast and watching them. I got the day nurse on the fourth floor at Memeorial. Oh no, that was all right, the shift had just changed, the early bird gets the worm, and Doctor Wager was much better and out of intensive care. Doctor Rashid had been in earlier and had told her that they would have to wait for a couple of tests to come back from Albany. Doctor Wager was awake, and he could have limited visiting after twelve noon.

Back on the tube, two New York State legislators were debating whether or not it was too earlier to call the situation in Iraq a civil war, and at first glance, the little crowd in the restaurant seemed attentive and dutifully grim about the distant goings-on in Samarra between the Shia and the Sunni. It wasn't until after they'd paraded before us a laughing bumbler of a weatherman, a two-minute people-in-the-news clip and about eighteen commercials, that I started to get the picture. Everyone, including my waitress, who had for forty or fifty seconds ignored what I was confident were my cooling hotcakes and sausage on the serve-up counter, was pointing his face or at least deferentially angling his head toward the twenty-three inch Sony mounted a few feet above the French-fry maker. But no one was really listening. I couldn't have really blamed anyone, considering the information overload that the modern world has brought us to. As a matter of fact, the only things that had registered with me were the color graphics on the weather map; there was a cold front moving very fast that would pass at midday. Temperatures in Massena and Watertown were already in the low forties.

At seven o'clock, the place started emptying out. Big V-8 engines roared to life, gravel was thrown clattering against the parking area guard rail, and outfitted in gear and clothing somewhat more heavy-duty than their various enterprises probably required, the people shook out the cobwebs and went about their business. I finished my second dollar-twenty-five cup of coffee and a last bit of buckwheats, then paid up and hit the trail.

* * * * * * * * * *

At Joey LeCourier's direction, I banged the left turn off Route 98 onto a gravel road going west. We were two and a half miles north of Keene and it was 7:45 A.M. After about a hundred and fifty yards. the gravel road veered left, and Joey directed me straight ahead, onto a dusty, two-rutted dirt logging path. Three car lengths past the Ingalls Cemetery, I stopped. I double clutched and played with different combinations of the gear shift, the accelerator pedal and the stub end of the broken transfer case lever, and finally managed to coax the old Wrangler into four-wheel-drive. We jerked forward. Our advance, though a bit more sprightly without the occasional spinning of the rear wheels in the dust, was now intermittently accompanied by a raspy, broken-toothed grind that seemed to emanate from the newly-employed front differential. I glanced at Joey. He managed a shrug of the shoulders, a raised eye, and a little nobody-ever-said-it-was-going-to-be-easy smile. Oh well, I thought, we were moving and it wasn't going to be that long of a trip.

"You wanna save time, mister, we can leave the main road right up ahead there and take a shortcut; that way we won't have to head up north and then double back," offered Joey.

"This is the main road we're on, then?"

"Well, this is about as main as it gets. Right – here."

I stopped the Jeep and looked up. Dead ahead. Pitchoff, Devil's and Sentinel. Just like the ranger had said. The haze blurred their outlines, but the three peaks were easily distinguishable from the surrounding range. If Landborg had been right about the distance, then forward visibility must have been four to five miles.

Still heading about due west, we left the logging road and plowed deeper into the shadowy forest. After another fifty yards, and before the rods and cones in the retinas had made the accommodation to the dark-

45

ness, I had to jerk the wheel to the left to keep from plunging down a steep bank into a pretty busy little trout stream about eight or ten feet below grade.

"That there's Nichol's Brook, mister. Now we just head along here for a ways – see those tracks, just follow them, maybe another mile or so 'til we get to Clifford Falls. Just below the falls, which ain't that big a deal, we gotta ford over onto the other side, 'cause the spring into Clifford Brook comes from the lake we're headed for. The lake's on the north side of Clifford Brook, about a mile and a half.

"I gotcha, Joey. Hold on tight there, Donald."

There was no need to hold on just then, because the path along the brook was surprisingly smooth and we weren't moving all that fast. But little eight or nine-year-old Donald didn't seem all that happy about something, and I wanted to get him into the spirit of the occasion, which was, after all, a bunch of guys in an old Jeep, out in the woods and on an important mission, for God's sake. Now that I'd thought about it, both of them had seemed a bit withdrawn from the outset. Furtive, even. Joey had brightened up since he began calling the shots on the navigation, anyway. I chalked Donny's bad mood off to the early hour, and concentrated on the driving, the sound of the branches brushing the old canvas top of the Jeep, and the smell of a lot of pine trees on an early morning in the mountains.

It was pretty slow going. In the entire fifteen minutes that passed before Joey motioned me to stop again, I had noticed only one time that the miles-per-hour needle behind the cracked and nearly opaque glass face of the speedometer had so much as bounced off the zero peg. The last vestige of the deer path we'd been following for the last few minutes now completely disappeared. Joey pointed off to the right, and gave me a take-'er-kinda'-slow hand signal. I eased out on the clutch pedal, and pushed into the underbrush to starboard. We broke through about fifteen feet of undergrowth and dead trees to find ourselves dropping down a boat-ramp-like declivity to the level of the streambed. Donald grabbed my shoulder from behind, and pointed to the far side. There was a small level area there, fifty feet to the right and downstream, which appeared to be out destination. I nodded, and eased the Jeep into the foot-deep clear water.

The stream was only thirty feet across, but our angled route was going to more than double the length of the ford. I kept it in second gear, low range. I wanted to keep the engine revs up, just in case the tailpipe went under; it did, but there was a reassuring pop-pop-pop as we bubbled and amphib'd our way past the mid-point and started up the other side. The front end was underwater for the whole seventy-five foot crossing, and the first thing I noticed when we got to the shallows on the far side was the absence of the last-legs grinding from the front differential. Either the noise had been a function of heat, and the cold water of the stream had put it in temporary remission, or there was a leak in the hubs or the housing, and the gears were now being lubricated by a combination of old ninety-weight gear oil and some fresh Adirondack stream water. Time would tell. And I'd have to talk to May about it.

The ford and the shortcut now behind us, we found ourselves on another logging road. Joey pointed up and to the left, and we pushed on. The slight southerly breeze was dying, and some occasional beefy gusts from the west and northwest signaled the approach of the cold front. The haze had dissipated, and I could discern actual shapes in the sky for the first time in two or three days. Gray buildups of cumulo-nimbus.

Except for the abruptness of the rise in the terrain and the occasional roadwide rock outcroppings, which made the short wheelbase and high clearance of the Jeep almost indispensable, you could have made this part of the drive in a conventional vehicle. Sure, if we had some ham, we could have some ham and eggs, if we had some eggs. I couldn't help but be reminded of my drive three or four months earlier, when Elmer Linthacum and I had assaulted the slippery red mud of a nine-thousand-foot mountain in central Montana in a 1942 weapons carrier. There was no question about this Adirondack area being rough and tough country, where a wrong move could get you in big trouble. It was just that in Montana, as you took a last hit of Wild Turkey, slowly got sleepy, and froze to death, or poured the last drop of precious water from the canteen onto your compound fracture and drifted off into delirium, you were probably a little less likely to see a discarded beer can in front of your nose or a 'Jim and Nora, L.P. High 83' Krylon-sprayed on a nearby rock.

Both boys were sitting up now, watching for landmarks, it appeared. I assumed we were getting close to the lake. Then I smelled the smoke. I looked over and noticed that Joey and Donald had picked it up too, if their wrinkled noses and unfocused eyes were a correct indication. The forest around us was thinning as we climbed rapidly up toward what must have been the tree line. Then the visibility deteriorated in a low cloud of brown and dust-filled smoke. We got to the edge of what was a pretty good little brush fire about a minute and a half after we smelled the smoke. I stopped. It was a brushfire right now, but unless something was done pretty quickly, there was going to be a forest fire.

"Mister, that lake's about a hundred yards farther – right up that way. We sure could use some water." He grabbed Donald by the arm and both boys bailed out of the doorless Jeep, ripping off their shirts as they advanced on the fire line. I banged it into third and jounced on up to the lake, which was just where Joey had said it would be. I emptied the rusty water out of the old five-gallon military gas can webbed and buckled onto the right rear of the Jeep. I filled it with water from what looked like a beautiful little fishing lake, doused my shirt, and drove back on down to the boys.

There was a lot of whirling-dervish, coal-faced, hotfooted stamping and flailing for the next fifteen minutes. It took three more runs up to the lake for water, but we finally got the damned thing under control. We watched it for a while, and, satisfied that it wasn't going to start up again, wearily trudged up to the Jeep and drove back up to the blackened lake shore. It was turning into a long morning.

"Where was it you picked him up, Joey?"

"Geez, I dunno for sure, mister. It's all different now with the burning and all. But I know it wasn't this close to the shore. It was down further to the right there. See that little washed out part there, where the path has to back off from the shoreline? Donald, isn't that about it?"

Donald nodded uncertainly.

"Yeah, that's it," Joey said. "It looked like he'd just stumbled down to the lake from where that little knot 'a pine trees is, hopin' to get a drink 'a water and maybe keep on goin' is the way I had it figured." We walked over to the washout as Joey talked.

"Well, Joey, if you think this is where it was, I'll go ahead and take some tests on the water. You can see it'd be better if we were sure this is where he stopped for that drink."

"Well, this is where it was, mister, I'm sure."

I got out the test kit, took samples in the eight little jars that came with it, sealed six of them, and did the preliminary litmus response test on the other two. There was acid all right, but not all that much, and almost certainly not enough to put someone in the hospital. I'd have to wait for the more conclusive acid, concentrate and bacteriological tests from Glens Falls before I'd feel comfortable about swimming in or drinking from what looked like a pristine mountain watering hole, with no oil slicks and no detergent foam spewing up from under the dead yellow leaves and brown pine needles that floated near the shore."

"Oh, by the way, Joey," I asked casually, "did you guys know this fellow at all? The one you picked up?"

"Oh no, mister, we never even seem him before," Joey assured me.

Donald nodded uncertainly again, and chimed in, "Yeah, and we thought he was dead, for sure."

"Well, you guys did really good work. By the way, how'd you know he was a doctor, anyway?"

"Whadaya mean, mister?" said Joey, a little choked up.

"Well, that Ranger Landborg said you mentioned on the trail phone that you'd found a doctor up in the high peaks area – he said you said a doctor."

There was a pretty heavy silence for a long minute or so, and it was obvious that the kids didn't know whether to look at each other or not. They were both a little flushed.

"I guess we better tell it true, Donald," said Joey.

"Yeah, I guess maybe so," Donald sighed.

"Mister, this is where it happened, honest to God. And it was all just like Donald and me said. And we did carry him down and all. He was really heavy, and we rigged a litter outa branches and dragged him all the way down and took a long time. And honest, we was goin' to give the note and stuff to his wife or the police or somebody; but after he gave us the money and all he passed right out – and –"

"Yeah, mister," Donald volunteered, "we thought maybe he was dead, and maybe it wouldn't make any difference if we kept the money. But, like Joey said, we were still gonna give the other stuff to his wife or somebody, for sure – and, and he himself, the doctor, even told us that it wasn't all that important, before he got unconscious and all." He was a little teared up, and it was tough to conceal with his smoke-blackened face.

"Where's the stuff he gave you, Joey?"

"Well, we got a little place back down by the Ausable where we keep things once in a while."

We stopped by their tree-stump cache on the way down. They had an old square lunch box, wrapped up in a Hefty trash bag for protection against water and bugs. There was a sealed brown envelope, with some scrawled words on the outside. It was tough to read, and it looked as though it might have been tougher to write. There was an address, and then a note, written with a different ballpoint pen. He must have written the note after he'd been reasonably sure that the boys were going to deliver it. It read:

"Deliver to Dr. Molly Wager, Keene, N.Y.
518-774-7714. Trial binary deliv. System
malfunc. Lot 33 Premature join. 200 mgs.
64/hr. Weds and 200 g.g this date no
effect. Claycombe maybe worse. Blow lid.
If Beck balks, use encl. And notify S.M."

"How much money'd he give you, Joey?"

"Fifty dollars, mister. I wish we never done it."

"You did more good than you did bad. I guess you maybe ought to give the money back, and if it's okay with you, I'll keep this stuff and make sure it gets to Mrs. Wager."

They thought that that would be just fine. They had the fifty stashed at home, and they'd get it back to him soon as he was better, even if they had to walk all the way over to Keene. By the time I dropped them off in North Elba and traded the Jeep for the BMW, it had started to rain and the temperature was dropping fast. Now all they had to worry about was if their mother, May LeCourier, ever found out.

IX

From the note on the manila envelope, it appeared that Wager might have been working in the lab at the Institute, and spilled something scary on himself and maybe on someone named Claycombe as well. They had probably done it while mixing at least two ingredients, if the words "binary" and "premature join" were any indication. He'd apparently been wrong when he had written that 200 g.g. had had no effect. "g.g." might have meant gamma-globulin, and they gave you that after you'd been exposed to something. Mumps, maybe. Probably after a lot of things. Or was it before? It had to do with the body's defense system, I thought. But here Wager was, feeling fine and accepting visitors over on the Fourth floor at Memorial Hospital. So the situation had not been so emergent as he must have imagined when he scrawled the terse note to his wife on the outside of the brown envelope.

I made the right turn from North Elba onto Route 73, and headed for Lake Placid. I headed for Lake Placid because that's what I'd been planning to do up to the point when I'd read Doc Wager's note to his wife.

So maybe now a recovering Wager would prefer that he'd never even written the note. Anyway, it wasn't my job to go around intercepting suspicious communications. My job was finished when I took the eight vials of acidic water from the little lake above the brush fire. The politicians could take it from there.

The hell with it. I'd drop by the hospital and go through the motions. I'd give Wager the chance to explain just what it was he'd been doing up by that little lake, how much water he'd drunk, just how he'd gotten there and from whence he had come, and maybe he'd even be willing to tell me a little about what had happened that had convinced him to write his message to Molly Wager and to entrust it to a couple of preteens who obviously had never seen a fifty-dollar-bill before in their lives.

I pulled the BMW up to a parking meter a block from the hospital, dropped a quarter in for a half hour, started walking in the light rain, and stopped. The hell with it again. I turned around and walked back toward the police station, went on by and went up the steps into the Carnegie Library.

To my amazement – in this seemingly remote backwater village, where I hadn't even gotten a cell phone signal for the last day and a half – they had a couple of internet stations. I went back out, and made the call to Miss Quantrell from the same old pay phone, across from the Alpine Motel, a half-block from the hospital. I gave my ident code for the day to a voice I hadn't heard before. She gave the correct reply indicator, and told me that Miss Q. was out for an hour, but that she could help. She made the switch to the scrambler and told me to proceed.

"Miss Q.," I began. "It's reasonably important that I get a little information on the following four subjects, info to be avail on the encoded company "public" site, a.s.a.p. Subjects are: one, Beckmann, spelled B-e-c-k-m-a-n-n, Institute of Biology, or something like that, in Keene, New York. Two, somebody named Claycombe who might work for the Institute. Three a doctor named Wager, Robert, who also works there. Four, something called the Mountaineers' Club, which has a yearly campout at a private forest preserve called Devil's Mountain Camp near same town of Keene. On fourth, most interested membership, in particular politicians, military and medical. Love, O'Toole. Sorry about the short notice, and don't tell Gregory."

The nice voice on the other end told me she'd get on it even if Miss Q. didn't come back. She said I could call her Seventy Four, if I liked. I thanked her and headed over to the hospital. I noticed that the Alpine Motel was still standing, but that the A-frame for the swings and the slide into the pool had buckled under the weight of the kids from Lowville. An elderly man with an acetylene torch and a red face was leaning on the crippled framework, scratching his head and trying to come up with a game plan to make what was left get the Alpine through to the end of the weekend.

* * * * * * * * * *

They say that hot water freezes faster than cold water. I've never checked it out. Maybe it's because I don't want to be disappointed. It's the same kind of phenomenon when you're recovering from a cold, an injury, and operation or even an accidental whiff, touch or swallow of some bad little microbe cooked up by a bunch of recombinating weirdoes trying to make something patentable in a backwoods genetics shop financed by the same government that pays your salary. I have checked this out. Anyway, when you're really on the mend, there's a rush that seems to carry you right on by the back-to-normal level and swoop you on up to a palpable physical high. There's something about the momentum, once the process gets underway, that gets the bigger job done faster, the further distance covered sooner. Same as the ice. And when two people are involved in the rebound, the same phenomenon can carry them quickly past the platonic. There had to be some reason for us to have made love on that third night. I'm not absolutely sure it was the third night. It was the night that the red emergency light shone and we were left alone for a few hours.

We weren't moving. It was cold. There were no sounds from outside: no shifts of gears, creaks, muffled conversations or electric whirrs. There wasn't even the trace of diesel exhaust smell that had previously disguised what was getting to be a pretty fetid atmosphere in Molly's and my steel bedroom. There was no ventilation from the outside, and the filtering system hadn't quite made it. We were recovering all right, but we'd been sick; and you could tell.

She'd untied me. I must have been out of it when she did. I could breathe, all my appendages had feeling, and somehow she'd arranged for what felt like a clean pillow. The light was in the rear, mounted over a four-foot-high steel hatch, and showing dimly through the red plastic with the steel cage around it. Our chamber was seven feet wide, maybe ten long. Steel sink, water bottle and cup dispenser at port quarter. Closet, possibly commode across to starboard. The kind of place you'd quarantine a couple of people whose comfort wasn't all that important, and who were infected with something you'd prefer didn't get around; or anywhere near you.

Moving my eyelids and eyes had been okay. Now, with the commode in mind, if it was a commode, I decided to risk the whole head and neck area. Could be worse. Roll slowly over to right side, probably overdoing the caution. Sit up. Maybe a big mistake. No. Just feel very weak and small and lightweight. Dizziness passes and I see Molly's form on the other bunk. Asleep. Okay, feet on floor, and very existential shift of weight to soles of feet, coordinated with sore muscle tissue forcing shoulders forward, then arching back and banging head on steel ceiling at about an inch-and-a-half-per-second vertical speed. Whole process not too bad, but calling for unaccustomed imposition on the amino acids, proteins, ribosomes, chloroplasts, mitochondria, cellular walls, connecting tissue and other floating components in the muscle and blood cells in the lumbar area. The little guys, let's face it. I learned the fancy words later.

I made it. It was a chemical commode, and it and I worked. I even regained enough of my presence of mind and my dignity to resent the lukewarmness of the water from the upside-down five-gallon bottle mounted on the bulkhead. There was a little stack of paper washroom towels next to the inoperative single faucet on the steel sink.

Back to the bed. I reversed the stand-up process, and made it back to the pillow with only one minor malfunction, that being the outrage to the atrophied stomach muscles when I absent-mindedly finished off the recline with a nonchalant lift of the legs from the floor over the railing and back onto the bunk. When that commotion died down, I lay quietly in the bunk, savoring the use of my restored senses. I felt the cold. I could hear Molly's quiet breathing, and I could see forms in the dim red light.

"I think we're alone." She said it in a normal tone of voice. After the initial shock to the brain stem and spinal cord, it seemed appropriate.

"Yeah, I think you may be right," I answered. Well, tried to answer. What actually came out sounded something like someone scratching the dust off a live phonograph needle with a rough thumb. She laughed a little

"You might wanna try that again."

I did and it finally got a little better. We both sat up and looked at each other across the two-foot space between the bunks.

"How do you feel?" she asked.

"A little better. You?"

"Yeah, I was. But now something's starting up again, I think. Different. I'm really weak." She shook her head as she spoke, and cupped her hands over her ears, like headphones. I got the picture. If they were taping or listening, there was no sense in letting them know our strengths.

"Water?" I asked her.

"Yeah. That would feel good. I'd love to just have my face washed and cool." She wheezed.

"I'll give it a try." I made it back over to the sink, making it sound harder than it really was for me. I wet some paper towels, and filled a cup. She drank some, offered it to me, I signaled no, and she finished. I mopped her brow, face and neck with the towels, and used a dry one to finish it off.

"That feels a lot better. Thanks." She said that, and she reached over and grasped my right wrist. She took my hand right over and down to her goddamned belt line. She guided my hand under her belt and waistband. They were not tight. She was lying down and neither of us had eaten for however long it had been. I felt the manila envelope and the papers. And something else. A bottle. I know, I know, but the bottle wasn't all that big. And it was really there, so what can I say. She let me go, and I pulled away, taking the bottle with me. I sat back on my bunk, and she sat up, facing me. She pointed at the papers, and shrugged; elaborately. I shook my head. I pointed to the bottle, and she acknowledged that she'd had something to do with that, and that I myself had had four, maybe five-times-five fingers worth of the contents, administered by her. I remembered the first ones, but didn't hold it against her. I mouthed 'antibiotics?' and she confirmed, with a mezza-metz move of the right hand.

And no one said anything outside, no one slid open the partition behind the almost one-way glass, the red emergency light seemed to be ever so slowly dimming, and one thing led to another. And Molly and I made love, because nothing else seemed to make any sense. It did. We were very quiet about it, and afterwards, partly because of the cold, we ended up going to sleep in each other's arms for a time.

X

Considering the avalanche of registration and billing forms that Lake Placid Memorial appeared to bury anyone with if and when he wanted or had to get into the place, it was amazing to me how little anyone know about that particular person once he had taken it upon himself to get the hell out. If, when, how or why, it was all a mystery. Having had occasion in the past to witness first-hand a modern-day hospital bureaucracy in "action", and the shuffling of puzzled, mortally-ill patients among a host of thumb-nail-informed, musical-chair physicians, to accommodate their tax shelter seminars, ski trips, real-estate closings and rebelling wives, I suppose that I shouldn't have been surprised by that anomaly. After a quarter-of-an-hour delay at Main Floor Admitting, I finally spoke with a capable-looking RN at the fourth floor-New Wing reception desk, who had herself never actually met or seen Doctor Wager.

"Mr. O'Toole, I'm trying to explain. I came on at noon. You see, my weekend was Thursday and Friday. And Doctor Rashid was only on call until last night at midnight, even though he stopped by early this morning. Doctor Wells can answer any questions you have, I'm sure. I'll se if I can do something about getting Doctor Wager's file back up from Records." I thanked her and she smiled with a well-every-so-often-it-doesn't-hurt-to-bend-over-backwards benignity.

Doctor Wells was a golly-gee-helluva-young-guy type who was sure to end up in hospital admin. Some day. He hadn't had the pleasure of meeting Doctor Wager himself, but he could read the chart.

"Let's see. Admitted on the twenty-second, Thursday, treated for infection... unspecified bacterial ... culture confirmed Albany, Friday the twenty-third, at six P.M.... anaerobic component ... Keflin and metranidazole controlled ... Steady improvement, released eleven-fifteen this morning at own request, further observation at infirmary, Beckmann Institute. Patient request and also written request of Doctor Peter Claycombe at the Institute ... which I believe we have here. Yes. "'Dear Doctor Rashid or Doctor on call. We have spoken with Doctor Wager, and he and I are in agreement ... simple and noncontagious agent, responsive to antibiotics ...' and, let's see, bup-bup-bup, oh yes, 'his work at this moment at critical juncture, requiring his presence, if at all possible. We will furnish you with updates on Doctor Wager's condition, if we see any change. Thank you', et cetera, et cetera, et cetera. So that's about it. Oh Sandy, excuse me."

"Yes, Doctor? Wait there, Mr. Bunton." She was a young nurse's aide, probably Filipino, pushing an i.v. rack along behind a slow-moving octogenarian, who appeared to have had a lower body replacement. He took fatalistically the interruption in his daily constitutional up and down the hall of New Wing, and balanced himself on his walker while she addressed Wells.

"Sandy, you came on at eight, right?"

"Yes, Doctor Wells. Well, actually, I was a little late. About fifteen minutes, and I'm really sorry – "

"No, no, Sandy, We'll talk about that later. Were you here when Doctor Wager, room four-twelve, was processed out?"

"Four-twelve – oh yeah. Yeah, about eleven or so. Doctor Salazar okayed it, I think. Two gentlemen helped him. They were very nice. And cooperative. They didn't want to upset our routine, you know. But they were in sort of a hurry, I'd say. Doctor Salazar, he left at twelve, and he'd probably know more. He'll probably be home after four or five – he golfs at the Lake Placid Club on Saturdays."

"How did Doctor Wager appear, Sandy?" I asked.

"He seemed fine, sir. Didn't even want a wheel chair, he said. And he'd been in intensive care, since a little after three. Twenty-four hours before. Hard to believe."

So it was. But that someone might want the hell out of this loony bin wasn't hard to believe at all. And Doctor Rashid, who had seemed to be the one person in the whole hospital who had his head on straight, had himself told me that Wager was improving fast. I think what bothered me more than the sinister aspects – kidnapping, forcible abduction, surreptitious injection with euphoric drugs, or whatever, -- was the never-ending runaround. And if it bothered me, think how it would affect a patient. Once you tell your story fourteen or fifteen times to what you thought might have been reasonably sympathetic altruists and there's been no payoff, you've got to start losing even more of any faith you ever had in the Hippocratic oath and the A.M.A.

It was time to move on. Outside, the rain had stopped. The cold front had passed, and there was a steady, fifteen-knot wind out of the northwest. I walked back to the library and got lucky with an Internet station. The librarian told me I had good timing.

"Another half-hour and you'd be waiting in line; when the early shift gets off at the high school they all head right over here and start surfing and checking email. Only thing we don't allow is instant messaging; we've got it disabled, at least that's what the tech guy tells me."

"You'll probably have wireless here before long."

"Yeah, I suppose you're right. Laptop city. But I'll be outa here before that happens, the way the board takes their time on anything having to do with spending money."

I got into the company-shared disk with the IDs and passwords I needed. It was soon apparent to me that old Seventy-Four had gone to the Miss Quantrell School of Concise Communication In A Limited Time Frame. Her abbreviations and emphases were carefully selected, and, as the library inkjet printer churned away next to me, I could even discern in her writing a close-reined sense of the sardonic.

The Mountaineers' Club had been founded in 1868 by a group of ex-war-correspondents who had had some time on their hands and hadn't had the NFL to fall back on. Its first president was a guy named Richard Hardin, who had covered Gettysburg for the New York Herald-Tribune. His tenure was cut short by a fall from the Hudson River Palisades during a thunderstorm. There was no need to limit the membership at the time, because nobody was crying to get in. They were newspaper people, their drinking cronies, a few politicians and a couple of naturalists, the common denominator being a desire for roughing it in the mountains for two weeks every August.

Without going into the detail provided by Seventy-Four, suffice it to say that things had changed. Building, maintaining and supplying the club's headquarters in Manhattan and in the bare-bones club facility in the Catskills had taken their toll; by the time taxes became more onerous, in the twentieth century, the war correspondents, Broadway beer drinkers, civil service hangers-on and theater people had become a minority in an organization run of, by and for the wealthy, the powerful and the con-nected.

Seventy-Four determined that the latest count had it that at least one director or officer from ninety-one of the top one hundred industrial corpo-rations in the United States was a member of the club, now headquartered on East 53rd Street in midtown Manhattan. That ratio rapidly declined as you continued down the list, i.e., in the second hundred corporations, only sixty-eight directors and officers were also Mountaineers.

There were some high fliers who shuttled back and forth between government and business; guys who took a sabbatical from the private sector every three or four years and worked for the government for six months or so as Assistant Secretary over at Interior, or maybe in Navy Procurement, or at least on a blue-ribbon panel of some kind. It was always a dollar-a-year and there was the blind trust requirement, but it was also some pretty good night life in Georgetown, an ego-boosting if short-lived bonhomie with people who could be seen on the network news, a little window-dressing for the bank or the law firm or the natural resources company back in St. Louis, and a continuing guest membership and guaranteed tee-off time at Burning Tree.

Most of the Mountaineers, though, were businessmen; who worked hard and did well, but who didn't get enough respect. Hell, these days everyone and his brother had a two-million-dollar house and a condo at Sanibel or Hilton Head or Naples, and it seemed that no matter how much money you had, it would always be tough to get into Le Cirque.

But here was a chance for the guys to get together out in the woods and to bolster their self-respect. Exchange a few Polish jokes, piss on the trees, actually get some use out of the new lightweight Nike hiking boots, renew the stock of friends, so depleted by death and forsaking, and maybe even reacquaint oneself with what the hell it felt like to have a lump in the throat once in a while.

At the very least, membership was a confirmation of The Belief – that success and status always meant something – that was shared by all these chairmen and presidents and CEOs of all these banks, railroads, utilities, universities, networks, cable-TV giants, realty trust, churches, oil companies, money funds, computer giants, publishers, developers and fast-food empires; all these chief justices, ex-senators, former Secretaries of Defense, former consultants, lobbyists and retired heads of the Federal Reserve Board, retired five-star Generals, diplomats and one-time you-name-its, and including a few high-placed investment-advising city-rescuing economists who could for four or five days just do the obligatory morning re-minding recital of "when bonds come down, puts go up", and stop worrying for a while about how to bamboozle some fixed income folk in Far Rockaway or Denver or the State of Washington into buying some new bonds that would temporarily prop up a bankrupt nuclear facility or transit system or sub prime mortgage originator whose financial straits were not yet the knowledge of anyone but a few insiders.

As a concession to tradition, the fifteen-man membership committee had chosen not to blackball one aging network anchorman who never really got tough with anybody, a former leading man on The Guiding Light who played to a four handicap and bought his suits on Saville Row, and even a Time-cover consumer advocate who had a reliable if piercing B-flat above middle C that was always needed and always used in every finale of every theatricale at Devil's Mountain. But membership was by invitation only, and there was a long waiting list. There were no women, and there would be none. The initiation fee and dues were a pittance – about a tenth of the cost of joining the right country club in Westchester, Orange or Marin Counties. There was a twenty thousand dollar one-time fee, then three hundred a month year-round, plus five thousand for a long weekend at Devil's Mountain Camp, everything paid except your seat on the company G5 or the Netjet – and for a few, maybe a low-ball Beech Baron – and the limo to and from Saranac Lake or Lake Placid. Any unscheduled, off-campus, intramural activity at the Holiday Inn Bar or the Lake Placid Club was your own business.

There had been fifteen hundred and twelve members way back in September of 1994, the most recent count Seventy-Four had been able to find, and this included twenty-one who could be classified as unpredictable. There were six Japanese, four of whom were with Mitsubishi, five Germans, including two former Krupps directors, a billionaire bottler from Manila, a Russian prince who had just turned ninety-one, four French Jews, and four blacks: two into Nigerian oil, one a hero from the First Gulf War, and the last, an ex-soft-shoe man who warmed up the crowd before the big show with what Seventy-Four said was a pretty funny routine, even if it had probably been stolen from Arsenio Hall.

Once you got accepted into the Club, the next problem was getting into one of the twenty-four individual camp areas at Devil's Mountain. These were of different sizes, and had names like Bald Eagle, Pontiac, Christian Brothers, Owl's Roost, Haven and Oak Leaf. Each camp had additional dues and assessments, depending on the ambition of the camp's capital fund managers; some had installed creature comforts that would probably have had old Richard Hardin turning over in his grave in Old Tappan.

The individual camps seemed to attract members of like mind. The Owls had their ex-state departments and academics, the Brickhouse Gang was known by everyone to be crawling with active CIA guys, the arts and crafts boys generally went to Silver Creek or the Bohemians, and the quizzical-looking white-faced Nobel types and think-tank denizens usually joined Birchbark or Norway.

Shangrila was probably the most prestigious of all. It was very selective, very conservative and very business. The furthest out they had gone was to admit a guy who had spent a year and a half at the Brookings Institute, and who now did soft-sell public relations for big oil on public TV. He was an exception and some on the committee were still suspicious of him. The rest were guys who did big things quietly. Unsung powerbrokers, who-me king makers, shadowy campaign funders. All hush-hush guys who insured loyalty and pulled strings with no dirty hands involved. Philanthropists. Guys with no labels on their shirts who didn't carry money.

In point of fact, the Beckmanns, father and son, might have been considered unlikely candidates for the Mountaineers, and especially Shangrila. But there they were. Old Steve had always had a knack for being in places people hadn't expected him to be. That's why the holding corporation, The Beckmann Group, Ltd, at last count had had assets rumored to be worth over thirty billion dollars.

XI

Steve Beckmann, Sr. had started out up to his elbows in garbage in North Jersey in 1945. He had kept it quiet, clean, convenient and cheap for his clients in Ridgewood, who could have afforded more. He'd gotten bigger fast. By 1948, his shiny, green dump trucks with the "Let's Keep Jersey Beautiful" slogan on the doors could be seen all over Bergen, Essex and Rockland counties, and Beckmann and Sons was the largest private garbage hauler in the state.

But the trouble with garbage was that you had to get rid of the damn stuff. And barge fees, tugboat charters, dockage and all the union wages and benefits that went with them were not in Steve, Senior's game plan. He followed the time-tested maxim, "if you don't like the way something works, buy it." Sludge disposal and landfill operations followed naturally, because you had to keep the new fleet of tugs and barges moving twenty-four seven. Most cities allowed the sludge hauler to estimate the amount hauled, probably assuming that the public would lose less that way than if another bureaucracy was created to oversee the sludge measurers.

Fifty years later, every expansion: from Beckmann and Sons to the present umbrella corporation, The Beckmann Group, Ltd, could be seen to have been a logical extension of vertical control, directed by a careful and frugal individual. Why pay some loudmouth, overpriced roughneck from Tulsa to drill for your oil if you could borrow someone else's money, buy a rig yourself, and lease it and others like it to someone else if there ever happened to be a time when they weren't busy? And why pay retail to Baroid for cement and drilling mud out of Denver when you could mine and bag the same stuff yourself for half the cost out of Clarksburg, West Virginia?

When it came to drill bits and tools from Hughes or Halliburton, why hell, buy Westmont Tools and Drilling Corp. for thirty cents on the dollar and sell them to yourself.

Before 1952, Beckmann and Sons was restoring piers on the Hudson River and disposing of poisonous chemicals in upstate New York. By 1980, it was recycling and selling used oil it had been paid to collect, and storing all the petroleum products the sixteen company-owned supertankers could ferry from the Persian Gulf at the two-hundred-acre Beckmann Oil tank farm in Hoboken. From seismograph trucks in Lagos in '90, to contract offshore drilling on the Louisiana Gulf coast in 1994, it was only natural that Beckmann and Sons would be laying soccer fields and pipelines and yes, even hauling garbage, in Riyadh in 1998.

The Old Man had been smart enough to stay out of nuclear. Too political. Just like coal slurry pipelines. You'd have to ask for, or at least listen to, the opinions of too many people, including environmentalists. But he was always willing to buy or lease your mineral rights. Well, he was if he got his terms, that is. You got your best deal if your minerals were not too deeply buried under the soil of some firmly ensconced, American-supported oligarchy where the buyer wouldn't have to worry about legitimate elections every four years or so. He was leery of oil shale, though he would pay three dollars an acre if he could get a ninety-nine-year lease and a maximum two-percent override for the cagey farmer from Alberta or British Columbia who thought he'd pulled the wool over the funny-lookin' eyes on the old dude from back East.

Now he was Chairman of the Board of the sixteen Beckmann corporate entities, and he was personally worth substantially more than six billion, as close as Seventy-Four could figure it. He was also remote, sentimental, and tearfully patriotic to a capitalistic, freeze-frame, 1965 America, i.e., before all that hanky-panky protesting in the later year of that decade. He liked his Jaguar XK120 roadster, and he spent a lot of time collecting and listening to records of old radio shows and wishing that there had been more than the one son. He lived for eight months of the year at the original Sears cottage on the north end of Devil's Mountain Lake. He didn't really need the stroking he got at Shangrila, but he hadn't missed speedboating across the lake in the mahogany Chris-Craft to the September Mountaineers' retreat for twenty-five years. Not even in 1985, the year his wife of thirty-five years had passed on at the age of fifty four.

Steve Beckmann, Junior, was now the CEO of The Beckmann Group, Ltd. He was a ruddy, beefy, back-slapping boozer, who had small eyes and golfed in the eighties, according to Seventy-Four. Something had changed under his aegis. Something about the soul of the business. Now, every meeting had a business potential, every man a price and every signed document a guaranteed hundred-percent profit for the Beckmann Group. Instead of staying out of politics, he jumped in feet first, and backed any and all leading candidates. If there were no obvious front-runner, he tended toward the conservative.

Additions to the Group since his taking over included the Eagle Shipyard in Norfolk, which built destroyers and patrol hydrofoil missile boats; TAC Electronics in Pascagoula, surface-to-air Repulse missiles; and ASW, Ltd. of Marseilles, which manufactured sonar and fire-control radar for any country that could come up with the cold cash. He had also fostered large Beckmann investment in banks and insurance, and organized a Beckmann-directed network of investment advisers and underwriters, necessary to lure the public whenever a particular financing situation might require some actual risk taking.

The Beckmann Foundation and the Beckmann Institute of Molecular Biology had been established in 1991, when the Old Man had still been in charge. Another natural evolution. The company's experience with oil tankers had shown them that there was money to made – and lost – in oil spills; and in cleaning them up. Research had already begun elsewhere on oil-eating bacteria, but Beckmann was confident that he could catch up, given an infusion of enough money. Seventy-Four also pointed out that the creation of the Foundation had followed shortly on the heels of a spate of bad publicity involving a Beckmann-owned and Steve, Junior-operated subsidiary, which had dumped a lot of oil and bad chemicals in the wrong place over a period of fifteen years. The companies and government entities that had paid big money to the Beckmann-owned New England Disposal, Inc., for a job badly done, were being sued by neighbors of the new Love Canal for big money. The defendants' move to implead the parent company threatened to involve the Beckmann Group in a never-ending financial debacle redolent of that which forced Johns-Manville to see Chapter Eleven protection in the bankruptcy court in '83, when the Supreme Court of the United States finally allowed as how there just might be a link between asbestos and the asbestosis that afflicted so many of J-M's asbestos workers. The Beckmann Institute, it was hoped, might offset some of that uncharacteristic notoriety.

It was also about the same time that Steve, Junior was reborn into the Mountain Friends' Church of Jesus in Tupper Lake. I don't really know if he was reborn. According to Seventy-Four, he joined the MFCJCTL in 1991. I made the inference. It figures, though. When the money gets beyond a certain point, as when the heat is on from the law, the only place left to turn sometimes is to religion. Like Charles Colson, or even Bob Dylan for a while. Of course nowadays it's just two or three weeks in rehab and a good press agent. And Seventy Four pointed out that she hadn't had time to delve into the possible tax-avoidance ramifications that might have been involved in Junior's return to Jesus.

There were twenty-three PhD's and medical experts employed at the Institute, with a support staff of over one hundred medical technicians, lab technicians, pathologists, chemists, animal handlers, service and security personnel. There had been some progress on changing the DNA of a plant bacterium so it would no longer produce condensation nuclei leading to frost damage, but there had not yet been a satisfactory test in the field. Reliance had been placed on something called the foreign-agent-mutant technique, which was a little too happy-go-lucky for even the FDA, which was then pushing for precise DNA snipping. In spite of the lack of technical breakthroughs, though, activity and spending were at an all-time high, and the Institute, which might have had a philanthropic beginning, was now showing a small profit, particularly because of certain undescribed and unspecified government contracts which paid off for research alone, whether or not there was any practical result.

Seventy Four had learned that the Institute was highly respected for its ongoing research into the sub-units of chromosomes, called nucleosome core particles, and for work on the structure of macromolecular assemblies, including viruses. There was no specific use for this work, but the knowledge of structure was apparently very important for continued research.

It was a very quiet Foundation that ran the Institute. There were no scholarships, no sponsoring on public television, no grants, and no modern New York City headquarters building. But Beckmann had made sure that the Institute and the Foundation were well-endowed, and that the efforts of the Institute continued to be dedicated to deep research and not to high profit; unless, of course, the two might sometimes coincide.

Finally, the only current contract involving the Institute with the Department of Defense was for "A Feasibility Study on the Likelihood of Natural Mycotoxin Occurrence in LaoShi Province in Cambodia." It was for $750,000, and Seventy Four thought it relatively insignificant.

The information on Wager, Robert R., whose illness had necessitated the extra six or seven hundred miles on my aging BMW, was sketchy. Born 1966, Calgary, Alberta; graduated Marquette, Biology, 1988; graduated University of Toronto Medical School 1992; continued at University of Toronto Department of Medical Genetics, specializing in DNA assembly, mammalian gene cloning, molecular immunogenics and membrane molecular biology. Married Molly Chisholm, M.D., graduate of University of California Medical School, Berkeley, 1993, who had apparently attended a U. of T. summer symposium chaired by young Wager, and presented a preview of a then soon-to-be-published report on research she had been conducting for Genentech in California. The subject of her paper had been "Excisionase And the Question of the Heteroduplex." The paper and Molly must have been to Wager's liking. They were married in September of '95, and Molly was signed on at the University of Toronto. The only other information Seventy Four had gotten was that Wager had left the University to go to work for the Beckmann Institute in April of 1996. Molly Wager followed two months later, and was engaged in private practice in Keene.

There was nothing particularly suspicious about all this. The move would have offered clean mountain air, reasonable housing, wood to burn and no suspension in Wager's research. And probably a good deal more money. So, except for the scary twenty-four hours in Intensive Care, everything seemed to have turned out just fine for Wager. Almost. He'd probably recover nicely at the Institute infirmary, and be able to go back to his nice life; liking his work, putting a little aside, and giving something back to the world. But Molly wouldn't be there. They'd been living apart for six months, and she had recently filed for divorce, according to Seventy Four.

I printed a few pages I hadn't read, signed off the company website and cleared the history on the browser. Seventy Four had done a yeoman's job, and someday I was going to find out why it was that yeomen had gotten such a good reputation. I stuffed the printed stuff into my pocket and walked out into the clear Adirondack air.

* * * * * * * * *

The new crew was in a hurry to get it all over with. The driver stopped and started with a sense of urgency, and kept the pedal to the metal in between. Instead of a safe and sane, expertly-piloted float over a straight and smooth Interstate that might have let a guy grab a diesel-induced snooze every so often, this one drove the way the Greyhound boys probably do after they drop the last passenger and deadhead it back to the barn, day-dreaming of ten-per-cent givebacks, disgruntled wives, and little ways to break the tedium and at the same time kick up the owners' weekly maintenance tab. And the man at the aperture was a real slam-banger on the sliding door. Open 'er up, put on the light, check 'em out, put out the light, and slam 'er home. Every ten minutes. I counted to six-hundred-Mississippi to check him out. It made it easier to measure time. Six slam-bangs equaled an hour. Also, the previous guy had invariably had the light on before he opened the door, and had always slid the door closed before dousing the light. I hoped

66

that the little things might add up.

And I knew it wasn't just the same guys in a different mood. Molly knew it, too. The red light had been put out when they started up the rig, about three hours after my epic journey from bunk to chemical commode in the after part of our chamber; but we were able to exchange a few, whispered communications, holding onto the bunk railings for support, as the trailer bumped, swayed and pitched like the back end of a double-articulated city fire truck negotiating a long downhill series of five-percent grade S-turns.

After her low-hurdling retreat from the shattered front windows at the farmhouse, Molly had grabbed the bottle from the dispensary cabinet in her office, filled it with a fistful of ampicillin and twenty or thirty Keflex five-hundred milligrammers and stuffed it all into her pants with the papers and the envelope. By then, the Uzi man had been spraying the room, and the guy in the white suit had chopped her behind the ear and dragged her back out of her office and into the living room. She had been feeling like taking a long nap anyway. Neither of us knew, but she'd been about twenty-four hours ahead of me all along. She'd diagnosed herself as well as she could, and she knew that the antibiotics, in combination, might have helped her husband. She thought that my twenty-four hours of delirium might have been a bit worse than hers.

After a while, I guess I knew what was pushing these guys. It was fear. The reason we'd been left alone for a few hours was that the first bunch had gotten sick. And, if they had had time, and some fortuitously located supplies of tetracycline, they probably would have sworn that they'd taken every precaution. It would have happened when they took off the white suits. Instead of the airlock, the incinerator, the chemical shower, the fluorescent chamber and the nice, soft new blues back at the Institute, they'd probably had to make a fast, makeshift change, somewhere on the two-lane highway between Keene and the ferry ride across Lake Champlain.

We did our best to keep up the pretense of weakness. It made for a rougher ride. You had to let yourself be thrown around a bit whenever the sliding door was open. After a while, I began to believe that it probably didn't make any difference to this guy whether we were getting better or not. He was going by the numbers, but I guessed that nothing we did could nave made him enter our chamber. Well, he'd been fairly predictable, but you never know. We kept up the act. There were no blithe trips to the john, or to the water jar, or to each other.

We got to the ship about two and a half hours after the new crew took over. If my theory about the one-way glass was correct, it was still dark outside. Neither of us had a watch, and I'll never know for sure how long that part of the trip took, but I think two and a half is close. There's something about movement in a vehicle, any vehicle – feeling the road, attending to the demands being made on the machine by a ham-footed chauffeur, and relating these inputs to an instinctual need for perspective when the other guys have got you strung up by the heels – that ended up giving me what I think was a pretty good mind's eye view of our trip from my swaying vantage point in the dark. And the ship part was easy.

It was the smell of the sea that came first. One of these days they may figure it all out, but so far they haven't to my knowledge been able to build anything so airtight that you can't smell jet exhaust, diesel fumes, or the full-of-life-and-death odor of the ocean. Pine trees, maybe; but not the sea. And after that it was the dampness, and the bone-deep chill that went with it.

It wasn't a big town. There had been only four or five minutes of street, block, corner and stop sign moves before we got to the pier. There were a couple of abortive efforts to get the rig turned around and tracking back alongside the vessel. The driver wasn't used to the semi; he knew the theory, but he didn't have the feel of when to turn opposite to the trailer and when to go along with it.

He finally got us into position. There were the footsteps of a man over our heads, the distant whirring of what I was sure was an electric winch on the ship, a metal clank, then two more, as he hooked up to three spaced at-tach points, then some more whirring as the winch man took up the slack. Then the slam-bang aperture man made his final move of the night; but this time he trained the light on Molly's face and gave three flashes right at her closed eyes. She opened them slightly, and he flashed three more times. She nodded, he shut out the light and slammed the door. I'll never know if he was telling her to hold on, or see you later, or what. I went for the holding on.

As our capsule – I now had it pictured as a bathysphere – broke free of the trailer bed, the imprecision of the winch mast placement over our center of gravity resulted in a sudden swing inboard. We crashed heavily into the side of the steel vessel with a resounding bong. I was deafened for thirty or forty seconds, and Molly was thrown from her bunk to the deck. She slid aft. One of the attach points had disconnected. After that, they got serious, and there were no more mishaps. They winched us up and over the gunwales, inboard for four or five feet – I thought – and put us on hold. I heard another electric motor, and imagined the hatch doors yawn-ing open below us. That is exactly what was happening, as it turned out, and I went to school on it. They had trouble fitting us through the hatch, and, although my estimates were even more suspect with the addition of the third dimension, I guessed that the hold was not a great deal larger than the capsule. And it wasn't very deep. It was all relative, of course, but I knew we weren't on the attack carrier flagship of the Sixth Fleet. The vessel moved too abruptly in the waters alongside the pier to be anything bigger than four or five hundred tons, I thought.

Then I'll be damned if they didn't pressurize the hold. For the rest of my life I'm going to be more aware of the five senses, especially when I'm down to two or three, and even if it's only temporary. The others take up the slack; and if they can do it then, then they ought to be able to do it anytime. This time it was the ears that told the story, of course.

It was still dark when they opened the door to the capsule and let in the beautiful, clean, salty, air that the topside compressor had pumped down into the hold. Then a new guy in another white suit found the right key, and switched on the white lights, which I hadn't been able to see before. They were recessed into the overhead, baffled, and very, very bright. He looked at us for a moment, shaking his head.

I didn't know how long we'd been in there. But the combination of sickness, antibiotics, a shrinking stomach and the anticipated arrival of the effects of a secondary infection had made me forget about food. But when I smelled the French fries and the burgers and saw the new spaceman deposit the cheerfully printed cardboard box from Wendy's on the little shelf by the sink, well, that was a different matter. I was ravenous, and prepared to be very cooperative. He reached back through the hatch and muscled in a fresh water bottle. He made the switch with the old one, moved the Wendy's tray to the foot of Molly's bunk, turned, and hastened back out of the four-foot-high opening.

The second man was about six inches shorter than the first, and his plastic gloves were green and semi-transparent. He carried a zippered musette-type bag over his shoulder. He opened it, extracted a syringe, inserted a large needle, and advanced on Molly. She turned away, toward the far bulkhead. He held her firmly by the shoulder, and when she looked back at him, he assayed a calming, no-harm-intended gesture with his empty gloved hand, and showed her the empty syringe with the other. She relaxed. He drew a couple hundred ccs of dark, red blood from her left arm, and cleaned the puncture with a wad of alcohol-soaked cotton. He even came up with the little round flesh-colored Band-Aid, even though it looked to me as though he missed the hole with it. He stowed the sample in his bag, joined a new needle and syringe, and turned to me. I groaned, turned toward him, onto my right side, bravely attempted to rise up in defiance, and finally gave up the show of force, overcome by what I hoped was a pretty authentic and infectious-sounding rack of a cough. I fell heavily back to my bunk, with spittle running out of either side of my mouth. I don't know which it was – the cough, the spittle, or maybe even the smell of the damn place that had finally worked its way through the charcoal filtering system for his spacesuit – but something made him stop and think it all over. He retreated back through the hatch. The lights went out.

It took a superhuman patience to wait for Molly to feed me in my weakened condition. The French fries were lukewarm and soggy, the Wendy's all-purpose hamburger sauce had been out of the refrigerator about and hour and a half too long, and the burger patty wasn't as much better than Burger King's as it once was. But it might have been the best meal I ever had, groaning stomach and no Beck's notwithstanding.

XII

"M. Wager, M.D.", was listed in the county phone book. The number was the same as the one on the manila envelope I'd gotten from the two boys. But all I could get was one of those particularly loud and insistent busy signals that begin immediately after you've dialed the last digit.

The address in the listing was simply "Gillmore Hill Rd., West of Keene." I headed out of town, east on 73. I didn't particularly like the sound of what I'd learned from Seventy-Four. But the fact was that Beckmann, Wager and Claycombe were doing what they were good at in a place that gave them the opportunities they needed. And they were making money, doing what makes the world go round. The only fly in the ointment was Wager's note to his wife, Molly. Why had he been so afraid? The only way to clear it up was to visit Molly Wager; at least, I'd have to try, before busting down the air locked (hopefully) doors of the Beckmann Institute and calling in the Army.

With "No Service" still blinking away on my cell, I stopped at a pay-phone in North Elba. Another busy signal. The cashier at the Cascade told me that Gillmore Hill Road was two, maybe three miles this side of Keene, and that Doctor Wager's place was down towards the end, Gillmore Hill bein' a dead end, and I should just look for the mailbox. On the left, she thought.

She'd been just about right. Gillmore Hill Road was an amply graveled, two-lane county road that ran east-northeast from Route 73, beginning about two and a half miles west of Keene. The six or seven houses on the road were spaced evenly apart, giving each family a good deal of privacy, at least for the time being. "Wager" was neatly lettered on a large red mailbox at the end of the road.

The dump truck must have had an extra half-load at the end of the gravel job. There was a twelve or fourteen-inch drop from the grade of the gravel down to that of the dirt driveway leading north into the woods behind the mailbox. I eased the BMW over the hump, hoping to stretch the useful life of the six-hundred dollar exhaust system for a little while longer, and drove slowly up the two leaf-strewn ruts that apparently served the Wager house for a driveway. About fifty feet up the road, a loosely strung log chain with a hanging "No Trespassing, Please" sign blocked my way. I stopped and got out of the car. There was a large Master padlock connecting the ends of the chain at the center of the road, and a hand-lettered not was scotch-taped to the bottom of the sign. It read:

"Sat. 12 noon. Mr. K: Sorry, out of town today. Can see you Monday, if you like. Use all of the erythromycin. Don't stop just because you feel better. Best, M.W."

I stepped over the chain and walked forward for another sixty or seventy feet. The road widened, and, ten feet further on, just before I stepped into what must have been the clearing for the house, I heard a dog barking. I walked into the open, and glimpsed the figure standing in front of the red house just before I heard the pffft! of the bullet about two feet above my head, and the crack of the high-powered rifle. I dropped to the ground, rolled back behind the trees I had just left, and thought over what I had just seen.

She was tall. She had darkish hair that may have been wet; but that might have been an extension I'd made because her light-blue terrycloth robe had looked wet. She had been standing in front of a two-story farmhouse that displayed a large bank of small-paned windows to either side of the three or four bannistered steps leading up to the front door. The color had been more like brick red. Between the house and me was a half-acre field, recently planted with what I guessed must have been grass seed. The dog was a black Lab, trying to sound mean, and guarding a graveled driveway that led up to and around the house.

"Never mind coming any further, mister. I'm a good enough shot to miss you, and I'm sure as hell good enough not to." She wasn't yelling, but she projected her low voice like a pro.

"Mrs. – Doctor Wager – I –"

"Yeah, I know, and I know why the phone is out, too. So you and your friends just mosey on out of here, understand?"

She fired a couple more warning shots from what sounded like an expertly wielded lever-action 30/06 or 30/30. The dog started barking again, a few gunshot leaves drifted down to the rutted road, and I opted for an ignominious retreat.

"You're making a big mistake, lady, and don't think you've heard the last of this," I warned. I didn't think she'd listen to an explanation, so it seemed wiser to play the part I'd been assigned. She put another bullet into the trees as I walked back up the road.

I trudged back up to the BMW, started it up, backed out and drove back toward Route 73. I made a U-turn about a half-mile further on, built the speed back up to about forty, put it in neutral, and freewheeled back toward the turnoff. There must have been a slight uphill grade. The car slowed quickly. I galumphed over the gravel and onto the dirt driveway at about seven miles an hour, coasted another twenty feet, and used the last few thousand foot-pounds-per-second of momentum to bury the car in the brush off to the left side of the road. I got out through the passenger door, closed it quietly, and listened. There was still an occasional indignant bark, but it sounded as though the dog might have been back inside the house.

I moccasin-footed and circled my way around to the back of the old house, which I could see through an occasional leafless hole in the hardwoods and low underbrush that covered the property. There was a barn and a beat-up garage in back. A never-washed, four-wheel-drive Subaru Forester of indeterminate color was nosed into the garage.

Just as I got to the back door, she let the dog out of the front. The lab announced his reappearance with a fusillade of throaty barks, generally directed at the still-remembered insult of my earlier arrival. The barking must have drowned out the noise of my advance through a creaky screened-in porch and a recently rebuilt but unlocked door into the kitchen. There was a pot of water nearing a boil on a huge, black, wood-burning stove to my left. I crossed the red-tiled floor of the kitchen, edged up to a door on the far side, and peered through. No one had recently dined in the dining room. It was in the throes of refurbishing. But it didn't look as though anyone had been working for a while. There was a pile of newspapers, a dusty stepladder, a few gallon paint cans, with rollers and brushes. All had been pushed to one side to clear a path from my vantage point, the kitchen door, across the room to another doorway into the living room. My perspective was limited by the intervening twelve feet of room, but I could see the broad expanse of small-paned windows that I had seen from the outside. And I could see Molly Wager.

She had leaned the rifle against the front door, and was in the process of changing from her old blue terrycloth robe, which lay in a damp pile at her feet, into something more in keeping with popping off warning shots at trespassers. She was about five-ten in her bare feet, and must have weighed in at about one-thirty. Runner's body. Long legs, slightly muscular, firm stomach and thighs, uplifted breasts. Her long, naturally auburn hair fell over her face as she bent to pull on some yellow panties. She didn't wear a bra. As she put on an oversize blue cotton work shirt, I noticed that here arms were tanned from above the elbows on down. No Easthampton chic here.

I got her at that tough time we all have: one leg in and one leg out. The toe of the second foot caught on its way through the knee-length corduroys. She lost her balance and hopped left, away from the rifle. I made my move on her second hop. She saw me coming at the last minute, realized she didn't have a chance for the gun and decided to hold her ground. She swung a powerhouse left hook at the side of my head. I parried, grabbed her wrist, spun her around and grabbed her by the shoulders. She went limp, and as I adjusted my grip to accommodate her dead weight, she came alive, left-elbowed me in the left ribs, broke my grasp, and dived for the rifle. I hit her just after the whistle, and lay on top of her, pinning her nose to the floor. The dog was barking but he was on the wrong side of the door again. She kept struggling, and when I turned her over onto her back, she even bit me on the wrist.

"Bastard!" she managed to get out. I slapped her twice, forehand, backhand, left cheek, right cheek. She surged under me and spat up at my face. I slapped her again and clamped my hand over her face. If looks could kill, I was long gone. She stopped struggling. I spoke.

"My name is O'Toole. I work for the U.S. Government. The Fish and Wildlife Department. I was sent up here to see if your husband's sickness had anything to do with water pollution or acid rain. I have a message from him to you. He had given it to the LeCourier boys when they found him by the lake. They didn't tell anyone about it because they wanted to keep the fifty dollars that went with it. I tried to call, but the line was – seemed busy." There were tears in her eyes. I took my hand off her mouth.

"I want to get up now," she said.

I took my knees off her arms and got to my feet. She lay there for a few seconds without moving. Her eyes were closed. Her face was swollen, slightly feverish-looking. She got up slowly, and I turned briefly away as she finished the job of getting into her pants.

"I'll be back," she said quietly, not looking at me. She turned on her heel and walked toward the kitchen, throwing her shoulders back and raising her chin as she entered the dining room. She had a long stride. I heard water running in the kitchen a moment or two later.

The rifle was a beautifully cared-for, lever-action Winchester 30/06,

Model 1895. There was an empty three-gun rack on the wall next to the Franklin stove. I put the Winchester in the middle slot.

It was a large room, well lit by the light streaming in from the huge, south-facing windows. Entering from the dining room, there was to the right a newly polyurethaned round oak table about four feet in diameter, covered with an eight or ten-inch-high pile of loose papers, unopened and unattended mail. The Franklin stove rested upon a four-by-five foot flagstone and asbestos base next to the west wall; a Rube Goldberg array of stovepipe, angled connectors, support arms, flanges and radiator clamps served to conduct the smoke and ash through a crudely-fashioned, six-inch hole to the outside, chopped through the center of the ceiling. Facing the stove, some eight to ten feet away, was a long, chintz-covered, over-stuffed sofa, which formed a boundary for that part of the room devoted to things social. On the wall behind the sofa was a series of board-mounted, black and white, happier-times photographs, of Molly and a dark-haired man in his late twenties.

The other end of the thirty-foot-long room had been converted to and reserved for her medical practice. A balustrade ran from the right of the front door to the rear wall, with an open gate at the center. There was a small waiting area, a desk, a couple of glass-doored cabinets, and a small area in one corner which could be shut off from the rest of the room by using a heavy white curtain hung from a chromed pipe on the ceiling. An open door at the rear corner appeared to give entry to an examination area, or perhaps a laboratory.

I heard an elongated clanking in the pipes as she shut off the water. She walked back into the living room. She had not looked into the mirror next to the dining room door, either going or coming. She stopped about six or seven feet away, and looked directly at me for the first time. There were drops of water on the shirt and her face was not so puffy as before. Her eyes were a deep, dark brown, her nose had been broken and almost perfectly set a long time ago, and her high cheekbones were in symmetry with her long, firm jaw.

"I put your nice old Winchester back in the rack."

"I'm sorry. I expected – something else. I – I really didn't aim at you out there. I guess I'm ready to see what he wrote." She was quiet and direct. Not resigned, but maybe tired. She would have made either a very good or a very bad poker player, I wasn't sure which. I gave her the manila envelope. She read the message, nodded, and turned the envelope over in her hands.

"You didn't read what's inside."

"No."

75

She turned to the table and cleared a hole in the pile of papers. She found a small pocketknife and used it to open the manila envelope. She laid the contents on the table, sat down, and prepared to read. There appeared to be four or five typewritten pages.

"Maybe you'd like something to drink," she offered.

"There was some water boiling – "

"No, I turned it off. I was going to have some coffee before. I've not felt my best today. There's been something going around, as we doctors are fond of saying."

"How do you take it?"

"A little milk, and a touch of Sweet 'n Low. It's all out on the counter."

"You read, I'll see what I can do."

The giant stove I had noticed earlier was a wood burner, but it was augmented by a couple of propane burners, one of which I used to boil the water for the coffee. The kitchen looked like the rest of the house. It looked like someone had had some good ideas about restoring it to an early American simplicity; but somewhere along the line something had gone wrong. It might have had something to do with time, it probably had nothing to do with money, and it surely had a lot to do with divorce. The fun, the faith and the caring were gone, at least for a time.

I took the two mugs of Martinsons' Instant back to the front room. She was slouched down in her captain's chair, knees to the table for support. She was kneading her temples as if to rub away a headache, and concentrating mightily on the first page of the contents of the envelope.

"Thanks."

"Are you all right?"

"I think so."

"You don't suppose you might have caught the same thing that your – uh, Doctor Wager did?"

"I guess it's possible. But the only occasion would have been when I visited him in the hospital. And that was almost two days ago now. I mean, I'm nothing like as sick as he seemed to have been. I haven't checked for a while, but at – what three or three-thirty, I didn't even have a fever. I do respect Doctor Rashid, and he told me that Robert did seem a lot better early this morning. Then I called again, later. I – I just – "

"You just aren't buying the pickup and delivery by the boys from the Institute?"

"Yes. But I overreacted, obviously. Even if you had been one of them. It's just that the coincidence of my being told that Robert had been taken out of the hospital only twenty-four hours after being in Intensive Care, then the phone going out, and the way I was feeling, I guess, well, I guess I got jumpy."

"Well, I can't say that I blame you. I made a few inquiries on my way over here. From some people in Washington, who, who are friends of mine and who can get information. It made me wonder about that Institute, and particularly about this Claycombe, who I guess is the Director of Research. But, first things first. I decided to deliver this thing to you. I thought maybe I could find out just why it was that your husband was as worried as he apparently was when he wrote the note on that envelope and gave it to the boys. I was hoping you might help me on that."

"Fish and Wildlife?"

"Most of the time."

"Here. Read along behind me. It's a copy of a report, or at least part of a report, that Doctor Claycombe must have been preparing for a general in the Pentagon. Robert must have been interrupted when he was doing the Xeroxing. See? He's scribbled 'no more time' on the bottom of the last sheet. But I think there's enough here to get a good idea of just what it is they're doing up there at Devil's Mountain. I've – I've known about some of it – for a while. I didn't approve."

"Is that – did that cause the breakup?"

"No. No." The second one sounded firmer. "We didn't believe in the same things. And after a few months, I got over being impressed by the, well, by the hero-worship thing. I mean, he was really it on virology, and I couldn't forget him and his knowledge after we worked together in Toronto. That's where we met. But – well, anyway, that's not really what did it. The hero thing, I mean. It was more a matter of – of time." She thought about it for a few seconds. "I guess you'd better look at this now. I think it's important."

"What do you call those pants you're wearing?"

"Jodhpurs."

"Right. It was on the tip of my tongue."

There were three Xeroxed pages. Some of the stuff was technical, but the report had been written to allow for exactly the kind of reader I was: a novice, who had to be led by the nose, one step at a time. Even so, I stumbled a few times. I read faster as I progressed, and it was important.

TOP SECRET   TOP SECRET

_____ Sep 06

Richard:

This is close. Check for
Current on-line routing
  Instructions, and check sp. We'll
  Need crypto Mon. earliest. P>C>

FROM : HIGHMONT
  P/W PCH1

TO: CLAMBED
    P/W JJH1
  3431/PENOFFSPECPROJ

Ref: My 1046 15 Aug   CC: SBJ1
        Yr   114 26 Aug   LPNY

Subj: Update, answer to second ref.

BEGIN SCRAM

Dear General Harrison:

1. Sorry about the technical language. I'm used to writing for
    medical journals, I suppose, where one is not hampered by
    the necessity for explanation of all but the most rudimentary
    concepts. This need makes it much more difficult to write

usefully about what are very complicated matters, even for experts. Nevertheless, I shall do my best. I do understand your position. I've always been in the same one vis-à-vis politics and the military.

2. To avoid interruption of the general exposition, and to thereby facilitate lay comprehension, I have relegated certain detailed conceptual discussions to the annotations on page --. Also, in describing the biological agent(s) involved, I will allude from time to time to the requirements for any biological weapon, to which you have asked me to conform in our efforts. To wit:

   a. The biological agent selected should have a logical alternative militating against the possibility of its existence. Ref: the possible natural incidence of mycotoxins in Cambodia, and resultant confusion surrounding attribution of yellow rain, as per our fonecon 8 Sep., about bee droppings.

   b. The agent should be quantity effective and area controllable.

   c. Ideally, the agent should disappear quickly, ref., responsibility for employment less easily assigned by world media, and further ref., safety of advancing forces. Cf. Gruinard Island. Incidentally, I resent your implied association of me with the failures there. I was strenuously opposed to deployment at that time, as the most cursory reading of the record will show.

   d. The agent should be a binary weapon. I know the pressures on you, with binary being the byword in chemical weaponry in the new millennium. For safety, storage, and longevity, it makes sense. But the requirement to delay the combination of the two agents selected until shortly before deployment has made our job more difficult and time-consuming, and will undoubtedly make field deployment more cumbersome.

e. The dual agents, or at least the secondary agent, should involve affliction not theretofore encountered naturally in the world. See Paragraph 7, infra."

It was heavy reading for a late Saturday afternoon in September. There were more and similarly delectable requirements for the perfect biological weapon, ranging from desirable symptoms to something called defensive characterizability. I skimmed the subparagraphs on reverse placebos and fools gold vaccines, and pressed on.

3. One note of clarification, on a subject that I infer to have been a cause of confusion on your part, General. You seem to have a more than rudimentary grasp of prokaryotic structure, the effect of antibiotics on bacteria, and the interaction of various therapies with natural human defense mechanisms. But you seem to have missed the points I made in our last fonecon with respect to viruses. Allow me to reiterate. Viruses seem to be impervious to antibiotics. Viruses are very small. The average E-Coli bacterium is about five-thousandths of a millimeter in length. One of the smaller viruses is only twenty nanometers, or twenty millionths of a millimeter in length. Hundreds of virions (individuals virus particles) can therefore occupy the same space as one bacterium. Unlike bacteria (for the most part), viruses are so small that they cannot be seen in an optical microscope. Therefore, except for recent development in transmission electron microscopy, viruses are only detectable by the presence in blood samples of the much larger antibodies "sent" by the human body's immune system to combat them. The antibodies are unique in appearance; they are recognizable as a response to the particular infection they were sent to fight. The identity of the virus, if is has been seen and recorded before, becomes apparent to the trained observer, but only when he recognizes those antibodies. Altering the antigenic characteristics of

the virus – its appearance – tends to "confuse" antibodies, or at least to tax more heavily the immune system.

4. There is some discussion in the scientific community as to whether or not a virus is even a "living" organism. Viruses lack the metabolic machinery needed to synthesize the components for their own replication. They must rely on the host cells that they attack for energy and such replicative machinery. I cannot overemphasize that point. A virion, or virus particle, consists solely of a nucleic acid core and a protein coat. It is the presence of the nucleic acid, either RNA or DNA, which is most cited for support by those who prefer to consider viruses as "living." I consider that discussion to be a waste of time. They do what they do, living or not.

5. A bacteriophage is a virus that attacks a bacteria cell. It uses the bacterial cell for:

    a. Its own propagation. Simply put, the cell becomes a factory for the production of hundreds of new virions. The cell dies, and the released virions spread to infect other cells. (This is called the Lytic pathway."

    b. A holding area. The virus injects its RNA or DNA into that of the bacterium, and all the progeny of the bacterium contain a duplicate viral DNA or RNA. (Each newly-divided daughter bacterial cell is at the mercy of the viral nucleic acid, which can dictate at any time that the bacteria resume the lytic-cell-destroying, multiple virion-releasing-pathway), and/or

    c. Transport. In this case, the bacterium becomes a vector, or transporter, and facilitates viral infection of other bacteria or other hosts, e.g., human cells.

NOTE: With respect to b., above, the latent virus, its nucleic acid faithfully reproduced by every dividing bacteria cell, is called a "provirus." Bacteria harboring a provirus are called lysogenic, meaning that they carry a property – a time bomb, if you will – that can lead to viral multiplication and the fatal lysis of the host cell. Exposure of such bacteria to ultraviolet radiation, X-rays, or chemicals such as nitrogen mustard and the organic peroxides can set off this time bomb, and the infection can proceed. See Note 12, infra for an amplified discussion."

I stopped reading. "Vectors" is one of those subjects – like "cash flow" and "data base" – that severely tries my attention span. I glanced at Molly Wager. There was a film of perspiration on her forehead and her upper lip. Her cheeks were redder than they had been a few minutes earlier. She looked up, and her eyes met mine. After about three seconds, she shook her head almost imperceptibly, and looked back at the report in front of her. The last two of the Xeroxed pages held my attention.

6. The selection of the first stage of our binary weapon – the initial bacterial infection – occupied most of our time up until early this past summer, as you will remember from our previous correspondence and from your visit to the Institute in May. We wanted the symptoms to be credible (see Para. 2g, supra_, and hence the only disease that the victims' attendants might expect. Serious, as we agreed, but not death dealing, particularly over a short period of time. This requirement ruled out the use of pulmonary anthrax, Q Fever, botulinus toxin and bubonic plague, all of which have fatality rates that are unacceptably high, considering our requirement that the initial infection be as care-intensive as possible. (The dead need no attendants.) For the bacterial first stage, then, we have elected to use a paste of Neisseria Meningitis bacteria, which have been:

a.   Genetically altered to produce milder, somewhat different symptoms than usual, and

b.   Subjected to random recombinant insertion of certain antibiotic-resistant plasmids (see Para.

5, infra) to further complicate the work of the victims' attendants.

The symptoms of the first phase bacterial infection, which we have called Bolivian Meningicoccal Meningitis, will include: flu-like body weakness, dizziness, diarrhea, nausea, meningitis-like headaches, stiff joints, lymphatic and blood circulation interruption and blockage, possible hearing loss and bleeding from various bodily orifices, incongruent skin eruptions, and pneumonia-like lung congestion in the more severely contaminated and/or susceptible victims. Our experiments on simian subjects at the Institute have confirmed these estimates, and my formal report will detail the dosages, treatments, effects when treatment was withheld, withdrawn, etc. The Bolivian Bacteria selected will be in the form of spores (as opposed to vegetative active bacteria) for the fir4st stage, so as to:

   a. make the bioagent less susceptible to environmental change (e.g., heat, cold, radiation, and/or enemy defense measures employing these and other phenomena),
   b. facilitate handling and storage, and
   c. protect our people and eventual military personnel.

NOTE: For the initial trials at BI, we have purposely attenuated the virulence of the bacterial infection, and have not always inserted the drug-resistant plasmids. The mechanics of delivery were giving us problems, as you suggested they might, and these precautions seemed prudent.

7. The drug-resistant plasmids prolong the life of the bacteria, of course, by at least delaying successful antibiotic therapy, but their prime function is to give the virus enough time, i.e., before the host bacteria are killed with antibiotics, to begin insertion into the bacterial vector cells. Remember, the nitrogen mustard gas used at the delivery point is not a capricious selection. It is uncomfortable for the victim, of course, and tends to relax his defenses.   He falsely assumes that

he has simply been exposed to another chemical agent, which can be defended against by donning his gas mask and other protective clothing. But more importantly, the gas offers a potential for spurring the activity of the provirus already infecting about one-half of the bacteria to proceed in the bacterial-cell-destructive (lytic) pathway, and to produce millions more virions. The other half of the bacterial cells and the virus selected – already combined shortly before firing or other deployment – are protected from the nitrogen-mustard agent by a separate, more slowly-dissolving beeswax envelope. They thereby continue in their latency for some time, with every bacterial cell division creating another potential viral factory.

8. The next problem was to select and/or manufacture the so-called second stage: the virus. It had to be one that would act the way we wanted it to, i.e., reacting predictably to nitrogen mustard stimulation, proceed lytically or latently in the desired proportions, be relatively stable in handling, and of course, produce further severely care-intensive, sometimes fatal symptoms. Again, we have worked with recombinant nucleic acid techniques, and selected a kind of retro-hybridoma that is both hardy and effective.

9. The virus we selected is a bacteriophage, of course – a virus that initially attacks bacterial cells – and we have called it Agent CX-2. CX-2 has been altered from the natural occurrence realm with certain recombinant techniques. It behaves somewhat like HTLV, which we discussed during your May visit, and, like HTLV, it has RNA for its initial nucleic core.   CX-2 is a hybrid of two other viruses: one, a Green Monkey Disease variant, and two, a mutant, highly unstable, heretofore unnamed, and extremely small (not filtrating out at 5 millionths of a millimeter) virus, which is quite likely to incorrectly and/or incompletely transfer its "normal" RNA to an infected bacterial cell. This instability is almost infinite in its complexity. The potential added difficulty in treatment should be obvious. With the recombinant techniques being used, one of the objections to Biological Warfare often voiced in the past, i.e., that

it was restricted to diseases which occurred naturally, somewhere in the world, has been removed.

10. Before discussing the effects of CX-2 infection on the human body and its immune system, I should describe another very interesting and useful characteristic of the agent. The protein coat of CX-2 is often the same as that of a non-pathogenic organism, and, although I cannot claim that we have been aware all along"

That was the end of the third page. I recognized Wager's scribbled "no more time" at the bottom. I put the page down by the others on the oak table. Molly Wager looked at me, gauging my reaction. It was then that I heard the chain on the drive pop, and jumped up to see the two SUVs juggernauting into the front yard.

XIII

If there's no way of finding out where you are, then it soon becomes extremely important to find out at least what the hell time it is. It was clear that none of our white-suited attendant-guards was going to be of any help. There were four of them, I thought. Big and Little Whitey changed the water bottle and checked us out, Bloodman took samples from Molly's arm, and Backupman worked swing shift. Whenever one man would clamber through the circular hatch at the rear of our chamber, we could see a partner back in the airlock, armed and alert, riding shotgun; ready to advance, or to slam the hatch, seal us in, and withdraw for reinforcement from topside. But none of them ever made a sound. There were no 'top a the mornins', or 'nice afternoons'. Big Whitey did give a little wave now and then, and he seemed to have a need to reassure Molly that he meant her no harm. But aside from the regularity of their appearances, we weren't going to learn anything from them.

Their watch schedules seemed to be something like four on and four off, with an extra four off every twelve hours; but before we could begin using the frequency of watch changes to measure the days, we needed a benchmark. We needed to know what time of what day it had been when they'd stuffed us into the ship's hold and bolted on the airlock. So we finally had to fall back on our shaky memories.

We came up with forty-eight hours; from the first shotgun blast through Molly's farmhouse windows to the gonglike crash of our fat cigar prison against the ship's side as they had clumsily lifted us off our trailer and into the hold.

I was better on remembering the first twelve hours. The muscle relaxant had worn off, we'd crossed the lake on the ferry and semi-trucked our way toward the sea, while Molly lay in feverish, retching, asphyxiating agony in her bunk, and before my headaches started coming on strong. She picked up on the next twenty-four, remembering the timing of the sliding-door man's moves and her jamming the antibiotics down my throat. There were other things – bathroom moves, beard length, hunger, her medical estimate of whatever our disease had been and how long it should have taken for the drugs to work. Anyway, we had to have a starting point, and that was it. They'd winched us aboard the ship sometime on Monday evening. We might have been off a day, but it was enough to work on.

And there we sat. For another twelve hours. Time enough for sixteen hisses of the airlock, four changes of the guard, and a tin apiece of old C-rations. Time enough to nickname the guards, to work on the time, and to consider just how much of a future we had if we didn't come up with some way to get the hell out of this space capsule they had us in. Until Tuesday morning, the only tactic I could come up with was my disease-ravaged, flailing-out-in-the-darkness, rapidly-failing, nobody-touch-me routine, and the only thing that that had gotten us was a few less needle holes in my arm than in Molly's. And who knew? Maybe in the long run these guys were working in our best interests after all. They seemed to be punctual and professional as they took Molly's blood, changed the water bottle and monitored our general behavior and appearance. Nah. There wasn't going to be any long run and we both knew it. Except for the aberrant Wendy's cheeseburger and fries, these guys were obviously more interested in the progress of the disease than in the progress of the patients. And one of the patients wasn't progressing all that well.

We were talking about her one visit to the Beckmann Institute, when her husband had taken the job the previous year. She was describing the setting – the gravel road leading down into the little valley, the three low-lying, wooden buildings. Very contemporary, she remembered. Her husband had worked in the main lab – research and experimental production. The infirmary, with its three wards, two private rooms and doctors' offices, and the service building, which had housed the motor pool, and the fire fighting and snow removal equipment, had flanked it. The compound was surrounded by a pine forest, and a pretty-good-sized mountain stream – Halfaday Creek, she thought it had been called – ran through the west end of the compound on its course to Devil's Mountain Lake off to the south. And then Molly Wager got one of those red-in-the-face coughing fits that eventually goes away. Most of the time. Molly kept on coughing. After a while there was some blood, and she got very weak. And when she finally stopped, she complained of a headache. She wasn't a complainer. She reviewed the symptoms and opined that she must have been suffering from either a relapse or a new, secondary infection. She took a couple of the remaining Keflex, but smiled ruefully, somehow knowing that the drug was probably not going to do the job. We'd both read the Claycombe report, and it was clear that she was going to need something more than the few horse pills we had left in the jar to beat off this Bolivian Meningococcal Meningitis with its altered nucleic acid. Sometime Tuesday, early morning, she lay back in her bunk and lapsed into a fitful sleep, punctuated by alternating fever, chills, and the kind of wracking coughs that jackknifed her sweating body and banged her head against the bulkhead if I wasn't quick enough to hold her.

It was about the same time that they finally got the ship underway. It was diesel-powered, and it had twin screws. We didn't need tugboats to get us away from the pier. It didn't take the sea so well as the ferry across the lake a couple of days earlier. Of course, that had been a lake and this was probably the ocean. All in all, I had it figured for seven, eight hundred tons. A thousand, tops, and bigger than I'd guessed. And ocean-going trawler, maybe. A bridge, a separate engine room, with a captain, a mate, and engineer and four or five crewmen, not counting the medical-security guys. Eight or ten knots. Good for weeks at sea. Not that that capability was going to make any difference to us.

After a half-hour to forty-five minutes of maneuvering through what I assumed must have been harbor traffic, we settled on course. The sea was on our port bow. I pictured the big low that had crossed the Adirondacks the previous Saturday, moving north and east and out to sea, with the counter-clockwise flow around its center giving the folks of northern New England a real ol'fashioned nor-easter. If that had actually happened, it would have meant that our course was to the southeast. I could have been a hundred and eighty off, but it passed the time.

The boys began to show up more often, and there seemed to be a growing concern about Molly. Especially with Big Whitey. Maybe it wasn't concern. Maybe it was just a professional and natural heightening of interest as a moment of crisis approached. It was tough to attribute anything nice to these anonymous, futuristic morgue attendants, as they hissed in and out of the airlock, sometimes two at a time, but always with Backupman hanging in behind the hatch. Now they would take her temperature, take the blood samples, wipe her brow, and once they brought her a new blanket. Finally – about four or five on Tuesday afternoon by my estimate – they hooked her up to an i.v. It was a made-up solution, with a hand-lettered label that I couldn't make out from my bunk. I kept up the moribund act, but they couldn't have cared less. It reminded me of what Seventy-Four had told me, about the Japanese experiments on diseased human guinea pigs during World War II. They would check the progress of both kinds – those they were trying to cure, and those in whom they let the disease take its course. Well, they sure as hell weren't trying to cure me.

About eight o'clock that evening, the seventh watch change since we'd boarded the ship, several things happened. The ship got to where it was going. Or at least to a holding point. We started steaming in circles, and the chop, the long swell and the constantly changing angle of hull to sea made for a nauseating ride. Molly's i.v. stand fell against her bunk and stayed there for quite a while. When someone came to change it, it looked like Backupman. He was by himself, and he looked worried. It's hard to say that about a guy in a white spacesuit with a mirror-finish glass visor, but he did. He moved as though he didn't have as much time as he would have liked. He looked at me a little more often. And there was no backup man doing what Backupman normally did.

The question was going to be one of timing. If something besides seasickness was affecting these guys, like maybe Big and Little Whitey weren't feeling all that chipper, and Bloodman, say, had a very bad head-ache himself, why, I'd just have to make sure that I made my move after they were weakened just enough for me to take them, but before the point where they couldn't open the airlock to let themselves in, or they simply decided it wasn't worth the effort.

No one came in at midnight. They usually did, and I thought I might have blown it. Not that I knew exactly when midnight was, but I could tell by the time it got to two or two-thirty, I was sure; it wasn't just impatience making the time pass slowly. When someone did come, it was Big Whitey. I didn't think he was due until the four-to-eight shift, and he was by himself, just like Backupman had been. Big Whitey was a sweet guy and all, but this time he brought a ship's-issue 45-caliber pistol with him, flapped down in a left-hip holster on a green web belt. He couldn't have been afraid of Molly. She wasn't responding well to the i.v. And whatever was in it. From the coughing, feverish movements of some hours before, she had lapsed into a kind of given-up-the-ghost semi-coma. So maybe he was worried about me. He looked at me for a long time. I managed to stare dully back through my half-opened eyes. He moved his gloved hand in front of my face, and I tried to maintain the fixed, disinterested stare. Finally, he turned to Molly, and wrapped a pulse and blood pressure cuff to her upper left arm. He had trouble with the Velcro connector tabs.

XIV

Big Whitey was moving with great effort. He was slow, and it looked like everything weighed a lot more than it had in the days before. He fumbled at the i.v. connections, fumbled at the squeeze bulb on the blood pressure device, and fumbled with the liquid crystal thermometer tape on her forehead. It was time.

I lurched myself up from the bunk, managed a guttural Bruce Lee hheeayyagh! that hurt my throat, and weakly clutched Big Whitey from behind, in what was supposed to have looked like a last-ditch but fruitless attempt at escape by a desperate, dying man. He bought it. He shrugged me off, and pushed me heavily back into the bunk, where I sprawled, trying my best to look insensate. He turned back toward Molly. I had been wrong about one thing. There had been another white suiter in the airlock, and it had looked like Little Whitey. It was too late to worry about it. I bounced back up from my bunk, grabbed Big Whitey by a fistful of white cloth at the scruff of the neck and another fistful at the seat of his pants, and, lifting and pushing, I bums-rushed him toward the back of the compartment. The ease with which he had repelled my earlier attempt had put him off his guard. He was a big one all right, but the surprise factor was doing him in. I don't think he realized that he was in any real trouble until we got to within about a yard of the aft steel bulkhead, and then it was too late. He wrenched himself halfway around, breaking my grip on the back of his neck and bending from the waist, preparing to stomp on me once and for all. But these maneuvers only served to make the collision with bulkhead more damaging than it would have been. He went down like a stone, with one arm hanging over the hatch opening. That arm took another bad blow a split second later, as Little Whitey slammed the hatch against it. And that was Little Whitey's mistake. He should have let the hatchway alone and leveled his machine pistol on my midriff. But, you never know; maybe that's what the book called for.

I didn't wait. I pushed hard on the hatch. Little Whitey pushed back. We both strained for a second or two, and then I gave him the old heave-ho. I pulled instead of pushed for an instant, which surprised him enough to relax his efforts for just that long; when I threw myself back against the hatch, I heard a sharp crack, a muffled cry, and then there was no more resistance. I scrambled on through the hatchway. Little Whitey was trying to cover his cracked visor with one hand and grappling with the outer airlock door mechanism with the other. His Mauser lay on the deck. I spun him around to face me. He was about five-six. The suit was too big for him, and I don't really believe he was feeling up to par, even before the run-in his visor had had with the steel hatch. I didn't have time to talk it over. I grabbed him by the shoulders, lifted and crashed him against the irregular outline of the airlock controls four or five times, taking the wind out of his sails.

Little Whitey's and my grappling with the inner hatch had not done Big Whitey's arm any good at all, and he was still out cold from the collision with the steel bulkhead. When I looked back on all the moves sometime later, I had to admit that these guys had been weakened by infection; their reflexes were slowed, and their judgment impaired. Then again, I wasn't all that strong, either. But I was on the mend, I admit, and that must have helped. I wrestled Big up and into my bunk, and carried a groggy Little Whitey from the airlock into the compartment, dumping him on top of his partner. Molly didn't like it when I lifted her from the bunk, maneuvered her as gently as possible through the hatch, and deposited her on the airlock deck. I got her plastic i.v. bag to stay put in a detent in the overhead, and made her a little more comfortable with two pillows and a blanket from the compartment. I retrieved Big Whitey's .45 pistol, went back to the airlock and dogged down the hatch, putting the two Whiteys on ice at least for a while.

"Molly, can you hear me?"

"Ugnuhhash."

"Listen, I'm going to get us out of here as soon as I can. You just hang tough, and I'll be back in a few minutes. Okay?"

"Beallright."

The airlock system had obviously not done its job – to protect against contagion – but I thought it might be a good idea to go through the motions. One valve voided the air chamber, pumping the contents back into the compartment. That operation must have been the one that had given us the salt air and the throbbing ears two nights earlier. I deployed the only other valve, and the fresh air from outside the airlock came in under pressure. At the same time, a bank of ultraviolet lights blinked on above my head, and a panel by the outer hatch lit up with the message "HOLD FOR DECONTAM" blinking on and off in red LED's. I bent over Molly. She was in that unhealthy-looking sleep again.

The panel finally displayed "OK FOR EXIT". An electric bolt slid back in the outer hatch mechanism, and I felt the air pressure suddenly diminish as I uncranked the foot-in-diameter dogging ring. It might have been a good idea to have put on Big Whitey's spacesuit, but it was too late for that now. I considered myself lucky to have both of them safely stashed in the compartment; any further carryings-on with either or both of them might have led to trouble. Pistol in hand, I kicked the outer airlock hatch open, backed against the inner bulkhead for a second or two, waited for the defensive fire that didn't come, and sprang through the hatch into the darkness beyond.

It wasn't really darkness. It was just that they hadn't had the time or the inclination to fully light the cargo hold. At first I saw nothing, my eyes still overwhelmed by the bright neon of the compartment and the fluorescent and ultraviolet glare of the airlock. Then I saw Backupman, lying on a cot next to the aft wall of the hold. He'd taken off his head and shoulder paraphernalia, he looked bad and he wasn't breathing well. I left him as he was, and turned to the bulkhead and the massive, wooden, ice-room door, with its plunger-type indoor-outdoor latch mechanism. The only trouble was that the indoor part had been removed. I was going to have to wait for someone on the outside.

It took about fifteen minutes. They had probably given Big and Little Whitey as much time as they dared, and now it was time to check up on them. I heard a scratchy voice from under Backupman's cot rasp out "Smitty, everything okay?"

Backupman managed to roll to one side, groping for the walkie-talkie. He groaned something unintelligible into the mouthpiece, sounding somewhat like I had a few days earlier when Molly had first asked how I was feeling. Then he began to get his voice together, and I took the radio away from him. He didn't look like he cared all that much.

"Smitty! What's happening in there?"

I wheezed and breathed a heavy "hurry ... hurry" into the mouthpiece. I took a position on the side of the butcher's door opposite Backupman's cot and in the poorest-lit corner of the hold.

He took just about enough time to get his white suit back on, and then he made his move. I heard the big plunger on the far side of the laminated, foot-thick door plunge home, and saw the door swing ponderously open, picking up speed and finally slamming home, held flat against the far bulkhead by a row of three aluminum catches. It was well I hadn't waited behind the door.

He did what I probably would have done under the same set of facts. Door open, back against the side of doorframe with weapon in ready position, count one-Mississippi-two-Mississippi, and then you dive through. I hung back in the darkness and let him go through his routine. He hit the deck, rolled to his feet against the airlock and came up with machine pistol at the ready. It was Bloodman, and he moved pretty well, white suit notwithstanding. He didn't see me. I guess he assumed that the good guys were still in charge. He relaxed his ready stance and walked toward the cot. His voice came out of a small speaker at his throat; it sounded like the battery was low.

"Jesus, Smitty, what the hell are they doin' in there? I mean, I know you guys aren't feelin' all that well, but –"

Backupman managed one last sit-up and gestured crazily at me as I came out of the shadows. Bloodman tried to whirl to his left and fire. I stopped his whirl and poor Backupman stopped the fire. Nine millimeter. Three, maybe four. Thug-thug-thug. A liquid sound. I don't think Backupman was going to have made it anyway. But Bloodman was another story. His white suit must have been doing a better job than the others. He didn't seem sickly at all as he went with my weight, added to the momentum of our fall with a twist of his shoulder, and sent me crashing down on top of the bleeding Backupman and sending my .45 crashing to the deck and under the cot. I leaned back against the rear wall of the hold, and, just after he'd managed one good swipe at my head with the skeleton stock of the machine pistol, I brought up my legs and pushed him off into the dark cylindrical outline of Molly's and my canister. He crashed into that pretty good, and I got him with a right shoulder on the rebound, sending his own pistol clattering across the deck. Then he got mad. He waded in, white fists flying; no parries, no thrusts, no defense, no finesse. I must have been getting a little tired from this game of ten-pins with the men in the white suits, and he damn well steamrolled right over me. I grabbed him by the ankle and hung on. For dear life. He broke free and stomped the deck where my hand should have been. I reached up, grabbed the white fabric, and ripped open his precious spacesuit from hip to knee. Bloodman, having lost his pride, his individuality, the integrity of his white suit and no doubt his health, gave up the fight and broke for the door. I grabbed up the .45 from under the cot and shot him once, in the back of the left knee.

He dived through the freezer doorway and sprawled on the deck in the passageway beyond.

I stepped over him, waiting for his reinforcements. They didn't come. There was an open door to a small, lighted stateroom on my left. It was a makeshift dispensary and laboratory. They had the blood samples from Molly, along with a raft of antibiotics that hadn't done the mob. I stuffed Bloodman through the door, tied his hands behind him, bandaged his leg and hitched him to a drainpipe under the lavatory.

The stateroom had been decorated in dove gray, complete with recessed indirect lighting, Pentagon-modern furniture, fireproof fabrics, a lot of chrome and a twenty-plus inch Mitsubishi LCD TV. The passageway outside ran for another twenty feet farther aft, past another stateroom – locked – and ended at a dogged-down watertight walk-through hatch to starboard and a reverse-direction ladder to port leading up to the next level. The bulkheads, decks, doors and hatches had all been carefully chipped free of old paint and redone in shades of gray. There was a recently painted legend stenciled on the hatch at the end of the passageway, which read: "Engine room – Second Deck – Auth. Pers. Only."

The engine room people were going to have to wait. I went up the ladder. Eight feet up, there was another walk-through hatch, labeled: "Weather Deck", and another ladder running up and aft. I spun the dogging circle to the left and opened the hatch a few inches.

XV

It was night. So Molly and I might have been a full day off, but not a half-day. Three, three-thirty, Wednesday morning. It wasn't all that dark. The moon was two points off the starboard bow and thirty degrees above the horizon. The haze layer had blotted out the stars and softened the light from the moon, but there was enough light for me to make out shape and dimension of various objects on the main deck. We were in a long, lazy, five-degree-rudder turn to port, and the apparent motion of the moon gave me a good look at the two sixteen-foot-square hatch covers and the little forecastle deck forty feet forward, silhouetted by the back glow from the baffled masthead light overhead. When the moon was eclipsed by the stern a few seconds later, I opened the hatch a bit further, stepped through, and looked aloft.

I was at the bottom of the twenty or twenty-five-foot-high forward wall of the superstructure, which was probably perched on the aft end of the hull, if my gut feeling of being close to the rudder and its center of turn radius was correct. My hatch was amidships, and there were weather-protected ladders, like stairwells to port and starboard leading aft and up into the superstructure. In the eerie red and green glow from the running lights over my head, I could see deep streaks of rust, pervasively eating through the paint on the front wall of the superstructure. Someone had either run out of money, or had wanted the outside of the ship to look different from the inside.

The turn to port was continuing. The moon reappeared to port, and I slipped to my right, ducking into the starboard stairwell off the main deck, and taking the first couple of steps up toward the 01 level. So far, I had seen or heard no one since I had hog-tied Bloodman to the drainpipe back on the Second Deck. I turned off the safety on the .45, levered another shell into the chamber, and continued up the ladder.

The rusted steel flanks of the superstructure rose some ten feet above the main deck level; access to the bridge from that point on was open to the weather. There appeared to be two more eight-foot-long ladders leading up to the starboard wing of the bridge. There were more signs of poor maintenance everywhere I looked; rust, lumpy and painted-over paint, encrusted bright work – a real scow. At the midway point between the two ladders up to the bridge were another landing, and a two-foot-wide steel catwalk, leading inboard to a door labeled "Captain – Weather" and then continuing aft. There was a four-by-five inch piece of weather-yellowed poster paper duct-taped next to the door handle with a neatly hand-lettered admonition: "Do not knock – See Mate for O.K."

As my eyes reached the level of the bridge wing, I heard a muffled voice from beyond the open door of the wheelhouse.

"Midships."

It was followed shortly by a churlish-sounding "meedsheep," and I felt the eighty-foot-long trawler steady on a northerly course. The moon was lower in the sky to port.

There was a stanchion-mounted gyro compass repeater with an uncovered alidade installed at the outboard extremity of the starboard bridge wing, but the lookout or quartermaster who might have used it to take sights for whoever might have been doing the navigating was sitting down on the job. In the subdued light from the wheelhouse door, I could see that he wasn't well. He was slumped to the deck, and shivering so violently that he appeared not to have noticed or cared that the Hudson's Bay blanket someone had given him had slipped off his shoulders to the deck. Whatever it was that Claycombe and Wager had spilled back in that Adirondack laboratory had made its way through a lot of air filters, white suits, airlocks and freezer doors. And despite the probable administration of a lot of gamma globulin and assorted antibiotics, at least seven or eight people had gotten some very bad, brain-lesioning headaches, plus assorted chills, fever, stomach cramps, dizziness and the kind of racking cough coughs that ulcerated their half-closed and swollen throats. Make it ten, or eleven, if Molly's and my theory about why we had been left alone for eight or ten hours on our cross-country trip had been correct.

All right. Crew. Figure two men in the engine room, two in the wheelhouse, a second lookout on the port bridge wing, and the captain; and add two just in case. Eight more folks who probably wouldn't approve of my walking around on their rusty little tramp steamer with the fancy insides. But they wouldn't all be healthy, and they wouldn't all be in the same place. The odds weren't great, but they were better than they'd been some forty-five minutes earlier, when I'd gotten lucky with a slow-moving Big Whitey.

The door to the wheelhouse had been secured in the open position. It was a warmish night, and our speed – as we circled around what I guessed must have been our holding position – was only three or four knots. With my left hand on the painted canvas-covered chains that served as hand-rails, and gripping the .45 with my right, I pulled myself up to the bridge level and sidled over to the wheelhouse door. As I looked forward and into the wheel house, I could see a man leaning on a red-lit chart table in front of him, slowly maneuvering what appeared to be a very heavy parallel rule, from a compass rose printed on the chart toward what I assumed must have been our position.

"Steady on zero-one-five." He said it quietly, over his left shoulder. He had a medium-heavy, but not comic Slavic accent.

"Staydee on piftee." The answer came from behind him; I risked moving forward a bit. The helmsman with the Hispanic accent was standing on a four-inch-high wooden grid and sagging against a three-foot oak wheel, struggling to push himself away, and to turn the wheel at the same time. He blinked back and forth, from the binnacled magnetic compass that moved ponderously in its gimbaled support a couple of feet in front of his beltline to the smaller gyro compass at its side. He shook his head in apparent amazement, as if he couldn't believe how hard it was to keep the thousand-ton vessel aligned with the lubber line that particular morning. I thanked my lucky stars that they had opted for a ship for holding Molly and me instead of an airplane. This was indeed a motley crew, and they could have done a lot of damage if anything were to require any moves faster than the three or four knots we were making.

The man giving the orders gave up on the parallel rule. He pushed the red light forward and out of the way, leaving it lit, and moved heavily toward a captain's chair mounted on the deck two feet to port of the chart table. He made as if to raise himself into the chair, but compromised on leaning his back against it. He raised a pair of binoculars to his eyes, panned from one of the four portholes across the face of the wheelhouse to another, and perfunctorily steadied on the moonlit expanse of two-foot seas dead ahead. The helmsman stared into the dimly lit compass, making fewer moves, but still blinking.

I was a bit bolder by now. Exposing more of myself than before, I looked through the wheelhouse toward the other bridge wing. No lookout on that side. A polished brass ship's telegraph – set at "ALL AHEAD

1/3" – to the right of the helmsman, and, to his left, a two-foot-high stack of state-of-the-art radio gear and a green-lighted radar console, flickering with the movement of its cursor.

I don't know how it would have come out if the starboard lookout hadn't sounded the alarm. He saved me the trouble of making a game plan – which could easily have backfired and most surely would have been a needless complication.

"Señor! Hombre en la cubierta!" he croaked out. He had mustered enough energy to get to his feet and make a run at me. The only weapon he had was his blanket, and it appeared that he was going to put it over my head and see what developed. The sight of his careening approach across the eight feet of bridge wing, blanket upraised and flapping in the five-knot headwind, almost made me lose my presence of mind. I sidestepped his slow-mo silhouette, and out of the corner of my eye I glimpsed the Señor limping toward the radio stack, trying to speed his meningitis-impeded movement by pulling with his arms on the chest-high brass rail that ran across the front wall of the wheelhouse.

The sound of the lookout bonging into the superstructure, and his despairing cries as he tumbled down the steel ladder toward the captain's landing, stopped everyone for a second or two. Well, at least it stopped the Señor and me. The helmsman stayed at the wheel; from exhaustion, disease-induced mental torpidity or death, I didn't know which. And if there was another lookout to port, he hadn't shown yet, either. The Señor forgot about his downed lookout; he pushed himself away from the railing, teetered toward the radio stack, and fell against the radar console. He grabbed the hand mike from its stowage cradle, keyed it and kept keying it as he slumped to the deck. He didn't seem to want to talk into it all that much, but it was obviously very important that he hold that button down for as long as he could. I had to stick the .45 into the waist of my trousers and use both hands to pry the right hand and fingers from the small microphone. It wasn't a death grip; he was still gasping. His hat had fallen to the deck. The sweat that covered his pale, balding pate, his weather-eroded face and the neck band of his khaki work shirt would have looked unhealthy in the reflected green from the radar even if I hadn't known that he was a very sick man.

So somebody else was out there. We were either waiting for them to come here or waiting for the time to come before we went there. And the Señor's insistence on keying that mike meant that he might have had hopes that they could more easily find us if he did.

I lugged the Señor back to starboard, and propped him into a sitting position, facing aft, between the chart table and the mounted captain's chair. He was breathing badly and asking for water. I told him that I didn't have any right now and he settled for my putting his hat back on his head. I looked aft and down from the starboard bridge wing door, and saw that the lookout was still a dark and unmoving lump on the Captain's landing. The helmsman made small and labored adjustments to the ship's course from time to time, but had so far seemed – strangely, I thought -- disinterested in the well-being of his commander. With one eye on the helmsman, I walked over to the chart table.

The Coast and Geodetic Survey's maritime chart for Cape Cod and Waters North of Cape Cod was pinned to the cork surface. A rhumb line coming from the top edge of the chart indicated to me that we had come from New Hampshire or Maine. The ruled dots along the penciled course line were spaced at ten nautical miles. The ship was probably good for ten knots. Our four-mile-square holding area was eight nautical miles west-northwest of Race Point Light house, perched on the northwestern tip of the hook of Cape Cod. The holding area was shaded with pencil, and neatly labeled "Event death drop point." I left any added speculation about just what the hell that was supposed to mean for later. Right now, I had to get Molly Wager to a hospital. Whatever their limitations, the people on staff at Hyannis or Falmouth Hospital would be better for Molly than anything I could arrange for her aboard the ship.

Cape Cod was behind us on our zero-one-five holding course. I walked over to the center of the wheelhouse. I stood just forward of the gimbaled compass. I took out the .45, and offhandedly ejected the unused cartridge from the chamber, checked the mechanism and casually rammed the next one home, as if the consequences of these acts were no great moment to me. Holding the gun with both hands, I raised it to shoulder level, and, facing aft, I aimed it at a small discoloration on the skin of the helmsman's forehead, just a shade to my left, to starboard in this case, of being exactly between his rheumy brown eyes.

"Left standard rudder." I said it almost politely, and stared into his face.

It might have been my size, it might have been my comparative health, and it might have been the .45. But I like to believe it was some time-honored, sea-going tradition, some unwritten maritime law known by all helmsmen, that the ship, like the show, must go on, even if the star is sick, and the producer has had a heart attack during the out of town tryouts, and despite the political goings and comings in the upper reaches of the hierarchy, that made that man shift his gaze to the rudder position indicator and begin to wheel and spoke the laminated oak circle around to his left. After a second or two, he held his position. I lowered the gun. He looked at me for a few seconds, checked the indicator, and spoke.

"Rudder ees left standard."

"Very well." I set the safety and stowed the gun back in my waistband, and walked out onto the port bridge wing. There was a flashing light on our port quarter. Some time later there was another, and in about fifteen seconds, yet another. Each had moved progressively forward, as the bow swung around the horizon under left standard rudder. The light approached the port bow.

"Rudder amidships."

"Meedsheep."

I walked back through the wheelhouse and looked at the chart. Race Point Light. "Fl ev 15 sec 41 ft vis 12 M." The bearing to the light in the port alidade was 185 degrees. The gyro repeater lubber line under the alidade showed out course to be 215 degrees.

"Come left to one-nine-five," I called out.

"Leff to won nine pive," he answered.

I walked over to the ship's telegraph, gripped the brass handle, and rang up "ALL AHEAD STANDARD." I looked at the helmsman. He looked at the telegraph. Fifteen seconds went by. Then we felt the throb of the diesel engines increase, as the ship began to accelerate. A minute later, as an afterthought, someone acknowledged the command from the bridge by adjusting the companion device in the engine room; the smaller black response needle on our annunciator blipped over to "ALL AHEAD STANDARD", accompanied by a short burst from a ringing bell. The helmsman smiled. I shrugged, and walked back to the chart table.

The ship's log was crammed into a wooden rack, mounted on the bulkhead in front of the table. The ship was the *S.S. Edinboro Star*. Liberian registry; registered owner: Hoboken Shipping Corp., Ltd., Hoboken, New Jersey. There had been no entries since September 9th, over two weeks earlier.

XVI

The little guy at the helm hung in pretty well. He lasted for another hour. With Race Point abeam to port, I told him to come left to one seven five, and he managed that. It was four-fifty A.M. Señor had a wrist watch. Race Point looked to be three to three and a half miles to port on the poorly focused picture on the G.E. radarscope. I noted the regular green blob that must have been the familiar north shore of Cape Cod. There was a break in the shoreline just left of dead ahead. It had to be Barnstable harbor. It was as good a place as any. The lubber line on the radar showed the harbor entrance to bear one seven two. I looked toward the helmsman, to tell him to make the adjustment in course. He was about thirty degrees off the vertical, falling slowing in my direction, taking the wheel with him. The ship veered lazily toward Race Point while I moved him to a more comfortable position near the port bridge wing door. I liked the little guy, and I wished I could have helped him. But the ship came first.

By the time I'd headed the ship back toward Barnstable and secured the wheel with the helmsman's and the Señor's belts, it was twenty-five minutes after five in the morning. No one had come to relieve the midwatch. I made a trial adjustment on the engine room telegraph, commanding "ALL AHEAD 2/3." There was no response on the telegraph, and no change in the steady throb of the diesels.

It was 16.5 miles down to the shallows around the entrance to Barnstable Harbor; we still had an hour and a half. I could have called the Coast Guard. But when I thought about the Claycombe report and the information from Seventy Four, the identity of the good guys in this real-life drama was no longer so clear as I would have liked. I could have been working against the best interests of my employers no matter what I did. And after I considered the time it would take to find the correct radio frequencies, raise the right people – and only the right people – at five thirty in the morning, arrange a rendezvous, and explain to some sharp-as-a-tack Lieutenant Junior-Grade career man just why it was that the legitimate crew and passengers of *Edinboro Star* had been reduced to ten or eleven sick, dying and dead men strewn throughout the little ship – well, anyway, I didn't call the Coast Guard. I had an hour and a half. If I couldn't do something in the engine room about slowing our ten knot approach to Barnstable Harbor – and its access to medical attention for Molly – I could always bring the ship back around to the north for a while.

There was a door to the inner superstructure at the rear of the wheelhouse. A short corridor, lit by a wire-enclosed lamp on the overhead, led aft to a short down ladder to the Captain's cabin. I didn't knock.

The captain was dead. He sat in his bunk, clothed, and partially wrapped in a blanket. His eyes were open, as if he were still interested in the test pattern and the loud, white sound of the 19-inch Trinitron moored to the tiled steel deck at the foot of the bunk. I opened the one porthole, and left him alone.

I found the wardroom and the galley on the 01 level. I helped myself to an unopened quart of Minute Maid, saving some for Molly. There was another sick man in the six-bed crew's quarters on the main deck, directly beneath the wardroom. He wasn't going anywhere soon. I dead reckoned my way back to the hold. Molly took a swallow of the orange juice, and even smiled weakly at me. Then she coughed some more. I felt her brow. Now it was cold, for God's sake. I adjusted her blanket and decided to leave her where she was. A bunk might have been more comfortable, but it was becoming obvious that there were different bugs for different people on this ship, that Molly was more susceptible to their attacks than I was, and that the last thing she needed was to be left in any room where any of the crew might have been sleeping while their mutating Bolivian microbes did what they had to do.

I didn't bother with the guys in the white suits. They weren't going anywhere until somebody else said so. And Bloodman hadn't moved from his tiedown under the lavatory in the stateroom. As I undogged the hatch to the engine room from the main deck, I felt the ship heel sharply to starboard. My belt-rigged automatic pilot must have given way. I left the hatch as it was, grabbed my Minute Maid, and made for the bridge.

The Señor was dead. But he'd managed to unrig the belts, and to let the ship take its head, before the last, adrenalin-aided burst of energy had been exhausted and the lesions had short-circuited his brain. He lay sprawled on the deck next to the oak wheel. His hand had been bruised by the spoke projections as the wheel had spun on our veer to port. I moved him back to his spot against the forward bulkhead of the wheelhouse, and headed the ship back to the south, with the belts back in place.

The radar showed ten miles to Barnstable, and that meant maybe eight or nine until we reached the shallow entrance to the harbor. Ten knots seemed faster and faster.

The sky was just beginning to lighten off to my left, and I thought I could make out a darker mass on the horizon ahead of us. I couldn't see any lights on the shoreline, but I knew they had to be there. I gave the helmsman a taste of orange juice and fitted him with an inflatable life jacket from under the chart table. He acknowledged these services, not gratefully, but approvingly – another seaman doing his duty sort of thing. I never did find out whether he made it through that long night.

It was right after I popped the CO2 cartridge on his life jacket that I heard the new sound over the diesels. It was the angry rasp of unruffled marine engines being pushed hard. It was getting louder fast, and it came from the starboard quarter.

It slowly took shape in the predawn haze, a thousand yards astern. It was gray, very military looking, and gaining fast. I got the mate's binoculars from the chart table. It was a hydrofoil, about forty feet long, skimming the two-foot seas at thirty to thirty-five knots, zigzagging at irregular intervals, as if somebody expected to be fired upon. There were no markings on the hull. There was a gun mounted eight to ten feet forward of the cockpit, and as I watched through the binoculars, two men emerged from a forward hatch and began stripping the protective covering from what looked like a twenty-millimeter cannon. Their clothes were gray and seemed to match, but they couldn't have been described as uniforms. An armored cover had been hinged into position over the windshield, so I was unable to see anyone in the cockpit.

His thirty-five knots and my ten gave me about sixty seconds to start doing whatever I was going to do. It was twilight now; the sun would be up in a quarter of an hour. I looked ahead. The dark mass was too big and too close to be the mainland. It was a low-lying offshore fog bank. Warmer, wetter air being wafted over the toe-paralyzing Labrador Current by the five-knot land breeze. Classic advection conditions. The distance was tough to judge, but the fog looked closer, and thicker, some ten degrees to port. I hurried back into the wheelhouse, and made the course adjustment. One six five. I resecured the belts, and went back to the bridge wing. There was some excited jabber from the radio speaker. Something about heaving to. I didn't have time to think about it.

He knew what he was doing. They always do. He'd altered course slightly to starboard, keeping station with ease, like a water skier making and instinctive adjustment to stay out of the wake of the boat. I was going to have to get very lucky, very fast. This guy could run circles around the *Edinboro Star*.

He slowed as he pulled alongside. The patrol boat lost the hydrofoil effect and settled on to its more conventional hull, as its pilot kept station on the larger vessel. He had to add power as the boat pushed its way through the water instead of over it, now behind the power curve. The two cannon men stood on the bow, poised, waiting to heave the grappling gear when the distance to the waist of the *Edinboro Star* got down to fifteen or twenty feet. The gap got smaller. Two standard-issue business suits appeared at the stern of the hydrofoil, each with an Uzi slung over his shoulder. The two sailors, after synchronizing their rhythmic warm-up swings, made it look easy. 1-2-3. Both grapples clanked onto the tween-decks area, and the sailors hauled them in until they caught – one on the gunwale, the other on the chained-off stretch next to the stowed accommodation ladder. Hand-over-hand, they pulled the patrol boat toward the ship's side. I heard the gas engines change pitch, as their helmsman made a slight adjustment to maintain station. The two business suits poised for the leap, and I looked over my shoulder at the fog. It was very, very close, looming and boiling up in front of us, and darkening what had become a lighter sky.

I trotted back into the wheelhouse, flipped the belts off the spoke, and violently swung the wheel, first to port, then, at the instant that I felt the ship respond, just as violently to starboard. The ship plunged into the fog bank. There was a cry, a splash, and as the ship responded to starboard, a crunch and a ripping of metal, then a final agonized clawing of metal against metal, as the patrol boat scraped back along the entire length of the *Edinboro Star*. I heard the revving of engines, and a couple of shouted commands, but all sounds from astern disappeared within a few seconds. We were alone.

XVII

Someone had gone into Cape Cod Bay, I was sure of that. It might have been one of the sailors. The C.I.A. types could be aboard the Star. But if they were, they weren't storming the bridge. I put the ship back on one seven five. It was ten minutes after six by the mate's wristwatch. A half-hour, maybe only twenty minutes, before whatever the ship drew would be too much for the shallows ahead.

The fog had a few holes. Every ten or twenty seconds, I could see as far as the main deck. After three or four misty, stop-frame views of the grapple-on area, I could understand a little more of what had happened. The hook on the ship's gunwale had held, but the sailor hadn't had time to secure the line to the cleat on the patrol boat. The bitter end trailed aimlessly alongside. The second man had done better, but the weight of the damaged patrol boat had been too much for the rusty chains across the accommodation ladder entryway. A ten-foot-long stretch of chain at the starboard tweendecks, the accommodation ladder and its davit had torn away and disappeared without a trace.

I was looking at the chart, trying to decide whether I should reverse course to give myself some time, alter course a bit to soften the soon-too-be-inevitable grounding, or let the damn thing plow on into Barnstable Harbor, hoping the fog would lift, and that it would be a little too early for unsuspecting fishermen to be out and about; just hoping for everything to turn out fine, as we do from time to time.

"Put the gun on the deck, very easily, Mr. O'Toole, if you will."

For a guy who'd gotten a pretty nasty blow to the side of the head, he'd made some fast moves. He must have known the ship, and what he was looking for. He'd probably entered the superstructure from the main deck through the same hatch I had first poked my head through some three hours earlier. Then he had to have gone down into the hold, and the airlock, then up through the inside of the superstructure; because he first appeared through the center door at the rear of the wheelhouse. And because he had Molly with him.

He had a nice, mid-western twang, heavy on the r's, confident, and strangely persuasive. I would listen to reason, now that he was here to acquaint me with the facts. I put the gun on the deck.

"Now let's slow this thing down, shall we, before anyone else gets hurt?" He gestured lazily toward the ship's telegraph with his unshouldered Uzi.

He was about six-two, maybe one-ninety-five, and had the neck, pecs and waist of a weight lifter. Molly was ashen and sweaty. She wanted to stand alone, but she couldn't have managed it. He supported her sagging weight easily with his left arm. I remember being angry with him for the way his hand gripped her breast through the soiled blouse. The side of his face was turning purple, and oozing blood from what was probably a crushed left cheekbone. The thought passed through my mind that he and his orthopedic surgeons, or whatever they are that go to when you have a crushed face, were going to have a lot of complications, when and if he ever got himself to a hospital in one piece. There were enough weird and ever-adapting bacteria wafting around that hell-hole of a wheelhouse to seriously infect the entire population of Massachusetts; they'd walk over one bleeding security type with his business suit from the discount men's store in Langley, Virginia, like army ants.

I walked toward them, and, when he raised the Uzi to his waist, I stopped at the annunciator. I looked at him, back at the ship's telegraph, and back at him. I chuckled, I think, and rang up "ALL STOP." No response. The ship plowed on.

"Same thing happened before," I said. "I think what we've got here is another failure to communicate."

He glanced at the radar, then turned back to me.

"Bring it left, easy, 'til I tell you." He backed off to port, giving me room to take the wheel. Molly's foot caught on the wooden helmsman's platform. He pulled her away. She grimaced. I unhooked the belts and turned the oak wheel a couple of spokes to the left. He switched the distance scale on the radarscope.

"Hold it. There. Steady on one-six-eight."

I did. I could see that the lubber line on the screen now pointed directly into the black area that was the entrance to Barnstable Harbor. The break in the bright green return from the coastline appeared larger now, with the difference in scale and the diminishing distance.

"All right. Put the belts back on. We're going back out onto the bridge wing. You first." I did as I was told. Again.

He had other options. Besides stopping, that is. But heading north could have endangered the patrol boat, if it was still afloat, or its survivors if it wasn't. East or west could have been even worse than south when it came to inhospitable waters. I think we both thought he had more time.

He picked up the .45 on our way to the bridge wing, and flipped it over the side. The ship passed through another "sucker hole", making things look more hopeful than they were. Give it just a bit longer. Maybe the fog would really lift. The sun will be coming up and the water can't be all that cold. Then we'll just steer our way out of here, tie up this O'Toole, and steer in circles 'til I get the old tub to stop.

We left a ringing bell to starboard. It was probably a buoy, and it probably marked the entrance to the channel. There was no way of knowing if it had been green or red. He waited a few more seconds.

"All right, O'Toole. Get in there and bring it around to port. All the way. We're going to need some time – "

We hit. Hard enough to slow the ship a couple of knots, as it scraped the top off the little sand bar. He dropped Molly, braced himself against the gyro compass stanchion, and shot a burst at my legs, as I fell through the hatchway into the wheelhouse on my way to reverse course. We were free for a second or so, and then we hit another one. It was bigger than the first. The ship heeled crazily to starboard, slowing almost to a stop in maybe a quarter of its own length. The life-jacketed helmsman banged against the captain's chair and grabbed weakly at its base. I was thrown to starboard. As I fell back into the hatchway, expecting another burst of nine-millimeter slugs, I saw him struggling with Molly and reaching for his fallen Uzi, which lay on the deck at the top of the ladder to the captain's landing.

I don't know what he was thinking. Too many plates in the air, I guess. Maybe Molly mustered up a last-ditch wrench that messed up his balance. Whatever it was, when the ship lurched another fifteen degrees, the two of them were thrown aft and to starboard. He pushed Molly away, windmilled for a second, and, to save himself, grabbed for the white canvas-wrapped chain that served for a railing at the aft end of the bridge wing. He should have relaxed and gone with it. His strength and coordination worked against him, combining with the momentum from the lurching vessel, a series of jolts from the changing consistency of the sandbar and the as yet undiminished churning of the two propellers and the thousands of horsepower from the diesels. He flipped up and outboard, down two ladders, off the upper edge of the steel plating that served to enclose the ladder that led up from the main deck, and disappeared down the weather stairwell. There had been too many ricochets and bad sounds for him to survive.

Molly, nearly unconscious, had simply collapsed against the railing on the bridge wing next to the Uzi. She was safe for the moment. As I bent to make her more comfortable, there was a muffled explosion below. Then another. The vibrations from the laboring propellers stopped abruptly. The reduction gears of the drive shafts had gone first. The diesels kept turning for eight or nine more seconds before they self-destructed, having suffered what I think is known in the trade as a catastrophic stoppage. Despite the soundness of all its parts, there had been no place for the whole to go. There was a series of small explosions, followed by a moment of silence. Then an ominous creaking. Then a prolonged groan of agony and the machine gun fire of hundreds of popping rivets, as the skeleton first shouldered and then buckled under to the writhing weight of the grounded vessel; the shifting fuel, ballast, and cargo, the sinking sands, the wavering push and pull of the tidal current, and the beer-can collapsing of its bilges, cofferdams and empty tanks had finished the *Edinboro Star*. A pathetic little cloud of steam and smoke belched up alongside – the botched finale of a small town fireworks display. By the time it cleared, all was quiet.

We were down by the stern and listed to starboard some forty degrees, aground forward, but slowly being reverse-clock handed around the sandbar by the current. The tide was coming in. If it managed to pull us off the sandbar and back into deeper water, the ship wouldn't float for five minutes.

There was a rectangular locker at the end of the catwalk that led from the captain's landing back around the stern. I shouldered the Uzi, lowered myself down the ladder -- my center of gravity now displaced some thirty degrees outboard --and pulled my way along the catwalk. The lookout and his blanket had disappeared.

A burst from the Uzi shattered the Master padlock. It took another ten minutes to force open the salt-encrusted locker cover with its rubber-turned-adhesive inner seal. There were a few flares, three old kapok life jackets – bearing the legend "U.S.S. AOG-62," and a large sealskin pouch, containing a yellow six-man rubber life raft, with "U.S. Army Air Corps, mark III" printed on an attached shipping tag from The War Surplus Warehouse, Savannah, Georgia. By the time I lugged the hundred-pound raft back along the catwalk and up to the bridge, the stern of the ship had been backed around almost ninety degrees, and it felt like the tide might well pull us off the little sand bar that had done us in, but which now kept us from sinking on the spot.

I tied the raft to the compass repeater stanchion, rigged the CO2 cartridges, and pulled the cords. I wouldn't have put any big money on what year the last safety inspection had been performed on the raft or the cylinders, but this time we got lucky. It inflated enough to bounce my hand in about forty seconds. I disconnected the cylinders, extended the attached collapsible oars, and let the raft hang down from the bridge wing railing, its far end almost touching the oily water below. Molly was coughing. Silently. Her brow felt dangerously cold. There were two more life jackets under the chart table. I put one of them on her, inflated it, and used the other jacket and the first aid pouch from the raft to raise her head up to the level of the Mae West collar.

By the time I fought my way below and forward, lighting my way through the pitch-dark innards of the dying ship with a flashlight from the wheelhouse, the water in the hold was two feet deep, and lapping over the sides of the foot-thick doorsill. The canister had shifted to starboard. The airlock end was alternately floating and quietly clunking against the side of the hold, as the water level rose, and the ship shifted with the current. He'd left the airlock hatch open after he'd gotten Molly. I spun the dogging circle on the canister and opened the inner hatch. I held the business end of the Uzi slightly in front of the light as a show of force. Little Whitey was standing in the space between the beds.

"The ship is sinking. Maybe a half an hour, maybe five minutes."

There was nothing more to say. I had to get back topside. When I left the canister, Little Whitey was shaking Big Whitey's shoulder. I untied Bloodman. He didn't seem to be affected by disease just yet, but the bullet wound in the left leg was going to keep him moving slowly for a long time, if he didn't go down with the ship. I dragged him into the passageway and left him the flashlight. He followed me with the beam until I was halfway up the second ladder to the main deck level. I forced open the hatch to the main deck, and four or five thousand gallons of seawater must have poured through before I was able to step out and dog it down behind me.

The guy in the business suit was sprawled, feet first, across the lower four steel steps of the weather stairwell. The water was sloshing at his ankles. When I felt in his jacket pocket, he stirred, and I forced myself to look at what was left of his face.

He opened the eye that still looked like an eye. He looked like had had a lot to say. But there wasn't going to be enough time. As usual. He got out one whispered word.

"Smith."

"Okay," I answered, after four or five seconds. Then he slumped, finally, just like in the movies, and he was dead. There was nothing in any of his pockets.

The life raft was chafing against a rusted upper deck drainpipe, which had been forced away from the ship's side. I pushed it out of the way and climbed back up toward the bridge. Halfway, at the captain's landing, I made a detour. Disobeying the mate's hand-lettered sign, I undogged and shouldered open the door to the Captain's Cabin.

His chair had toppled over against the starboard bulkhead, and the weight of his upper body was now supported by the side of his head and an unbending neck. His open eyes still stared intently at the dead television. I got a blanket for Molly, and a sports jacket, slacks and two clean shirts for myself, from a large, upright, sliding door locker at the aft end of the cabin. There was a lump in the left-hand jacket pocket. A 38 caliber Police Special, short barrel, and a business-size envelope, stuffed. Hundred-dollar bills. Eighty, maybe a hundred. There wasn't enough light from the porthole. The ship moved, seemed to teeter for a few seconds, and then lurched to starboard yet again, losing its hold on the crumbling sandbar. I grabbed up the clothes, the .38 and the envelope. The doorway from the cabin looked sprung, I noticed, as I hurried back up to the bridge.

The bottom end of the raft was now in the water. I undid the tie line from the bridge rail, and lowered the raft as far as the line would allow. As I was about to retie the line, the ship broke free from the sand bar, and swung slowly out into deeper water, settling and listing even more, as the water poured in through the rents in the ship's side, now opened directly to the sea. Just as the stern began to pick up speed, it crunched into another bar. The line was jerked from my hands by the shock. As the ship's bow began to come around with the tide, I could see the beginning of a new cycle: the stern would be pulled off its bar, the bow would ground, and the tide would walk and crunch the *Edinboro Star* from sandbar to sandbar until there was nothing left. I picked up the clothes, the life jacket, the blanket and a disturbingly frail, silent and lightweight Molly, hipped myself over the rail, and dropped the five or six feet into the water.

We went under for a second, but Molly's lifejacket corked us back up. There was a pretty strong current. I kicked us downstream and overtook the raft. I threw the gear in, and put Molly's hands on the snare drum-taut bulge above the grab ladder at the stern. I put my right hand on top of hers, raised myself up and in, and pulled her up behind me. By the time I got her aboard, the ship had disappeared behind us in the fog.

XVIII

We might have gotten to dry land a lot sooner if the fog had lifted, or if I hadn't started rowing after fifteen or twenty minutes. The tidal current was pushing us toward what I thought was the western end of Barnstable Harbor. If that was indeed the direction we were moving, it could have been a long trip; two, maybe three hours, assuming that we weren't slowed by encounters with the several small islands along the five or six mile length of the Harbor that I remembered from the chart on the *Edinboro Star*. I didn't feel like making that trip on that morning. I didn't think Molly would have lasted that long. And after being bounced off several two-bit sand bars, and scuffing the skin of the raft on the broken clam shells, the disintegrating skeletons of the fiddler crabs and the sharp edges of various other marine detritus that covered the bottom until I feared for the integrity of the neoprene and the vulcanized seams of the World War II-vintage rubber raft, I got tired of doing nothing.

I moved Molly forward a few inches, then hand-inflated the after thwart. I headed the raft so that the current came from the port side, put my back into the oars and hoped that we were headed south. We got into deeper water almost immediately, and it got difficult to keep the boat oriented across the stream. I needed the occasional submerged sand bar or the black, undulating clump of eelgrass to gauge the direction of the current. And as the water got deeper, the fog thickened, making it impossible at times to see over my shoulder to the forward end of the raft.

I didn't think we were going around in circles or headed back out to sea, but it was taking a long time. After what seemed like at least an hour, we entered a stretch of shallower water. If my instincts had been correct, we were approaching the south shore of the harbor. We high-centered a few times, but I was able to pole us along, helped by the still-flooding tide. At about the point that I estimated that we'd go permanently aground if the water got any shallower, we plunged suddenly into a narrow break in what might have been a muddy shoreline at low tide. We were in a channel, six to eight feet wide. Long, greenish-black marsh grass grew from its flooded banks, reached up into the fog and leaned in over the stream. I saw a few cattails, and at irregular intervals the long, saw-toothed leaves of green sedge would claw at the lifelines on the sides of the raft as floated through the misty tunnel.

There were occasional rustlings in the reedy growth alongside, but the only wildlife I saw was a pintail duck, causing more commotion than necessary. Broken wing sham and all, she skimmed the water in front of the raft and disappeared into the fog. Alone again, I let the current push us along, not comforted by the thought that there were probably hundreds of other channels like the one we were in, all leading to nowhere.

I fended us off the banks with the oars from time to time, and let the current push us through the myriad twists and turns of our river through this great maze of a marsh. I could have pulled us into the bank at some point, picked up Molly, and slogged my way overland, but I didn't like the odds; and I didn't like the land. There was no way of telling which way was south, and I was no longer even confident that that was the direction I wanted to go. There was another reason. As we got further from the center of the harbor and deeper into the marsh, the fog began to burn off. Besides the occasional hole, there was a general brightening now; there couldn't have been more than fifty feet of sea mist between us and the clear sky above. I'd give it another half-hour and see if we got lucky.

The banks of the channel were broken down now, the current slowed, and the water shallower, as we approached what I guessed might be both the time and the furthest reach of high tide. At one point, I had to get out of the raft. That gave it enough buoyancy for the six-inch-deep water. I followed along behind, pushing the raft, and helping it over the shallower stretches. I would sink into the muck half-way up to my knee on every step; then, still sinking toward some deeper firmness that I never plumbed, I'd break the suction, fall forward, and, at the last second, muscle my trailing leg up with its three or four pounds of caramel-like ooze, just in time to save me from falling flat on my face into the stagnating salt water. After a couple of hundred feet of this, and after a series of turns, all slightly to the right, the water got deeper again, the channel narrowed and the current picked up. I fell back into the boat, and dangled my legs in the water astern.

It took me a few minutes to wash off the mud, and I'd just finished putting my Adidas back on when we nudged something up forward – once, then again. It seemed to have blocked our progress, and I clambered over Molly to the bow to remove the obstruction and send us on our way. It wasn't an old tire, a rotting tree trunk, a barnacled, stove-in lifeboat from the Andrea Doria, or any other reasonable hunk of flotsam or jetsam. And it was strange how a little shaft of light had just at that moment pierced the lifting fog to hit his broken face like a follow spot.

It was Smith. His misshapen corpse had stiffened, and his left arm, which I had last seen raised back above his bleeding head on the weather stairwell of the trawler, braced now against the bow of the raft, barring our path. The blood had been washed away, but the sea – or one of its denizens – had taken some of the flesh along with it. Smith was not a nice thing to see in his wavering shaft of sunlight. I shuddered, roughly pushed him to the side of the channel with one of the oars, squeezed by, and poled us along downstream.

It was about thirty seconds later when I heard the car door slam. By the time I had heard the second door, the three joyful barks from the dog, and the quiet voice of the man, I had a pretty good sense of where the sounds had come from. Forward, and to port. I pulled the raft into the left bank, and held it against the pull of the current by grasping a couple of handfuls of marsh grass; I avoided the razor-sharp sedge. There was a wiry, winching sound, then the flex of the metal carriage as the boat floated off the trailer. Once I had the idea, all the sounds made sense; the snap of the released footbrake, an old straight-six engine doing about twelve hundred r.p.m. as he pulled the trailer back out of the water, then the ratchety reset of the foot brake, the door slam, the footsteps, the gear, the oars, and silence.

I waited about ten more minutes. I trampled down ten or twelve square feet of marsh grass, and, with Molly still aboard, I grabbed the wrap-around lifeline and hauled the raft out of the stream and up onto the springy undergrowth. It was going to stay put for a while.

The sounds were gone, but I had a bearing. I pushed forward and left, as slowly and as quietly as I could, trying to keep the undergrowth between my feet and the muddy water to avoid the quicksand effect. It wasn't all that tough maintaining my heading. The marsh grass, washed and weathered by the tides and the winds, tended to lean in one direction, like a flock of grounded seagulls on a golf course. As long as I kept my angle of attack fairly constant, I could avoid going around in circles. I stumbled into a smaller channel after twenty-eight measured paces. One foot caught in the undergrowth as the fragile right bank gave under my weight, and I tumbled into the shallow stream. There were no wrenches or sprains, and I managed to weather that particular run-in with nothing worse than a few scratches; my hundred-eighty pounds had ground my face and upraised arm into the sedge grass that guarded and cushioned the opposite bank. Eleven paces farther, the sun had gone to work with a vengeance. The steaming fog boiled up around and ahead of me, and I saw the bulbous old Fraser with its ludicrous, standard, British Racing Green paint some fifty feet away, perched on a hummock at the side of a damp dirt roadway, and still attached to the homemade boat trailer that dangled down the back of the hummock, presumably to the boat launch. The old man – by the look of the Fraser, he'd had it from day one, say fifty-some years – and his dog were nowhere to be seen.

I watched for five minutes. Then I reversed course, checked my angles, and padded my way back into the marsh. I took my thirty-nine paces, avoided the fall into the small stream on the way, and hit Molly and the raft on the first try. I rewrapped her in the ship's blanket, put the captain's clothes on top, lifted the hundred and twenty pounds as gently as I could, and left the raft for good.

It was a little slower going. With the combined weight, we tended to sink through the marsh grass and into the silt. But the trail was pretty well marked now by my repeated passages, and by the time we got to within twenty feet of the car, the visibility was up to a hundred feet or so.

I laid Molly in the back seat of the Fraser. I chocked the wheels of the old, welded angle-iron boat trailer, and made the disconnect from the hitch on the car bumper. I walked down the ramp, stripping my clothes off on the way. I bathed quickly, dried myself with one of the captain's clean shirts, donned another, and slipped into the slacks and the sport jacket. I ripped a sleeve from the wet shirt and wrapped it around the snub-nosed revolver. The wrapped gun and the hundred dollar bills went into the side pockets of the jacket. The fit was a little tight and a bit short, but I would look ever so slightly less suspicious when we returned to civilized society in what I hoped would be a very short time.

The owner of the Fraser was interested in function, not cosmetics. The paint was old, but a couple of rusted areas on the left rocker panel had been carefully reamed out, leaded in, primed and sanded. The windshield was clear, the wipers were fresh. The front seat was low, and I didn't discard the extra cushion. The rear seat had a dog hair-strewn plastic cover, and looked like new underneath. The keys were in the ignition.

I got out, slipped a bill out of the captain's sheaf of hundreds, folded it, and wedged it into the wooden handle of the winch on the trailer. As I turned back, I saw the boat through the fog, some fifty or sixty yards away. The man was facing me, and rowing lazily in my direction. It was a twelve or fourteen-foot skiff, with lap-straked wooden sides, and a Golden Retriever mix in the bow. I got back in the car. The gas gauge read three quarters of a tank. I looked back over my shoulder. He stopped rowing and he stared, as I ground the wheel-post-mounted gear shift into first, engaged the clutch, and idled our way back up the narrow dirt road over the easily visible tread marks from the old man's earlier approach to the boat ramp. I thought I might have heard the dog bark once.

There were signs after a while. And it was a good thing. There were no landmarks and no structures, no water towers, nothing to key on. This made it especially difficult if your last fog-free encounter with topography had been three hundred miles to the west, among the four-thousand-foot-high Adirondack Mountains. Our road became Salt Meadow lane, and we turned left onto Route 6A maybe a mile south of the boat ramp, as the crow flew. Of course, we hadn't been able to travel in a straight line. We had followed the road as it meandered, zigged, jogged, hair pinned and circled its way through what was indeed called The Great Marsh. It had been twelve to fifteen minutes before I saw the salt marsh heather, then the scrub oak and wild grape vines that bordered the dry gravel, and finally the pavement of Salt Meadow Lane.

There was another sign indicating "Hyannis – 6 miles", then a turn onto Route 132. After three or four miles, we passed the first signs of urban sprawl, then the Sheraton Regal, the Cape Cod Mall, and a rotary near the airport. I caught sight of a blue "H" sign pointing left from the one-way street I was on. I made the turn, and pulled the smooth-running Fraser up to the Emergency Entrance to Hyannis Hospital about twenty minutes after we had left the rubber raft.

With a blanketed Molly in my arms, I climbed the stairs next to the ambulance dock, and shouldered open the swinging doors to the emergency room lobby. An intern and a broad-shouldered female nurse were comforting a young man on a gurney who had somehow gotten a screwdriver implanted in his left palm. He kept yelling "take it out, take it out!" which sounded like a wise first move to me; then again, I wouldn't have known all the complications that might have arisen from such a precipitate act, either. The doctor noticed me, looked at Molly, and brusquely directed me to an adjoining room with an operating table at its center.

"George, we'll be back to you in a few minutes. Cathy, I'll need an i.v., oxygen and the standard tray. And call Doctor Cates while I do the workup."

He moved fast, taking her temperature and blood pressure, checking her eyes, hooking up the i.v. and giving her a shot of something. Another, older doctor joined him, and the big nurse and a younger woman worked alongside, cleaning Molly's face, removing her damp clothes, and wrapping her in an electric blanket. They put the soggy manila envelope and the nearly empty bottle of antibiotics with her clothes on a service cart to one side of the operating table. They opted against the oxygen.

I sat in a chair by the door. The only sounds were an occasional moan from the guy with the screwdriver in his palm, and the never-fail calls over the paging system. The younger man was referred to as Doctor Driscoll. After fourteen minutes – it was eight-ten A.M. on the wall clock – they put her on another gurney and wheeled her into an adjoining hall. Doctor Cates stayed with me, and shook his head when I tried to follow.

"All right, young man, we'll take it from here. She'll be in intensive care. Suppose we sit down over here and you tell me what happened to your young lady." He smiled and led me toward a desk near the swinging-door entrance. I stopped abruptly, and politely but firmly removed my arm from his grasp.

"Doctor, I appreciate your concern, and I like the way you people work. But I don't have a lot of time. Her name is Molly Wager, W-A-G-E-R. She's a medical doctor, from Keene, New York. That's near Lake Placid. Five days ago, she was kidnapped from her home in Keene. At that time, she was coming down with a case of something I think you'll find to be called Bolivian Meningococcal Meningitis. She's had very little food for several days. She received a shot of what I think was a muscle relaxant on the first day. She treated herself with Keflex and ampicillin, a couple of which are still in a bottle that you took from her person. She recovered for a day or two, but encountered what she diagnosed as a secondary, more serious infection, which has not responded to sporadic, continued treatment with Keflex. In the past four to six hours, she's been lugged up and down the steel ladders of a sinking ship, now aground near the entrance to Barnstable harbor, and now infested with similar but never identical bacteria from several sick, dying and dead men aboard the same ship. She spent two hours in a forty-year-old rubber life raft while I felt our way through the Great Marsh, I think you call it. It was foggy, cold and damp out there and I don't think it helped. I –"

"Hold on now, son. I've got the picture. Now don't you worry about her. We're going to do everything we can. We knew she had an infection, but we were going to wait for a culture before we gave her an antibiotic. Knowing that the Keflex worked for a while should be helpful. We'll try another one of the cephalosporins, and then switch to something else. I'll tell Doctor Driscoll about all this. You wait here, all right? We're going to have to report this to the police, I'm afraid, and they'll want to ask some questions. Barnstable Harbor, eh?" he addressed the last question half to himself, as he entered the hall and headed toward what I assumed was the Intensive Care Unit. I walked over to Molly's dirty, wet clothes at the side of the operating table. I left the Keflex bottle, nearly empty. I took the envelope, although I wasn't sure why. The Fraser purred to life on the first turn of the key. I liked the way the old guy treated his machines.

XIX

It was a sunny and still warming September morning by the time I got back to the traffic rotary by the Hyannis Airport. If there had been any fog there, it was all gone by 9:30 in the morning. It took me two circuits of the rotary – much to the dismay of thirty or forty impatient Massachusetts drivers – to determine that there were at least two terminals. The one to the west had the larger stuff – an unmarked BAC 111, four large, yellow, oil company helicopters, a Nantucket Air Cessna 402, an old Gull Air Beech 18 with oil on the tarmac under the left engine, and a couple of turbo-Navajos loading at the break for Gate Number One, in the green vinyl wire fence that appeared to engird the entire two square miles of the airport. To the south side of the field, I could make out a line of tied-down light singles, with what looked like a twin-engine Baron at the end. I risked my life for one more circuit, edged and coaxed my way to the right, and escaped toward the south ramp.

Hyannis Aviation was a Cessna dealer, and it looked like a nice, clean operation. The maintenance hangar was spotless, and the two youngish men who were working on a partially dismantled V-tail Bonanza wore clean uniforms and moved with purpose. Although the sales staff hadn't arrived, there was a young guy behind the counter to answer phones, pump gas, and maybe sell something from the well-stocked Pilot's Store to the occasional early-departing transient. I used the restroom, took a cup of coffee from a fresh pot near the lounge area, and strolled outside.

There was a line of six little 152's, a couple of four-place Skyhawks, a retractable-gear Cutlass and a big turbo Centurion, all looking clean, well maintained and for sale. A second line had a 152 Aerobat, a Decathlon, and a red, white and blue CAP 10B; the CAP 10 was the one that caught my eye.

French. Aerobatic, and pretty fast. Maybe two hundred horsepower. With the low-slung midwing configuration, and the sliding canopy, they look like little fighter planes. You used to see them at air shows, usually trailing smoke and doing four-point precision rolls and near head-on collisions, ending in hammerhead stalls and self-induced spins. They seat two people, next to each other. And if I remembered correctly, parachutes were required for aerobatics.

I sauntered up to a red and white 152, looked inside, window-shopping, and perfunctorily registered that it had two navcom radios and an ADF. A little on the old-fashioned side with no GPS, but serviceable. I moved on to the back line, avoiding any direct moves to the CAP 10. The Aerobat and the Decathlon looked a little beat up; probably privately owned and on leaseback. I finally walked over to the CAP 10. A red-haired, eighteen-year-old girl pulled up behind me in an electric golf cart. I heard the quiet whisk of the fat rubber tires against the pavement as I rounded the right wingtip.

"Hi there. Can we help you, sir?"

"No, no. Just killing a few hours between planes over at the other side. Thought I'd come over and see what the real people are flying these days."

"Oh. Well. If you need a ride back over, just whistle when you're ready. It's complimentary."

"Thanks, anyway. I've got my car. Nice airplane."

"Oh yeah, everybody likes the CAP Ten. It belongs to Doctor Hardy, in Osterville. He's a dentist. It's on leaseback, though. Rents for one forty an hour. Wet, I think."

"Little steep. Mind if I look?"

"No, that's okay. It's locked, probably, but you can look in under the canopy. One of the instructors'll be here pretty soon, and he'll probably show you the inside. See ya' later."

"See ya'. Thanks."

I stepped up onto the black abrasive walkway at the inboard end of the right wing, avoided the flap and its "No Step" decal, and peered through the tinted canopy at the instrument panel. Nice new radios, electronic flight display, GPS. I put a hand on the canopy to reduce the glare on the plastic. Two orange, sit-on parachute packs had been thrown onto a recessed shelf in back of the seats. All right. It would do.

`A young man wearing a white, epauletted, 60-40 short sleeved shirt, a black, clip-on, four-in-hand tie, and indestructible black waiter's trousers stepped out of the office, stubbed out his cigarette on the brick wall, and field-stripped the butt as he walked over toward the CAP 10. He touched his tongue a couple of times with a bottle of Binaca, and worked up two sticks of Doublemint before he got within speaking range.

"How ya' doin'?" he offered.

"Morning," I answered.

He walked by the prop, popped open a five-inch door on the left cowling, and checked the oil. He went around the left wingtip, climbed onto the left wing walkway, inserted a key, and pulled the canopy back. I looked at the instrument panel for a few seconds, and with a head shaking, awed appreciation I thought appropriate to his reverential, expectant silence. I scanned the rest of the cockpit: G-meter, angle-of-attack indicator, heavy, criss-crossed shoulder harnesses, and the simple stick controls for ailerons and elevator.

"What kind of cruise speed you get?"

"Well, it's not bad for a hundred and eighty horsepower. One-fifty, at sixty-five percent power. Knots."

"Quick."

"Course, that's not their real strong point, I guess you know."

He had one of those universal, country-western, airline pilot kind of voices that almost concealed the familiar Massachusetts sound.

"Yeah, I understand. I saw one at an air show a few years ago. French couple."

"Yep, I remember them. Outa Poughkeepsie. They were the dealers for the whole East Coast. Somethin' else, isn't it?"

"Yeah. Is she booked for the day?"

"Yeah, Doc Hardy's goin' down to a fly-in in Delaware, eleven-thirty or twelve. Overnight. You a pilot?"

"Some in the military, maybe eighty, ninety hours in small planes. Never one of these."

"Oh hell, you'd be right at home. They fly real nice. Ya' got any time tomorrow afternoon? Give you a half-hour demo; see if you like it. Or Friday morning, early. I've got a couple hours from seven to nine."

"Nah. Guess I'll have to wait. I'm catching a Gull Air flight up to Boston. Leaves at twelve. And even if we could go up for a half-hour or so before your Doctor Hardy gets here, I don't have my ticket or my logs with me."

He didn't say anything right away, and I thought I might have gone too far with the hopelessness of the situation. He pushed a button, then another, on his watch, and scrutinized the face for a few seconds.

"Tell ya' what. It's – what, quarter to ten, and I got a student comin' in at eleven. That'd give us, say, fifteen minutes for indoctrination stuff, an-

120

other ten for preflight and screwin' around, then a half hour or so in the air. Hey, if you can make Mrs. Chroughwell in the office okay it without your license an' all, it's okay with me."

Ben Franklin is the one who did it. I had nothing much going for me; no major credit cards, not even a driver's license, much less a pilot's – and Mrs. Chroughwell wasn't a cheerful person. What did I expect, anyway? Well, I understood her position, and if I had ever imagined that I might have been going for an indoctrination ride in a CAP 10 that morning, I would surely have brought my papers, et cetera, et cetera. It was all pretty lame; but she perked up a bit when I mentioned cash, and the hundred dollar bill did the trick. John, the instructor, was on my side, and the need to get the whole operation underway and finished – if it was going to be done at all – before eleven, giving Doctor Hardy a half-hour leeway and John's student his due, added just the touch of urgency that any half-decent scam depends upon.

Operating manual in hand, I followed John back out onto the tarmac at three minutes before ten. We did a standard preflight walk around; he led, I watched and listened. Sumps, tanks, prop, gear and control surfaces.

"Shit. Somebody filled the rear tank."

"Is that bad?"

"Well, it's just that it's not approved for aerobatics. Musta been Doc Hardy. We'll just have to burn off a few to play it safe."

We lowered ourselves into the cockpit, slipped into the chutes, adjusted the harnesses and buckled ourselves in. He was in the left seat. He gave me a ninety-second rundown on the flight characteristics of the CAP 10; best angle-of-climb speed, best rate-of-climb, the cruise configuration; speeds for entry into various maneuvers and the like. Then he looked at his watch, and broke off the indoctrination lecture.

"Hell, we've gotta move. I'll give you the rest in the air; we won't have time to do all that much, anyway."

He looked around. There was no one near the plane. He switched on the electric fuel pump, watched for the pressure indication, called out "clear prop", and turned the key in the switch. The Lycoming sputtered, caught, and came to life. He switched on the radio, tuned the communication side to 123.8, and turned up the volume. He reached back over his shoulder to pull the canopy forward while we listened to the prerecorded airport information.

XX

"This is Hyannis Airport Information Bravo. Time, twelve hundred, Zulu. Sky partially obscured, five hundred scattered, visibility two and one-half in fog. Temperature is five seven, dew point fifty, wind, three zero zero at eight, altimeter, three zero point two six. Landing and departing runways two four and three three. NOTAM, runway two four threshold displaced six hundred feet due construction at approach end. Advise Hyannis Ground, one-two-one point nine, that you have Hyannis Information Bravo. This is Hyannis Airport Infor –"

He switched the com frequency to 121.9, picked up the microphone from its hook at the bottom center of the panel, and called ground control in the tower.

"Hyannis Ground, this is Mudry Three-One-Five Juliet Papa, at the south ramp; taxi VFR, with Information Alfa."

"Ah – good morning Mudry Five Juliet Papa, this is Hyannis ground." The voice from the tower crackled through a small speaker behind us. John turned up the volume, as the tower man continued. "Taxi to runway three-three, and be advised new numbers: wind is three-one-zero at ten, altimeter is three-zero point three two, sky clear, visibility twelve in haze."

"Three-one-five Juliet Papa."

We taxied out to the hold line for 33 and he did his run-up. Mags, fuel select, full control travel. He switched to 119.5, and spoke into the mike.

"Ah, Hyannis tower, Mudry Three-one-five Juliet Papa is ready for takeoff on three-three."

"Mornin', John. Five Jay Pee is cleared for takeoff on three-three. Watch for jet traffic reported five west for right downwind to two-four."

"Three-one-five Jay Pee."

He rechecked the latch on the canopy, looked at my seatbelt, and I gave him the thumbs-up. He accelerated smoothly down the runway, adding throttle as we picked up speed. He kept a little left aileron, and used what seemed like a lot of right rudder to stay on the centerline. At full throttle, the noise was deafening. We rotated at about sixty knots indicated, and climbed steeply up into the haze.

At five hundred feet, when we had left the departure end of runway 33 a few hundred yards behind us, he started a coordinated turnout to the left. I kneed the stick back to the center, and when he gaped at me in astonishment, I tugged the sleeve-wrapped .38 from the captain's jacket pocket, unwrapped it, and pointed it at his mouth. It was a little more dramatic than necessary, maybe, but you never know how a guy is going to respond to these things.

He actually stopped chewing on the Doublemint for a second or two. I switched off the radio. I unplugged the microphone from its jack under the switch panel and put it on the floor. I had to yell over the sound of the exhaust and the prop, and still had trouble even hearing myself.

"Sorry about this, John. We're going on a trip. It's going to inconvenience you and Doctor hardy, I'm afraid. I am a pilot, that part was true. Let's start by coming right to three-five-zero, okay?"

He didn't do anything for a few seconds. I knew what was going through his mind. Heroic Hyannis Flight Instructor Foils Hijacker With Dogfight Maneuvering.

"Don't do anything foolish, John. It's not going to work, and I don't want to waste the time. It's very important to me that I make this trip, and if I have to shoot you in the knees, I'll be willing to do it."

Maybe it was the mention of the knees. It might have been my face, which probably looked less friendly than usual, with the six-day darkness of the beard, the deepening lines of exhaustion underneath, and the added intensity from making myself heard over the giant chain saw in front of us. Or maybe he pictured an alternate headline in the Cape Cod Times. Airplane Thefts On Rise in Northeast. Local Flight Instructor Still Missing. He brought it right to the northwest.

"All right, just hold it right there. Level at six hundred," I shouted.

In sixty seconds, we were over the south shore of Barnstable Harbor. I saw the trailer, and the boat moored beyond it. The fisherman was gone. There was the yellow raft, forty or fifty yards to the east, and there was the tidal stream where we'd bumped into Smith. It all looked smaller and less threatening than I would have guessed from our experiences in the fog. The sedge and marsh grass-covered channel that broke the south shoreline and encircled the shmoo-shaped, three-square-mile island, was only a muddy ditch now, the tide having retreated in the past hour and a half.

The three pieces of the *Edinboro Star* lay half-submerged on a series of sand bars at the tip of Sandy neck, the long, west-to-east peninsula that protected the harbor from the waters of Cape Cod Bay. I had John do a three-sixty at six hundred feet.

The superstructured aft quarter and the large midsection of the ship were within a hundred feet of each other; the small forecastle deck was a couple of hundred yards away, being rolled eastward by the ebbing tide, back toward the harbor entrance. There were three police launches and four or five fishing boats around the superstructure, which lay on its side in five to six feet of muddied salt water. A harvest of uprooted eelgrass clung to its new waterline. A man on the lead police launch was working with someone on the wreckage to rig a highline. There were two more boats, smaller than the launches, moored to the midsection, a hundred feet up harbor. I wondered if Big and Little Whitey had made it up from the hold; and I thought about the helmsman. I pointed to the directional gyro on the instrument panel, and John steadied the plane on 350 degrees.

After ten minutes, with Provincetown abeam to starboard, I had him begin a climb to twenty-five hundred feet. He eased back on the stick and increased power to 2600 RPM. He settled on one hundred knots and showed twelve hundred feet-per-minute vertical speed. I smiled at him, held the gun where he could see that it was at the ready, and reached across him for the light blue sectional chart that was stowed in a vinyl pouch on the left side of the cockpit.

It was the only map on the airplane; a New York Sectional. Keene and Lake Placid were just barely on it, a quarter of an inch below the top edge of the back side. From Keene north, I would have needed a Montreal Sectional. No matter. I had a feeling that I could navigate without radios if I could just get us as far as Keene. From there on, it would be over the same country that the LeCourier boys and I had covered on our jeep ride the previous weekend. Pitchoff, Devil's and Sentinel Mountains would be the only landmarks I'd need.

It was a length and a half of the .38 up to Ogunquit, Maine, then a turn left to about 315 degrees, and then three and a half more gun lengths to get us near Keene. The gun measured about 45 nautical miles on the distance scale at the bottom of the chart. 225 nautical miles. The wind at Hyannis had been out of the northwest at ten knots. Unless there was another system to the west, the wind at altitude would be from the same general direction, but stronger. Figure a headwind of twenty knots. Maybe thirty. At least an hour and three quarters, maybe two. That would get us to the Keene area before one. But not by much.

"All right, John, let's go up to forty-five hundred; and keep the nose right on that headland, please." Visibility had risen to twenty or twenty-five miles. I could still just make out the tip of Cape Cod over my right shoulder, and Cape Ann and the famed North Shore were dead ahead.

"Listen, Mister, I don't like this, and I don't mind sayin' so. But as long as we're doin' it, we might as well do it right. You go up to forty five hundred around here and you might have a military jet or two on your tail. This is a National Defense Area we're about to go into. You wanta' stay outa trouble, stay at twenty five and head further west. We're okay in the Boston TCA below three thousand, long as we don't get too close."

I checked the chart. It jibed with what he'd said.

"Okay, John, looks like you might be right. Let's make it three three zero for a few minutes."

We left Cape Ann to port about fifteen minutes later. We climbed to four thousand, five hundred, and headed just west of due north, staying a mile or two off the shoreline. He leaned the mixture until the engine began to run slightly rough, then enriched it until it was just smooth, comparing his seat-of-the-pants adjustments with a fuel-flow indicator to the left of the radio. With the aircraft level at 4500 feet, and the engine leaned to best power, the airspeed indicator showed a hundred-forty knots indicated, one-forty-six true.

After passing Portsmouth, New Hampshire, we cruised on up the coast for another five minutes, then made the left turn to the northwest. I switched the radio back on, and tuned the Nav side to 113.7, which was the frequency shown on the chart for the Lebanon omni, eighty or ninety miles ahead of us. Even at forty-five-hundred feet, it would be a while before we got a usable navigation signal at that range. Now all I had to do was to will myself to stay awake.

The noise and the vibration in the poorly-insulated cockpit of the CAP 10 threatened to beat me down; it had been five or six days since I'd had more than an hour's sleep at one sitting, and there had been none at all for the last twenty to twenty-four hours. John was going cooperate, it appeared, and the sun shining through the canopy on the back of my head was very relaxing. The .38 was getting heavy. It was only when John suddenly jerked himself awake after what must have been a five or ten-second catnap, and, with a guilty glance at me, sneaked the plane back up to forty-five hundred from forty-three-fifty, that I was able to shake off the drowsiness.

"Hot," I offered. He looked at me, not hearing. I pointed back at the sun, and fanned my face. He nodded. He reached below the panel, closed the heater valve, and unscrewed the fresh air vent. The outside air temperature gauge read 41 degrees Fahrenheit. It was cold in the cockpit now, but there was no longer any danger of falling asleep.

The off-flag on the omni radio receiver head flickered, and I concentrated for a time on what were simple – but in my case long unpracticed – procedures of radio navigation; tune in the frequency, identify the station, turn the bearing selector until the needle centers, fly the course indicated at the top of the omni head, and correct for wind by turning in the direction of needle deflection from center. Actually, John was doing the flying and the correcting; and doing it without asking questions.

The folks back at Hyannis Aviation wouldn't even begin to worry until eleven-fifteen or eleven-thirty. They might be a little angry, but they wouldn't have been expecting any trouble. About eleven-thirty, they'd make a no-panic call to the tower. No, Mrs. Croughwell, the takeoff was normal, far as they knew; no word since. Finally, at about noon, say, with Doc Hardy chomping at the bit for his delayed trip down to the Delaware fly-in, they'd maybe send someone to look for us, and, by one or two, the FAA and the police would be in on it. Someone might even compare notes with the people who'd been investigating the wreck of the *Edinboro Star*, and if anyone was still alive on the ship, and they took them to the hospital in Hyannis – well, then things would start to add up. And Doctor Cates would probably remember the business about Keene, New York. And it had probably been dumb of me to have said anything about that part of it. Chalk it up to wanting the doctors to know anything and everything that might help Molly; and to my resentment for Doc Cates' patronizing self-confidence as he had led me to the desk back in the emergency room.

John tapped my knee and pointed ahead at a line of fair-weather cumulus at just about our altitude, ten or fifteen miles distant. I nodded, and signaled that he should go above them. He looked at me, shrugged, eased the stick back, and added power. We shot up to five thousand feet in fifteen or twenty seconds, sacrificing airspeed for the small increment in altitude. He let the speed build back up to a hundred and forty knots indicated before reducing power. I knew that our westerly heading dictated a cruising altitude of even thousands of feet plus five hundred, and that the next notch up would have been sixty five hundred, but I decided to let the five thousand ride for a few minutes. I plugged the mike back into its jack, turned on the Com side of the radio, and tuned to 122.0, the frequency shown on the information panel of the chart for receiving inflight weather briefings. The speaker behind our heads came to life with a conversation between a Jet Blue 737 on its way to Newark and something referred to by the jetliner as Albany Flight Watch. After Jet Blue had gotten the information, that Newark was three hundred broken, visibility a quarter mile in fog and heavy rain, I spoke into the mike.

"Albany Flight Watch, Piper Six Two Three Echo."

"Six Two Three Echo, Albany Flight Watch."

"Yeah, Albany, Six Two Three Echo is enroute VFR from Kennebunkport on up to Saranac Lake for a long weekend. We're about ten north of Lebanon and we see a line of clouds up in front of us. We're at forty-five hundred and so are they. What do they have up at Saranac for ceiling and visibility?"

"Ah, Six Two Three Echo, standby one."

John gave me a long, emotionless look, disapproving of my making a mockery out of the system by using a made-up call sign and a position twenty miles from where we actually were.

"Six Two Three Echo, Albany."

"Go ahead, Albany."

"Well it looks like you'll be all right once you get up past lake Champlain. They've got some lake-effect build-ups that run forty, fifty miles north and south of Burlington. But Saranac lake is showing ten thousand scattered, big dew point spread, fifty-twenty-eight, winds at three five zero, twelve gusting to eighteen. They're using runway, let's see, runway two seven, I guess. Looks like it'll be okay if you can get yourself over those build-ups near the lake. If you try to go under, well, you might have a terrain problem on the west side of the lake. What type aircraft are you, Six Two Three Echo?"

"Uh, Six Two Three Echo is a Piper Arrow."

"Okay, Two Three Echo, anything else?"

"Uh, yeah, do you have the Saranac Lake altimeter reading?"

"Three zero four five."

"Three zero four five. Thanks."

"Have a good flight, sir."

"Six Two Three Echo, see ya."

John had been looking at the mike, and I thought he might have been thinking about being a hero again. I switched off the com side, pulled the mike, and put it back on the floor.

"Okay, John, you heard the man. Let's get on up to ten-five, all right?" he vented his anger by jerking back on the stick and ramming the throttle all the way forward. We climbed at twenty-five hundred feet-per-second for about twelve seconds, then fifteen hundred, then a thousand, then six hundred feet-per-minute. At ten thousand, we were still climbing, but only at seventy knots and three hundred feet-per-minute. The gasping Lycoming engine was only able to generate 1750 RPM on the prop. We finally reached ten thousand five hundred he gingerly adjusted the trim and left the throttle full forward. We dropped just a bit, but held ten-four at a hundred fifteen knots indicated after he readjusted the mixture. I had us some twenty nautical miles northwest of Lebanon, with sixty miles to Keene. We were heading 325 degrees to track outbound on the Lebanon 310 radial I knew we'd lose the signal before we got to Keene, but it would be good for a while. I was just glad we weren't going down to Newark.

XXI

It was seventy-six nautical miles from the Lebanon omni to Keene, but the time-speed-distance computation was going to be less straightforward than usual. Our airspeeds had varied from the 140 knots indicated out of Lebanon, while we cruised at 4500 feet, to the diminishing climb speeds as we struggled up to 10,500, and the 120 knots we were now indicating as we held that higher-than-optimum altitude with what I guessed might be about fifty percent of the oxygen-starved engine's rated horsepower. I threw in an average headwind of twenty-five knots, and arrived at an average ground speed of a little over ninety-five knots; forty-eight minutes from Lebanon to Keene, twenty-three of it already elapsed. There were a lot of variables, and the need to watch the man in the left seat had been one of them. Well, garbage in, garbage out. I subtracted five minutes for general purposes and a possible lesser headwind element. In exactly twenty minutes, we would be over the village of Keene.

By the time the twenty minutes were up, at 1:07 P.M. by the eight-day clock on the panel, we had been forced even higher by the tops of the graying cumulus clouds building up below us. We were skimming some, dodging others, clinging to our 11,200 feet and trying to hold an average heading of 314 degrees. The clouds stretched to the horizon to our right and left and had risen several hundred feet above our altitude behind us. We could see a couple of darker areas that might have been holes in the overcast some fifteen or twenty miles ahead. But even if they were holes now, they might not be by the time we got there. The people at Flight Watch could only go with what they had, I knew, but it was hard for me to believe that it could be clear at Saranac Lake, only twenty miles ahead of us. The mountain weather was playing tricks, and was obviously more serious than forecast.

"You instrument rated, John?" I asked.

"Yeah."

"All right. Start a shallow seven-twenty to the right, while we talk."

He banked the CAP 10 fifteen degrees to the right and began the mile-wide circles, holding altitude with a touch of nose-up trim.

"We're over the spot I want to get to, John, or at least close. The highest peak within fifty miles is Mount March. Five thousand feet." I reached across to adjust the altimeter to the 30.45 setting Flight Watch had given us for Saranac Lake. The altimeter now showed our altitude to be a touch over 11,300.

"So which airport are we lookin' for? And just how do you plan to get us down to it without filin' IFR with someone?" He continued the turn past the one-eighty mark, still holding the altitude, and gesturing triumphantly at the blackening clouds boiling up over Lake Champlain.

"No airport, John. You're going to descend through the clouds to six thousand feet. If we don't break through by then, we'll head west toward Saranac Lake." I dialed in 111.2, the chart-listed frequency for the Saranac lake omni, on the Nav side of the radio. "If we do break out, we're going to look around for a while, find a nice, soft spot for me to aim at when I jump, and you'll be able to go about your business. You should have an hour's worth of fuel left, maybe even an hour and a half."

The enormity of these instructions struck him dumb for a few seconds. He continued the shallow holding turn, back through the three-sixty mark, and on into the second go-around before he could trust himself to recite, in order of increasing seriousness, the crimes I would be committing if I forced him to do what I had proposed.

"Mister, you've got another think comin' if you think I'm going to drop this airplane through these clouds –"

"John, I'm in a hurry, remember? I know what's involved. We won't hit the ground at six thousand feet. I'll worry about the jump, if and when we break out. We're nowhere near an airway, so the chances of hitting an IFR aircraft in the clouds are slim."

"How about some dude tryin' to fly in or out of Lake Placid direct, off the airway?"

"We're going to have to take that chance, John. And let's do it now. Steady on north. You watch the instruments. I'll watch for holes."

He didn't like it at all; and neither did I. But he reached down, switched the fuel selector to the front tank, and brought the power back to 1400 RPM.

The moment we entered the clouds, the relatively smooth ride was over. The moisture-laden air from the northwest was being thrown up at us by the lifting effect from the mountains below. If the air had been wetter or the day hotter, we might have been descending into the beginnings of a full-fledged post-summer thunderstorm. We had continuous moderate turbulence, and John was having trouble holding the five hundred feet-per-minute descent he had opted for. The deepening darkness, the angry drum of the occasional rain on the plastic canopy, and the little missiles flying around the cockpit – cigarette butt, gum wrapper, pencil, lock washer, broken piece of protractor, dust and Cape Cod sand – made for an interesting few minutes. I saw a brighter spot off to the left, just as we passed through eight thousand feet.

"Standard rate turn to two eight zero, John, and continue the descent."

He banked left and brought the nose around to 280 degrees. The airplane seemed to be a fairly stable instrument platform, bumps notwithstanding, and John was very, very good.

We broke through the upper deck at 7300 feet. Below us was another layer, but now there were a few holes, through which I could glimpse the shadowy terrain below. And it didn't look all that far below.

John pointed to one break in the clouds, looked at me, and I nodded. He brought the power all the way back, put the stick hard right, and kicked in full left rudder. Our rate of descent went up to 1200 feet-per-minute, but the sideslip he had put us in kept us from gaining airspeed. He held it on seventy knots indicated as we dodged between two railroad-car-sized wisps and plunged into the hole. It wasn't wide enough. He pulled back on the stick, and kept in left rudder; our forward motion dwindled rapidly, the airspeed needle bounced off the zero mark, steadied on fifty knots, and we began a tight spin to the left. We went through five thousand feet, and the ground and the wispy walls of the hole through the cloud layer panned crazily, left to right, across the Plexiglas windshield. At 4200 feet, we broke out. He relaxed the backpressure on the stick, kicked in full right rudder, and stopped what had been a fully developed spin in three quarters of a turn. He came back up on the power and steadied on a course of 260 degrees. Five miles ahead, the sun was shining down on the blue waters of what looked like Lake Placid. A half rainbow led from the near end of the lake up into the dark clouds in front of and above the CAP 10. John and I looked at each other. I nodded and he smiled.

"Okay, John, let's see if we can sneak back under those clouds and find me a place where I won't have to walk so far."

He brought the nose around to the right and I stopped him when we were headed 082 degrees, a little left of due east. There they were. The three mountains. Five miles. We were coming in from the west side, and Sentinel's peak was in the clouds to our left, but I was sure they were the ones. I pointed at Devil's Mountain.

"Head for that middle one. Stay as low as you can. Circle the peak counter-clockwise and be ready for a quick turnaround if I say. By the way, you do nice work."

He knew it. And I think he also knew that this hijacking was not going to have a tragic ending for him. Anyway, he cooperated. He dropped us down to 3500, below the tops of a few smaller mountains on either side of our easterly course. The valley we followed led just to the right of Devil's Mountain, and he maintained three or four hundred feet above the dirt logging trail that followed its gently rising floor. There wasn't going to be a lot of room to maneuver. The cloud deck was only twenty five to fifty feet above our heads, and the terrain came up to meet it a mile or so to the east of the mountain.

"I suppose you know, mister, that you're not supposed to open this canopy in flight except in an emergency."

"Well, I didn't actually know that, but –"

"Yeah, I know mister, you're gonna do it anyway; that's what I figured. What I was gonna say is, for Mrs. Chroughwell, and Doctor Hardy, and me, last but not least, I'd like to slow-fly the aircraft down to about fifty five or so before you jump so I stand the best chance of keeping in one piece for the hop over to that little airport in Lake Placid."

"Okay, John. You can start slowing any time you want."

He brought the power back just as we started the left circle, about five hundred yards away from the peak of Devil's Mountain. By the time we got around to the north side, he had the flaps down, the nose up, and almost full power back in. We were plowing along at fifty-eight knots, banked thirty degrees to the left. Then I saw the lake, just ahead of the left wingtip, coming into view from behind the northwest slope of the mountain. There were a few structures at the north end. We were too low to make a decent aerial reconnaissance, but I assumed that they were a part of Steve Beckmann, Senior's lakeside estate. I signaled to John, and he brought the nose back around to the right, keeping the bank shallow. What had to be the Beckmann Institute was just visible, about a mile north of the lake, nearly hidden behind the notch between Devil's and Sentinel Mountains. This was close enough. I didn't want to overfly the grounds. I signaled John to continue the turn, and unfastened the shoulder harness.

"Hey, mister, you can't jump from this altitude. You pick your spot and

I'll get up into the clouds right over the top of it. Give you a thousand, fifteen hundred feet more feet, anyway."

"Okay, John. This'd be just fine. Right about here." Even at fifty or sixty knots, we had already reached the side of the mountain opposite the lake.

He brought the nose up, bled off the flaps, continued the turn, and built his speed and rate of climb. We reentered the clouds at thirty-six hundred and he made one more standard-rate climbing turn before leveling off at forty-five hundred, heading north again.

"This is it, mister. We'll head this way for thirty seconds while I get'er down to sixty knots again. I'll make the turn, you open the canopy, wait fifteen more seconds, and you should end up pretty close. I put a little northwest wind into it. Twenty knots. What'd you figure comin' up here?"

"Twenty five average."

"That's good enough for me. Jump on twelve, say. You ought to have about two thousand feet."

With the plane at sixty knots, the canopy safely back, the noise making my previous complaints seem picayune, a protesting John rejecting but finally taking the two hundred-dollar bills, the count at five, the .38 firmly jammed into my beltline, and the parachute straps checked and rechecked, I looked at him over my shoulder.

"Nice flyin' with you, John."

"See you again, mister. Be careful, now." He gave me the thumbs up sign. I waved, stood up in the seat, took a deep breath of the sixty-knot relative wind, and pitched myself over the side and into the mist, hoping that I wouldn't get conked by the tail.

XXII

I counted to one and pulled the cord. The pilot chute deployed; the main was orange and it worked fine. I broke out of the clouds about five hundred feet above the northeast slope of Devil's Mountain. I heard the plane's engine, then lost it as it receded to the west, beyond the mountain.

The bulbous, thirty-foot rectangle of bright orange had decelerated me to eight or nine hundred feet-per-minute, but it seemed like the ground was coming up very fast. I worked the rectangular lift hole around to the south, and aimed for lower ground. There was a clearing to the northwest, but I wasn't going to make it. If I'd jumped from twenty thousand feet, say, with no clouds to fall through and a target selected prior to the jump, I might have been able to work the shrouds and the lift hole enough to move upwind a few hundred feet. But in the twenty-five or thirty seconds I had after I broke out of the clouds and before I went into the forest that blanketed the slope of the mountain, all I could really do was to marvel at the windless silence and the smell of pine trees after a rain. It was nice while it lasted.

They say that if you lose all power in a single-engine airplane, and you're over a forest, with no better emergency strip in sight, then to barely maintain flying speed and pancake into the tops of the trees is not the worst thing you can do. If you have a twin, well, then you probably won't have to worry about whether this is true; though there are those who say that the extra engine will only serve to get you to the scene of the crash a little sooner. Anyway, I've never had occasion to try the pancake-into-the-forest maneuver. But if you do, I think you're going to need something with a little more surface area on its underside than a human body has.

I don't know what the result would have been if I had been dropping straight down; some scratches, a ripping chute, maybe a couple of broken bones, maybe worse. But no matter what I did with the nylon suspension lines, I was still moving over the ground at ten to fifteen miles-per-hour when my instinctively raised legs caught the tips of the first tall trees. My initial thought was that these little wispy slaps at my ankles didn't hurt that much and might well defray my groundspeed; a landing more orderly than the one that seemed to be developing might still be possible. Then I was up to my waist; that particular treetop gave, bent, and then released me, all in the space of a second. But it was enough for the chute to move on down wind. The lines relaxed, then snapped taut, plucking me off my temporary perch, back into the air, and banging me into the next one. This happened three or four times; I can still remember the indignant recoil of the upwind virgin treetops behind me. At first I tried to time the impacts and brace myself accordingly. After the first two, I relaxed. Better. At last, I was dragged into a tree that wouldn't give way. The chute and the persistent fifteen-knot wind were pulling me around the top, but I managed to hold on with my legs as I snapped off the quick-release buckle. The chute went south and I went north.

After three or four crack-the-whip oscillations, the tree steadied. I could relax my death grip on the hay bale-sized bundle of sticky pine needles that was the treetop, to assess the damage. The tree was none the worse for wear. There was a little blood here and there from my face and hands, but it wasn't so abundant that it could have come from anything but superficial wounds. The .38 was long gone. I was sore. But I was safe; if clinging with arms and legs to the top of an eighty-foot-high White Pine can be so characterized. I looked down. The long needles just below me were still wet from the rain. Several rectangular, green, non-coniferous leaves floated down toward the shadowy forest floor. They all had pictures of Ben Franklin on them. I grabbed for the captain's pocket, which had ripped away from the coat; the bills were spewing out of the envelope, two by two. I managed to save forty or fifty of them, and nearly dislodged myself from my precarious holding position in the process.

The landing had not been a total disaster. I was able to get a flying squirrel's-eye-view of my surroundings, which would have been impossible from the ground. I was facing south; the peak of Devil's Mountain loomed up before my right shoulder. I wrestled myself around to face the other way, dropping down a couple of feet when I sensed that my weight was threatening the soundness of the treetop. The upper third of Mount Sentinel was still in the clouds, two miles to the north. The notch between the two mountains was like a bridge between them; though below my vantage point, or crash site, the notch was several hundred feet higher than the several interconnected valleys that hemmed the bases of the two mountains. Beginning at the center of the notch, and running down and east, there was a barely discernible interruption in the continuity of the forest. A road, a stream, maybe just a fault line.

I shinnied down the tree, circling the larger branches and picking up a few hundreds on the way. I selected a line of trees to the northwest to maintain my orientation. Just as I got to the bottom, the sun broke through overhead. It was only a temporary respite from the gloom of the low overcast; looking up through the trees, I could see more clouds to the north and west. But it cheered me up a bit; I forgot about my stinging, blood- and sap-encrusted hands and face for a while. I picked up the few more bills I could see, and struck out downhill and across the slope to the northwest.

After few hundred yards, I altered course to the right a few degrees. I had been aiming for the notch between the mountains, but I wanted to come in below its crest; and if I were to cross the break in the trees en route, well, so much the better.

XXIII

I came to the road about a half hour later. It was only a mile or so from my drop point, but the downhill traverse had proved to be slow going. It was slippery, and there was a lot of ankle-threatening dead wood buried under the pine needle floor of the forest. I intercepted the road about an eighth of a mile below the crest of the notch. Looking downhill, to my right, I could see the road dropping away, weaving further right and out of sight, generally headed east, down into the valley toward what must have been a connection with the road along Nichol's Brook that the LeCourier boys and I had followed the previous Saturday morning.

So someone had mowed down a few thousand pine trees, and gouged out a cut from the rocky topsoil leading up to the notch between the mountains that was some thirty feet wide and at least four or five miles long. Then they'd trucked in a couple million dollars worth of gravel and spread it over the clay underburden to a uniform depth of two and a half feet. There were thin spots and some corrugations, but it looked like it would suffer the passage of fairly heavy equipment without damage. I headed left, uphill, hugging the side of the road.

The stream must have paralleled my course down and across the mountainside. It met the road about a hundred yards farther up the slope. It tumbled down from the south, pooled up at a small, man-made, earth and cement-sided dam, ten feet short of the road, then poured more sedately down an aluminum sluiceway and through a metal culvert that the construction people had installed under the gravel roadbed. I took off the torn jacket, rolled up my shirtsleeves, and went to work on my face and hands. The silt from the slow-flowing stream bed below the dam made a pretty effective cleanser for the dirt and the dried blood, but I was going to need something chemical to get the black pitch marks off my hands. The water wasn't so cold as I might have expected, nor so clear; I blamed the recent rain. It tasted fine.

I followed the road uphill for another hundred yards, until I was just below the crest; then I struck back into the trees to the left. I crossed an ancient foot trail that appeared to run along the crest of the notch and on up the north slope of Devil's Mountain. The terrain dropped sharply away from the trail on the Institute side, but there were too many tall trees for me to see the compound below. I doubled back, and followed the trail to the south and uphill, hoping for a sightline with the higher elevation. Fifty yards up the trail, I realized that I was going to have to climb another tree if I wanted to see anything. The trees weren't so high on this, the windward side of the notch, but they were closely spaced enough to halve the light from the dark gray sky and to obstruct every sightline within twenty or thirty feet. I selected a fifty footer that looked like it might have been a bit taller than its neighbors, hoisted myself up into the lower branches, and began the half crawl, half clamber through the thicket above me. At forty feet, the neighboring tops had dropped away with the terrain; I could see the compound, a hundred and fifty yards to the northwest.

The Beckmann Institute was closer to the crest than it had appeared from the cockpit of the CAP 10. Maybe three small city blocks. Fifteen or twenty acres of mostly level land had been cleared of trees, except for a decorative survivor here and there, to accommodate the buildings; and another five acres had been denuded to facilitate the construction of the last eight or nine hundred feet of access road. The sharp falloff from the notch had required a system of switchbacks, built-up roadbeds and wooden beam and concrete retaining walls that had probably added fifty percent to the cost of the road up from Nichol's Creek.

Molly Wager had had it about right. There were three buildings, they were definitely contemporary, and there was a lot of wood and glass. But it was not the bustling place she had described.

There were no vehicles or people to be seen in or around the service building. It was to my right. It could have been a very expensive, sixteen-car garage owned by an edge-of-the-cliff, Northern California lumber magnate who had a taste for angles and dark-tinted glass. Its two, hangar-sized, folding panel doors were closed. There was an empty, quarter-acre asphalt parking area to the left of it, and, further left, a pumping station, two large electrical transformers enclosed by a wire mesh fence, and a twenty-five-foot-long cylindrical propane tank, mounted on its side on a series of cement-anchored wooden x's.

The center building – main lab and administration, according to Molly – had probably been featured in an architectural journal or two, and no doubt graced the first page of somebody's I-did-this book. It was a hundred feet or so to the left of the service building, separated from the parking lot and the power and fuel stations by a fenced, half-acre field, longer than it was wide. Two horses grazed at the far end of the small pasture.

I'm sure that the reviews of the main lab just have said things like "A Triumph of Angle: Form Reflects Function." To me, it looked like three misshapen prisms that had been forced into too small a space. But it worked. The triangular faces of two, long, low pyramids, underground at their outer ends, sloped upward toward the center of the structure. They were transected by another, larger pyramid, lying on its side, with its triangular base soaring toward me and the front of the building. The overhang from the off-perpendicular base of the larger pyramid served to protect the all-glass front entrance from the weather. The bases of the two flanking wings almost touched, and appeared to be straining to do so. The various lines – the bases, sides, and altitudes of the three pyramids – were formed by cedar logs, arranged so that their smaller ends pointed up toward the center of the building.

The outer walls – the plane sides of the pyramids visible to me – were inlaid with progressively smaller triangles of varying woods; all were no doubt of Adirondack origin. The inlays and the strategic placement of the windows left the impression of another dimension; in fact, it was the only dimension that seemed to have survived what must have been a conscious decision by the architect to avoid any angle or line that might have suggested the square, rectangle, perpendicular or parallel. The dimension remaining was depth; level upon level, without end. Even though I knew the size of the surrounding mountains, the height of the tall trees in the forest that surrounded the clearing, and the approximate distance from my tree to the road and down to the Institute grounds, I found it difficult to estimate with any confidence the size of the pyramided main building; or even the lengths of the stripped but untreated, weight-bearing logs that formed its outlines. It was like looking at something through a telescopic lens of unknown focal length; the kind of confusing perspective that took your mind off the obvious and made you think of other things. I imagined that this was probably a good thing for a micro-biological research laboratory, where things probably aren't over even when they're over; just about the time you think you've seen the smallest thing there is, you notice first that it has a leg, and second, that something is burrowing into that leg. I was reminded of the confusing moments I had spent in Molly Wager's eighty-year-old farmhouse, when the two SUV's – filled to overflowing with big, business-suited men carrying small but deadly Uzis – had chewed up her newly-planted acre of a front lawn a long few days before. I mused over these architectural and philosophical dead ends as I watched the only signs of life in the whole compound.

A three-axled, two-and-a-half-ton army truck, made to military specifications by an anonymous manufacturer, and painted a kind of non-hue – grayish green, maybe – that would have looked the same in color as it did in black and white, was parked on the graveled main access road at the entrance to the driveway that circled up to the main building. Just in front of the truck was a large, pine-cone-shaped wooden sign, hanging from a rustic log frame. It was too far away for me to read the yellow lettering. The canvas that covered the ribs over the box of the army truck was reefed up a couple of feet from the bed; there were personnel benches behind the ribs, and there was some movement. As I watched, a slightly built, olive drab-but-with-no-markings-clad soldier – or at least a soldier type – wrestled a large coffee urn out onto the laid-down tailgate. He went back into the tarp-covered truck box, and came out with a red ice chest. As he dropped to the ground, I heard the rumble of heavy engines. The soldier heard it, too. He looked eastward, back up the hill toward the switchbacks and the notch.

Two large Mercedes diesel trucks, with fourteen-foot-high boxes, the width of which would have scraped the trees on either side of the graveled road up from Nichol's Brook, lumbered into the notch end of the gouged-out clearing, geared down, and carefully negotiated the wet surface of the graveled switchbacks, down toward the service building. They passed the parking lot, the pump station, the transformers and the propane dump, and moved on toward the main building. The coffee man ran around to the cab of the six-by-six, started it up, and jerked forward about twenty feet, clearing the entrance to the driveway.

The first Mercedes cut the corner a little too closely as he made the right off the access road. The moving-van-sized box lurched over to the right and the double wheels on the right rear axle slowly sunk down into the transplanted sod that ran up to the edges of the driveway. The driver, another young olive drab, shut down the engine, lowered himself gingerly to the sod on the left side of the driveway, tight-rope-walked himself back along the edge, and walked casually around to the right rear to survey the damage; he gave the driver of the second truck a what're ya' gonna' do kind of shrug as he passed out of my view. The second driver got down, walked around the front of his cab, and joined the first. After a minute or two, they reappeared, and walked, laughing, over to the army truck. The coffee man poured them each a cup, pointed to the red portachest, and, with a third

140

cup in hand, walked down the slight incline in front of his truck toward the infirmary.

The infirmary would have been a fairly conventional custom contemporary, even with its uneven sides and its oddly shaped windows, had it not been for the flat, sloped, trapezoidal lean-to roof, which was separated vertically from the more traditional structure it sheltered by a system of stilts. Of course, the trapezoid wasn't really a trapezoid; the bases weren't parallel. And if I knew the guy as well as I thought I did, he'd had abbreviated triangle on his mind when he designed it. Again, the outlines of all the plane surfaces were formed by untreated logs, possibly pine in this case, and there wasn't a square, perpendicular or parallel in sight. There was the same illusion of unplumbable depth as with the main building. Without accurately describing its dimensions, I could safely say that the infirmary was about one third the size of the admin-lab building. The oddly shaped windows stretched across the front of the building, and maybe ten feet back along the side I could see. Like the other buildings, the infirmary and its sheltering roof were backed to the weather from the northwest. A stream ran through the western end of the compound, presumably to feed into Devil's Mountain Lake to the south. Molly had called it Halfaday Creek, I remembered.

A single soldier stood at a loose parade rest in front of the entrance to the infirmary, feet apart, with his M-16 moving lazily in and out of the one-o-clock position at his right. He faced the building, apparently more concerned with keeping people in than keeping them out. The coffee had been for him. The slightly built driver of the army truck, with his delivery made, ambled back over to join the Mercedes drivers at the portachest.

A lone crash of thunder rang out from the north. It was followed by a surprisingly vigorous fifteen-second-long downpour that caused the three soldiers to abandon their lunches from the portachest and seek cover under the tailgate. There was a sheet of lightning, then, eight-Mississippi's later, another clap of thunder. The heavy overcast in the eastern two thirds of the sky moved another half degree, and the sun, going the other way, broke out to stay, bathing the area in a squint-provoking brightness that made even the colorless army truck look like a thing of beauty.

XXIV

By putting one foot in front of the other, without some unifying master plan, I had somehow managed to get myself from Cape Cod Bay, imprisoned in the airlocked cylinder in the hold of the *Edinboro Star*, to the Adirondack Mountains and the top branches of a fifty-foot pine tree, overlooking the humanitarian research facility that had made everything possible. Most of the moves in the preceding four days had been reactionary – getting Molly and myself out of some predicament someone else had put us into. Beginning with the hijack of the CAP 10, however, I had had something more definite on my mind. I wanted to talk things over with the good doctors Wager and Claycombe. Maybe Molly's constantly mutating infection was going to be impossible to cure, I didn't know; but I couldn't ignore the possibility that those two men, if they were still alive, would be better equipped to direct the course of her treatment than the crack staff back at Hyannis hospital, who might themselves be experiencing at that exact moment some of the initial headachy symptoms, desperately popping tetracycline and boning up fast on everything from cerebrospinal and Bolivian Meningitis to Lyme Disease.

Hell, maybe Wager and Claycombe had some sort of an antidote by now. If Wager's quick recovery hadn't been a lie, they must have known what to give him to bring it about. The bacteria must by now have infected quite a few more people than Molly and me, the men in the semi-truck as we drove across New England, and the passengers and crew of the *Edinboro Star*. There had probably been a public outcry over the strange new Asian flu that no one had predicted like they had all those other years.

There had to have been some pressure; maybe even a few calls to and from the CDC in Atlanta. And they'd had five or six days.

If Wager and Claycombe were on the premises, they were probably in the infirmary. If they were there, they were there under armed guard. That was a problem; I was unarmed. But even so, I felt that I could circle around to the rear of the compound, come up behind the infirmary, distract the guard, sprint the twenty feet to his position, and take him before he would see me, or at least before he would pull the trigger. I knew I was bigger than he was; and I was probably madder. Whether or not I could do all that without attracting the attention of the people outside the main building was another question. But at worst, I could break into the infirmary, armed with the guard's M-16, find Wager and/or Claycombe, tell them the facts about Molly, and let them take it from there before anybody barged in after me to put me under house arrest. Let Wager cut through the inevitable red tape to get whatever it was that they had down to Molly in Hyannis. If they had anything. If Wager was still alive. If the guard was as young and as good-natured as he looked from a hundred and fifty yards.

I had already started back down the tree when a mud-spattered, four-wheel-drive Volvo C-70, and then a military personnel carrier with ten or twelve men in the back, appeared at the top end of the compound. They sped down the access road, taking the switchbacks at twenty miles per hour and spraying loose gravel over the log-reinforced concrete retaining walls. A few seconds later, an unmarked military ambulance followed them, taking the downhill turns with somewhat less urgency.

Everyone snapped to. The sentry at the infirmary straightened himself up, the truck drivers bustled over to the sunken right rear of the first Mercedes, and the coffee man busied himself around the tailgate of the six-by-six.

The station wagon pulled to a stop behind the coffee man, and the personnel carrier slowed and idled up to a respectful distance behind the Volvo. A khaki-clad soldier jumped from the rear end of the personnel carrier. He reached back, retrieved a large pack, and hurried up toward the station wagon, struggling to deploy the antenna on the portable field radio as he ran; the ambulance passed the other vehicles, picked up speed, and slid to a stop in front of the infirmary.

Five men had emerged from the Volvo. There were only two, from the rear seat, who seemed disinterested enough in military protocol to be senior officers. Casually waving off a salute from the agitated coffee man, they walked toward the mired Mercedes truck, engaged in animated conversation. A third man from the Volvo trailed them, never more nor less than three and a half feet behind, looking warily from right to left. The two remaining men stayed near the car.

After disappearing behind the Mercedes for about thirty seconds, the two officers, followed by the bodyguard, reemerged. The smaller of the two had made up his mind. He started giving orders. As if by magic, four men jumped from the personnel carrier and ran toward the disabled truck. Two more trotted down the road toward the infirmary, in step with each other, checking their M-16's on the way. And finally, six more, similarly armed men headed back up the access road, climbing the switchbacked hill to the notch. One of them was in charge; he broke off two men half way up the hill, and directed them into the forest, in my direction. He and another man from the remaining four fanned out into the forest just as they got to the edge of the clearing, and the other two continued up the road and out of my sight.

I didn't know if they were looking for me, but if they were, they wouldn't have far to go. I waited. The officer in charge seemed to have established communications with someone on the field radio. One of the soldiers backed the second Mercedes diesel into the other end of the driveway, up against the snub nose of the first, and two others rigged a log chain from the axle of one truck to the other. The ambulance driver and a helper unloaded a wheeled stretcher, and pushed it toward the three soldiers in front of the infirmary. The helper flapped open a long, green, plastic body bag as he approached the entrance. Several other soldier types began the deployment of what looked like some kind of decontamination paraphernalia from the boxes of the two Mercedes. The three sentries drifted to my left some ten or fifteen feet; just enough to get the best of both worlds; still at their assigned duty posts, but just upwind of any funny microbes that might accidentally slip out of the infirmary doors.

The odds against my getting into that infirmary had gone up; and now I wasn't even sure that was what I wanted to do. It wasn't just the number of men and M-16-s that were changing my thinking. There was some something so – military – about all these newest arrivals; their bearing, their deference to authority, their clear-cut chain of command. All right, that would be exactly what you would want if you had yourself a crack private security force; military doesn't have to mean <u>military</u>. But the absence of insignia, this studied rejection of any traceable identifying markings on the gray-green vehicles and the uniformed men, forced me to consider just what it was they didn't want somebody to know. And why they didn't want somebody to know it. There was another thing. They looked young. Late teens, early twenties. Not the officers; the grunts. It was more than a hundred yards to the little knot of vehicles, but I could see well enough to feel sure that this wasn't a posse from Saranac Lake, a Beckmann Institute security force on practice maneuvers, or a pickup group of cynical mercenaries. They looked like recruits. Intuition. Body language, maybe.

But what military? U.S.? If so, why not go down to say hello; arrange for a confirmation from Washington on me, explain the whole thing and go over to talk with Wager and Claycombe with the blessings of the commanding officer on the scene? Well, I'd been in the business long enough to know that the important thing about an unknown force is not its nominal "identity", not "who they are," but simply whether they're friendly or unfriendly. My experiences of the last four days, the studied anonymity of this small force, and the apparent urgency with which they were staking out the forest, possibly searching for me, made it very easy for me to make that decision. Unfriendly. They – assuming that these guys were the same "they" – hadn't cared much about Molly and me in the past few days – "event death drop point" indeed – and there was no reason why they were going to start now.

The Claycombe report had made it clear. Instead of the garden variety acid rain poisoning event that had brought me up to these mountains, we had a garden variety biological warfare production facility financed by a maniacal oligopoly and probably fully supported by a federal government just going on habit and preparing a response to a non-existent but at least more traditional threat to the country than the amorphous and slippery terrorism that was the real one. The Beckmann Institute was manufacturing a state-of-the-art biological weapon. The military was involved. And the whole project was supposed to be top secret hush-hush. That was enough. The skullduggery that the various branches of the services would involve themselves in in the name of secrecy – from arrest, imprisonment and torture, to blackmail and umbrella tip-piano wire-potassium cyanide in the banana daiquiri-assassination plots – was no longer even front page news. Even if Claycombe himself had died after mishandling a component of some doomsday bug-bomb being financed by the Pentagon, the Institute press release would spin his passing as a testament to scientific dedication and the place for philanthropy, and it would be only one step further to not report his death at all. Maybe they couldn't do that with Claycombe, but they sure could with me. Or Molly. A lot less messy. Ever so much less media coverage. Instead of six to eight years of juggling subpoenas from various congressional committees, they would be out twenty or thirty bucks for a couple of body bags. And the secret's still a secret.

My thoughts as I sat on the upper branches of my second tree of the day were not political. I didn't like what they were doing down there. Not at all. But right then my feelings were strictly personal. Get some help for Molly Wager, and get it fast.

But the frontal attack was going to have to wait. It couldn't help Molly to have me out of action. And even if I could have gotten to see Wager or Claycombe, it was more than likely that their wishes, even if humanitarian, would have taken a back seat to the military need for secrecy. I heard the dull snap of a pine twig, off to my right. It was time to make my move.

The opportunity for taking a reasonably careful stroll back down the gravel road toward Nichol's Brook Road, the cemetery and Keene, where I could make some phone calls and maybe even get myself some firepower, had been lost when the six forest-beating soldiers had cut me off from the access road. Now, it was going to have to be cross-country. I'd have to circle around the west side of Devil's Mountain, skirt the lake, and head south toward Route 73, the highway that ran between Keene and Lake Placid that I would eventually have to cross, assuming I didn't lose my bearings. If I could find it, I might even be able to follow the logging road that I had seen from the air as John and I had flown back up the valley toward Devil's Mountain after our spinning descent through the clouds. I shinnied down the tree, looked and listened, and dropped down the hill into the forest, leaving the game trail and the crest behind me. The sun was about thirty degrees above the horizon, which was unevenly formed by the tops of the mountains to the south. It was probably a little after three. It was getting to be a long Wednesday.

By now, I was getting pretty good at moving through these Adirondack forests; expertly gauging my direction by the angle at which I crossed the downward slope, cleverly spotting the softer-looking piles of pine needles which invariably made for bad footing, athletically jumping or fording the occasional streams and rivulets that poured down the mountainside every two or three hundred yards, confident that I had successfully eluded my pursuers, even if they didn't know that they were my pursuers. In fact, I was so pleased with the way I had been handling myself, that after crossing Halfaday Creek, a mile or so downstream from the Institute, and climbing ten feet up the steep bank on the far side, I decided to give myself a five-minute breather before continuing the climb. I lay down, leaned my head against a tree, and, raising my feet, braced them against another.

"Mister, don't you even think of movin' even one inch if you don't want any holes in that sorry lookin' sportcoat a yours."

I opened my eyes, hoping that that wouldn't count as a move. Another thirty-eight caliber revolver; in ham of hand attached to big arm bulging through man-made fiber of yet another business suit. Nice face, a drinker, used to taking things seriously. Big body, possible difficulty in holding chest and shoulders up, gut in. Pants legs stuffed into new leather hiking boots. Nice ones. The reason I hadn't heard him was that he didn't have to make much noise when he just sat in one spot and simply waited for Natty Bumppo to bull moose his way through the forest and lie down within five feet of where he was sitting.

"All right if I sit up?" I asked, doing it just before he gave me the okay.

"Just make it nice and – I said make it nice and slow, y'hear?"

"What's the meaning of this, anyway? Can't a man go for a walk in the woods on his day off anymore?" I stalled, brushing an imaginary wood tick off my right ankle.

"Not on private property, he can't, mister, and somepin' tells me you ain't on any walk in the woods that's gonna do anybody but yerself any good. Suppose we – "

"Look, whoever you are, we can straighten this whole thing out in about ten minutes. I'm Doctor Driscoll; I work at the Beckmann Institute, back up the hill. Just call up there, or better yet, follow me back up, and I'll save us both a lot of trouble. I didn't know that this stream wasn't on the Institute property. I – "

"We'll see just who knew what when I say, and we're gonna do it my way. If you're who you say you are, there's gonna be no problemo at all. Hell, I'll even apologize. But I'm just doin' my job and they'd fire me like a hot potato if I let somebody come traipsin' in around here without checkin' up on 'em. All right, you lead; we'll go on back up there and talk to somebody at the Institute."

With this kind of a guy, thinking doesn't do a bit of good. Neither does finesse. It's all action and timing. Hit them while they still think that you just might be a doctor and on the up and up, before they start remembering that maybe somebody told them that the Institute was closed down for a few days, and that those guys never go for walks in the woods anyway, not being outdoors people. I struggled to my feet, groaned, grabbed my back in mock old-timer dismay, and turned back toward the stream below us. I listened for his first step, stumbled, braced myself against a tree, and simply continued the turn, raising my left leg out from the hip, and punching with it as it swung on around to knock his feet out from under him. He bounced off another tree as he went down, or the one shot he got off might have hit me. He wasn't as slow as I'd imagined. The shot would have been heard by everyone within a mile or two, and that would certainly have included the six soldiers back up toward the crest. There wasn't time for the struggle over the gun, or the exchange of splattery punches, the bruised and broken knuckles, or any more talking. I had to stomp on his neck. While he was down. He went out without a sound, not dead, but very likely to have a bad crick when he woke up. As long as I was being mean, I took the boots. They were a little big, but they beat the Adidas Cross-countrys I left with Slambang Porky, which were just about to fall apart. I retrieved the .38 from his limp right hand and jammed it into my belt.

I headed back up the hill, moving west, altering a few degrees to starboard to give a wider berth to the Beckmann estate, just in case there were any more security men out beating around the bush and trying to make themselves look important. Or looking for the big guy and wondering what the single shot from the small-caliber pistol had meant. I felt a bit sorry for the fat man. But hell, I might have saved him from a bad case of meningitis. Or worse. Who knew?

XXV

I followed Halfaday Creek to the south, hugging the tree line at the top of its steep banks, and making as little noise as possible. Quieter meant slower. It took me a good half hour to reach the upper end of the hundred-foot-long straight stretch of stream bed that dropped on down to the north end of Devil's Mountain Lake; it was no more than a mile from my run-in with the fat man. When I saw the still surface of the slate-blue lake ahead of me, I made a forty-five to the right and headed almost due west.

There were three shots from some distance behind me, fired at half-second intervals. I heard voices, and I assumed that one of the soldiers had stumbled onto the security man, fired the signal rounds, and been joined by the others. If the fat man was awake, and if they believed him when he told them he wasn't me, they'd know that I was armed, and that I had a half hour on them. If they didn't believe him, I would have more.

I picked up the pace as I trotted up the gentle slope away from the lake. After two hundred yards, I turned south again. I paralleled the west bank of the lake, which I could glimpse through an occasional break in the forest. I kept up the trot, knowing that I didn't have to worry about being heard. At least not by the people behind me.

By the time I got to a point abreast of the south end of the lake, it must have been four or four thirty in the afternoon. The terrain, fairly even for the last two miles or so, began to rise again, sharply at first, then steadying on a one-degree incline to the south. I was beginning to picture myself climbing the side of Pitchoff Mountain at midnight, stumbling around in the leftover snow banks, and dodging the playful but hungry outlaw black bears that no doubt roamed these environs, when I came to what looked like the logging road. Well, a logging road. It angled off downhill to the southwest; it was south of Devil's and still north of Pitchoff. It hadn't been used in a long time.

Through the narrow break in the treetops above it, I could see that we were going to have one of those mountain sunsets; when the sky stays bright for a long long time after the sun disappears behind the mountain, when it gets darker and darker under the trees, and when the people on the western slopes have to wait for another two hours before they can pour the first martini.

Even if the road wasn't the one I'd seen from the CAP 10, it seemed to lead in the right direction. I'd at least be able to see the stars in what was going to be a clear night sky, so I wouldn't be floundering aimlessly around the forest. And the road had to go somewhere. I turned right and headed downhill. The ruts were covered with pine needles. After the first few steps, I resumed the trot, seeing that it was going to be much easier going than the forest floor. And that was when I heard the moaning. Behind me and off to the left. I stopped to listen.

It was distant, it was mournful and it was eerie. And there was something vaguely familiar about it that I couldn't place. The black flies and no-seeums that Pete of Pete's Amoco had spoken of were just beginning to wake up from their afternoon siestas. I had already bludgeoned a couple of mosquitoes on my arm and neck. Maybe there was some vast spawning ground, some watery swamp hole below the lake, where they lived and reproduced in the billions, buzzing this song of ecstasy before launching their first twilight attacks on the other denizens of the forest. I turned toward the sound and took a few hesitant steps back up the road, trying to gauge the distance and guess the nature of this strange, dirge-like music of the forest. It continued, rising and lowering in pitch and intensity. I thought for a time that it could have been a machine; a generator, maybe, or a grease-starved submersible pump for some backwoods retreat, whining away in its last hours of life. It seemed to call to me, and I couldn't resist. Yes, it was going to get dark under the trees. But I wasn't going to be under the trees. I would be padding down the soft ruts of the abandoned logging road under a still-bright sky, within an hour or two of a return to civilization and all it meant: telephone, food, and sleep. I could afford a fifteen-minute sidetrack.

I followed the road back uphill for another fifty or sixty yards. Then I had to leave it; the sound was coming from somewhere farther to my left. Then it was downhill, away from the sun, and I didn't like it. I was headed back toward the south end of the lake. Maybe that explained it. The light, northwest breeze blowing through the rushes along the shore;

or some other freakish, but natural, resonance formed by the waters of another stream and a beaver dam, say, or an accidental buildup of debris that had jammed against the bank in such a way that when the waters hit it . . . I broke off speculating. I wouldn't be able to head toward the sound for much longer. If I had any pursuers, that was where they would be coming from. Even if I had to forgo some personal experience with the mating song of the Giant Adirondack Frog, or the Lesser American Loon, or whatever, I was going to have to turn back. I'd give it another fifty feet. Then I smelled something like burning incense. Fifteen seconds later, it smelled of musk and melted wax.

And then I broke out of the forest onto the upper edge of a giant, natural amphitheater that ramped down to a partially sunken, hundred-foot-long band shell dug into the ground at the south shore of Devil's Mountain Lake. The flickering from a thousand candles held by a thousand men was reflected in the gold mirror that was the late-afternoon surface of the lake.

There was a lone figure on the softly lit, sixty-foot stage. He stood, head bowed. He was spotlighted by a follow-man off to my right, who, as I watched, inserted a pink gel into the slot in front of the lens, and fine-tuned his focus. There must have been a hundred citronella smudge pots ringing the perimeter of the amphitheater; the resulting smoke screen seemed to have driven off the insects, but softened the outlines of the scene in front of me, so different from the dark solitude of the pine forest.

Everything made sense. The Mountaineers. Their encampment. One of their theatricals. Maybe an invocation of some kind. The enormity of the final truth took me another few seconds. They were humming. Quietly. In unison. There were tears in the eyes of the men closest to me; and I didn't think it was because of poor intonation. The sound. It hadn't been insects, pumps, generators, frogs, loons, beaver dams, bulrushes or haunted burial grounds. It was this hillside of safari jackets, this acre and a half of golf swings, reddened jowls and nascent corpulence, humming that old Tinpan Alley, Hollywood-Irish chestnut, "Too-ra-loo-ra-loo-rah." Half humming, half crooning. A few more venturesome actually sang the words; maybe they had been authorized, I didn't know. They'd been humming and singing that old Bing Crosby warhorse for at least ten minutes, and there was no sign of any letup.

I couldn't turn away just then. I'd been noticed by a group of men about eight feet in front of me, on the outer fringe of the throng in the sharply-tiered amphitheater. They wore similar, Black-Watch flannel shirts under their multi-pocketed, Brooks Brothers' war-correspondent jackets; each man had a lighted candle in one hand and a glass in the other.

"Psst!" one of them beckoned me, peremptorily, but with a conspiratorial playfulness. I looked to either side, and ambled over to them.

"Where's your candle?" the same fellow asked me, in a stage whisper that must have been heard by everybody, humming or not, within thirty feet.

"Bad wick. Kept going out."

"Here, take this one. I've got a couple extra. Which camp you from?"

"Uh – Evergreen." A shot in the dark. He bought it.

"Know Rog Trumble?"

"Hell, yes."

""Too bad."

"Yeah, too bad."

He let his buddies know that I was okay, that I was from Evergreen, and that I knew poor old Rog Trumble. We were hushed by a couple of men in another knot of hummers off to our left. Somebody slipped a drink – Jack Daniels, stiff – into my hand, and gave me a teary nod of understanding and a long squeeze on my candle arm. I'd seen him before, I was sure, but only in two dimensions. Television, probably. He looked bigger in person.

There were at least eight more times through "Too-ra-loo-ra-loo-rah" before the guy on the stage lifted his hands to the pastel sky, and, with palms down, slowly brought them down to his sides, leading the teary-eyed chorus into a decrescendo and what I felt was to have been an end to the humming coincident with the final relaxation of his hands at his sides and the dropping of his head to his chest. But a few stalwarts hung on for one more chorus. They happened to be pretty good hummers, though, and their fading echo was like a time-softened memory of a harsher fact. By the time even they petered out on the "I—rish Lul—laaaaa-bye" high notes at the end, I was a little bit touched myself. Then there was a minute of silence, broken only by an occasional clink of ice from the thousand crystal glasses.

The man on the stage lifted his head. In the two seconds before he spoke into the cordless microphone clipped to the lapel of his safari jacket I heard the hum as an unseen technician brought up the gain on the p.a. system amplifier, and I spotted several large outdoor speakers mounted in the trees at the back edge of the amphitheater.

"Thank you, gentlemen." His voice, conversational in tone, had a crispness that only the finest sound systems can produce. "I know that Steve would have liked that." He forced himself to speak though a frog in his throat. "And I'm afraid that even if I did have more to say, I might have trouble getting through it." There was a dutiful chuckle from the grieving men. Someone must have gone on to the big boardroom in the sky, I thought. He continued. "We have a member who wanted to say a word or two. He – he – let's just say he doesn't need any introduction at all."

The hum conductor walked stage right a few feet and met a beefy six-foot-two newcomer, who had stepped out from behind a surprisingly three-dimensional-appearing forest-green flat in the right wings. They wrung hands, and the conductor exited upstage right. There was no applause.

The big guy walked downstage and center, stopped, and looked up. He shifted his gaze from one section of the crowd to another, then to the darkening sky, to the forest, and back to the crowd. He touched the outer corner of each eye with a popsicle-sized right index finger; not dramatically, but long enough so that the gesture wouldn't have been lost on anyone. I heard the gain come up again as he opened his mouth to speak. The sound man was a pro.

"Whaddaya say we blow out these damn candles, before they burn on down to the stub ends and somebody gets hurt, okay?"

His voice had a studied gruffness; a one-a-the-boys, give me another double, do unto others before they do unto you kind of boozy raspingness that the others seemed to understand. There was a good deal of laughter, and I heard the relieved sigh of a thousand breaths blowing out the Too-ra-loo-ra-loo-rah-shortened candles. As the candles were doused, the master electrician brought up the house lights just a tad. There were dozens of small spotlights, trained – through a haze of citronella smoke – onto the trees at the rear of the amphitheater. The reflection from the pines, with the fast-dimming mauve sky, gave enough light to see your neighbor by, but not so much as to distract you from the main event.

"One thing the guy loved was this damn pine forest, bugs n' all." He continued, "and it wouldn't make any sense to burn it down, 'specially at his own memorial service. But really, fellas, that was something. Talk about yer grown man crying, I wanna tell ya.

"Funny thing, that old song. Never knew quite what it was made Dad like it so much. Y'know, lemme see now, fifty-eight, maybe fifty-nine, he even chartered a Boeing 707 from American, which wasn't that easy to do back then even if you could afford it, and up and flew the whole damn family over to Shannon there, then limo-ed us all down for a weekend in Killarney. He didn't have all that much interest in Ireland now, don't get me wrong, and he sure as hell didn't know sh – 'scuse me, beans, about Killarney, but seein's how that was part of the words to that song, and it was his favorite even then I guess some 'a you know even better'n I do, well, he just had to get over there where they first started that too-ra-loo-ra stuff;

and that was the way he did things that he loved. Big. Not showoffy, but big. And fast.

"Now as I remember, it rained for forty-six hours straight over there, but by God, the family had got to Killarney, and that's what counted."

There was the kind of a laugh you never hear at funerals for people who died too young. In my own group, the half-hearted laughers were matched by a number of sotto voce mutterers; apparently old Steve Beckmann, who must have been the one who'd passed on, was not so universally beloved as Steve, Junior, presumed.

"An' I'll tell ya another thing he loved and that was comin' down across the lake in that old teak Chris-Craft every year to hook up with you guys. I don't think I need to say any more about that. There're people here knew him longer and, let's face it, closer'n I did, and I just wanted to let you know that the family appreciates what you've done, and what many of you have said, and what I know all of you have thought about from time to time over the last thirty-six hours. Be sure that we won't be doin' anything different with the camp, the family place or anything like that. Things're gonna stay just like they were. Thank you again, and – oh, I did want to mention one other thing.

"Y'know, Dad was proud as he could be about the Institute, and all the good work that they're doin' up there. And for some reason, we just didn't feel like it should be business as usual this week. A lotta good folks up there had grown to love him as we all did, and we've decided to just close the doors for a few days up there as one sign of all our feelings for the old man. So, I'm sure you understand; there won't be that tour of the labs an' all that we had on the program for tomorrow and Friday. I'm sure we'll be back on schedule for next year's camp. Thanks again, gentlemen. It meant a great deal to me; and I gotta feelin' it meant a great deal to him."

He stood in place, acknowledged the swell of applause, and slowly walked off to his right. The emcee met him again, they held each other's arms for a time, and Steve Beckmann, Junior, walked off into the wings. Someone clinked the cold neck of a quart of Jack Daniels against my hand and my half-filled glass, and topped me off before I could refuse.

"Thanks."

"One for the gipper." He was the man who had first called me over. His eyes were drier now.

"Steve," I said, lifting my glass a few inches.

"Steve, Senior," he corrected me.

"Senior it is; I'm with you." I took a sip, then faked a longer one. I hadn't eaten anything since Monday night, and the last thing I needed was a light head, if and when I finally walked out of this literal vale of tears and headed back to the logging road.

"Do they know – I mean, are they sticking to what they said yesterday about how it happened?" I asked him.

"Far as I know, yeah. Bad cold; flu thing. Same's those people down in Lake Placid, I guess. High temperature, bad headaches, whatever. Hey, let's face it, he was an old man."

"Yeah; guess it's just sad that it had to happen when everybody's up here and all," I ventured, falling into the obligatory woodsy delivery that seemed to go with Mountaineerdom, and thinking about viruses, altruism, unmarked uniforms and irony. I heard the emcee announce that there would be a half-hour social break before the show; the stage lights dimmed and he walked off, as our conversation continued.

"I know what you mean. Makes you think twice about just what it is money was s'posed to be good for. Course, if yer gonna go, ya might as well go out in style, and that burial at sea's gonna be something, with that lit-up speedboat and all."

"I'll be up for it, that's for sure," I answered. "Wha'd they say .. Midnight?"

"Well, I'm sure it'll be midnight before they get it ready, no matter what they're sayin' about eleven thirty sharp. Hell, they got the show to do, then they gotta set up along the shoreline an' all; it could be one, one thirty before they light that thing off."

Then I saw the fat security man. He was standing about fifty feet to my left, looking incongruously dainty in my beat-up Adidas, and talking animatedly with two other large, business-suited bouncer types. They were looking over the assembly, and one of them spoke into a walkie-talkie. I looked off to my right. There were several uniformed guards coming up the far right aisle of the amphitheater, still forty or fifty yards away. They reached the back corner, made the turn, and walked casually in my direction, stationing one of their fellows every twenty feet or so. They, too, looked down into the crowd as they moved along.

"Listen, fellas, thanks for the candle and the drinks; I guess I'd better mosey on around to Evergreen for a while. Who was it I was drinking with, by the way?"

Instead of answering, several of them softly double-hooted at me, raising their eyebrows, and smiling in anticipation. I nodded, feigned a dawning awareness, and held up my hand to forestall any further explanation. Smiles all around. I waved, lifted my glass again, and retreated.

"Hey. Evergreen's down in C-3 this year, aren't they?" challenged the guy I'd remembered from television.

"Right, I know. I've got to stop by and see a couple of friends from Birchbark for a few minutes. Later."

That seemed to satisfy him. I walked deeper into the throng, toward stage left. My movements would not have appeared suspicious, I thought. A lot of others were milling around, sector hopping, during the half-hour break. I stopped when I came to a group of twelve or fifteen men who appeared to be the only people in the amphitheater besides myself and the security force not wearing safari jackets. They all looked very wise, and at least ten of them were smoking small pipes. There wasn't a lot of drinking going on, and they weren't all that friendly, to me or to each other. I decided that this must have been a representation from what Seventy Four had called the think-tank bunch. Norway, I thought she had said. Well, it was a good stopover; at least, no one would get excited if I didn't say anything. I just stood there, sipped my Jack Daniels, and tried to look thoughtful.

It was no good and I knew it. Even if the fat man didn't spot me, they could always use the p.a. system. 'Gentlemen, we have an interloper; an alien among us. Be calm, but notify one of our uniformed friends if you have seen anyone who might not belong.' Then the hootowl boys would add things up and blow the whistle. The Mountaineers would think it was just another gate-crashing photographer or investigative journalist; the search and discovery might liven up the evening. However it came about, it would be a rough ride for me over to the Essex County jail; these guards might have been dressed like park rangers, but they wouldn't be above a little nighttime forest roughup of the guy who had caught the fat man when he wasn't looking.

So when a couple of portly, tweed-jacketed members of my new group, who looked only slightly less disheveled than I, made for the center comfort station exit at the top of the amphitheater, I strolled along behind them. I was still fifty feet from the fat man as we reached the top, but one of the uniformed guards had taken station near the exit. He was young, maybe twenty or so, and he looked like he might have spent some time on a football field. He scanned the dozens of smiling red faces as the Mountaineers, bull of booze and full of themselves, filed out of the amphitheater and into the aisle way into the forest. When his gaze fell on me, I could see something register. I walked directly to him, and spoke, just as he was about to ask me a question.

"Excuse me, young man." I enunciated very carefully, put an arm around his shoulders, and breathed a little Jack Daniels into his space. "I was told that Evergreen was to be in D-3 this evening, but it now appears that my informant had had one to many. Could you –"

"Uh – no sir, actually they're in C-3. C as in Charlie. Right down the left aisle and over –"

"Ah, yes. Perhaps I heard my friend incorrectly. Would you by any chance happen to have an aspirin?"

"No sir, I'm sorry, I don't; but the man at the restroom cabin should have some."

"Thank you, young man. What is your name?"

"MacLaine, sir. Richie – uh – Richard."

"Thank you, Mister MacLaine." I made as if to rejoin my partners, and strolled unevenly toward the aisle way, leaving him to remember what it was he'd wanted to ask the nice man, who might have been a little loaded, but who had turned out to be the only Mountaineer who had ever asked his name, and actually called him by it, too. I suppose I had been lucky that they hadn't yet had time to circulate a description of me to the park-ranger types on that side of the amphitheater.

The wiring for the trail to the comfort station was jury-rigged, but probably reliable and safe enough for the three or four weeks a year it was needed. Forty-watt bulbs, screwed into rubber-insulated sockets every five feet, with a new extension every twenty-five feet or so. After passing two extensions, I got to a curve in the trail where I couldn't see anyone going or coming. I reached up and pulled the plug, throwing the downstream end of the trail into darkness, and precipitating a lot of grumbling and good-natured calls for assistance some fifty feet ahead of me. I left the trail and slipped into the forest.

I headed due south, found the logging road after a quarter of a mile, and turned west onto it, downhill. There was a bright loom over the top of the eastern mountains; it wouldn't be long before moonrise. After a few minutes, I could no longer hear anything from the Mountaineers; the only sounds were the soft wheeze of my new boots crushing the three-inch-thick bed of dried pine needles into the rut of the abandoned road, and the triumphant buzz-saw attacks on my head and hands by the vengeful, citronella-maddened black flies of the Adirondacks.

XXVI

I had been right. Every road had to go somewhere. The only trouble was, the place that this road went to was about a mile and a half to the west of where I'd joined it. They'd close-cut the side of a small mountain between me and Lake Placid, and, with the easy stuff exhausted, pulled up stakes some years before. I could see a few scrawny, foot-high pine seedlings in the bright light from the newly risen moon, but someone with some know-how, some equipment and a lot of nitrogen was going to have to take charge if they ever wanted this to look like a forest again. The bug attacks suddenly became more frenzied; they loved it when I slowed down or stopped, especially out in the open, where they could quickly build their dive speed up to redline without fear of having a head-on with an overhanging branch. I struck out downhill, keeping the moon to my left, and the pointer stars at my back. The logging operations had ended a few hundred yards to the south; I left the barren, close-cut hillside and plunged back into the forest.

The flies kept me motivated, the boots were a plus, and the moonlight filtering through the treetops helped me avoid any serious falls. There might have been an easier way to get from one point to another, but I didn't find it that night. It took me another two hours to get to Route 73. It was unlit, except for the headlights of an occasional passing car, which I used to orient myself as I trotted down the last downhill mile through the thinning forest.

I followed the blacktop of Route 73 westward, toward Lake Placid, and ducked back into the trees whenever I sensed the approach of a vehicle. The moon was well above the eastern horizon when I smelled the steaks, then saw the familiar lights of the Cascade Motor Lodge Restaurant a hundred yards ahead. They were doing a brisk business for a Wednesday night. There were fifty or sixty vehicles in the parking area. I turned north at the green "Entering North Elba" traffic sign, cut through the woods behind the Twin Peaks Motel, and walked the last quarter mile down to Dan's Trailer Park, at the end of the winding gravel road.

A light shone from a rear window of May LeCourier's Airstream onto the dusty hood of the old jeep, still sitting right where I'd left it so long ago the previous Saturday morning. A dark-colored Plymouth Horizon was parked in front of the trailer. Maybe she had the night off. There was a light on in a twelve-by-thirty-six mobile home two spaces down the line, but that was the only other sign of life in the camp. I walked over to the back of the Airstream, squeezed into the space between it and the jeep, and looked into the window.

Wendell LeCourier must have been pretty good with his hands in his better days. He'd built a sixteen-foot-square extension onto the port wall of the trailer, and cut a six-foot-wide doorway into the aluminum wall and wooden bulkhead for an entryway. He had an extendable, insulated fabric door for privacy, and, from the looks of the connecting devices spaced around the neatly fitted doorway, the original wall could be quickly rein-stalled. If they needed to, they could fill up the tires, kick out the concrete blocks, latch onto a trailer hitch and move on down the road, leaving the square addition behind. The result of all the fitting, carpentry, heliarc weld-ing and interior work was that the inside of the trailer didn't look like one. There was room to move around; and not everything had to be fold-up and stowable.

To my left, with her back to the addition, May sat in a faded, bent-wood rocker that looked like it might have been someone's family for a while. Her eyes were closed. There was steam coming from the cup on the small table at her side, and she hadn't yet removed the teabag. The Baby Ben on an inner wall shelf showed it to be ten minutes to twelve. It was hard to believe that only twenty or twenty-one hours had passed since Big Whitey had filled in on the mid watch aboard the *Edinboro Star*. I heard footsteps in the gravel, approaching the front door of the trailer. I ducked down between the jeep and the back wall. Someone knocked on the front door. Then again. I heard a muffled "just a minute" from May. I felt move-ment through the trailer wall, and she opened the aluminum screen door.

"Hi, Dan. 'Nother phone call?"

"Yeah, May, hospital again. Said it was important."

"Okay. I'll walk back up with you. Maybe he's feelin' better, 'dthey say?"

"Naw. They never say nothin' to me."

"Sorry, Dan. I know it's a lot of trouble." The door slammed. "Maybe next month I'll be able to get a phone again."

"May. How many times do I have to tell ya' not to be worryin' about that?"

Their voices receded as the two people walked back up the hill toward the first trailer. I slipped out from behind the Airstream and watched until they were out of sight. I swatted a particularly voracious, but now logy and engorged black fly on my left wrist, moved quickly over to the concrete block step, opened the aluminum screen door, and stepped inside.

I waited for thirty seconds in the half darkness near the door. Nothing. I moved back through the narrow kitchen, by the bathroom, and into the living room area, where May had been sitting. Then I heard the bad-sounding breathing. They had opened up the back of the trailer so it could be one big living room, and put the two bedrooms in the addition. The smaller bedroom had a pair of bunk beds along the outboard wall, and the older boy, Joey LeCourier, was asleep in the lower one. The upper was unoccupied. Joey looked flushed. His nose was completely stopped up and he breathed through a phlegmy obstruction in his swollen throat. There was a pitcher of water and damp washrag on a small reading table built onto the head of his bunk. I wiped the perspiration from his forehead. He groaned, tried to turn over to his side, failed, and fell back onto the damp mattress. I heard the door. I stepped back into the living room and stopped by a lamp next to May's rocking chair. I gave her a little wave as she walked into the room. Her hand went to her mouth, and she blinked her gray eyes. She'd been crying.

"Hi, May."

"O'Toole. Jeez, you really scared me. I – how'd you – well, sure, I left the door unlocked, that's how. I – I – "

Then she started to sob, and I could see she'd been through too much lately. I held her for a minute or so, and she didn't seem to mind.

"It's okay, Mrs. LeCourier; cry it all out and then we'll talk it over and see what we can do."

She nodded; it kept on coming for a while. Then she was still, and I just held her in my arms for another minute.

"Okay, I think that's all over now. Sorry," she said. I backed away. "Jeez, I don't know what brought that on, O'Toole." She armed the tears away, sniffed mightily, caught her breath short of another sob, waved to me to sit down, and disappeared back into the hallway. She ran the water in the bathroom and yelled to me that I could get a beer out of the fridge if I wanted. I did. Utica Club.

She looked a little better when she came out. She walked into the bedroom, and looked at Joey for a long minute in the half-light from the living room. Then she rejoined me, half-closing the accordion partition behind her. She removed the teabag from her cooling cup and laid it alongside a couple of others on a wadded-up paper towel on the table.

"Looks like he's been a pretty sick boy," I said, as she sat down in the rocking chair.

"You should have seen him a few days ago; I know he looks bad, and his breathing isn't all that good, but I think he's coming around." She spoke in an exhausted half whisper, not wanting to disturb the boy. "They gave him all the medicines at the hospital, and they seemed to take on him, anyway a lot better than they have on Donny. He's the one I'm worried about. That Doctor Rashid called a few minutes ago – oh, that's where I was when you came in. He's been working like twenty hours a day for the last three or four days. They just keep coming in, he says. Some folks are worse off than Donny, too. Like Mrs. Bockus – she's – well, she was – a lady lived up north of Keene – with her husband – and he's sick as can be, too – well, she didn't make it. Last night. She was only sick for twelve, fourteen hours, and that was it. Fifty-seven, maybe fifty-eight. He's sixty. And we didn't even know them. I mean at first Doctor Rashid thought that it might have been Joey and Donny who gave it to her; but now he says no. Even old Mr. Beckmann is very sick, I guess, and they can't even move him down to New York or someplace with the fancy doctors and the facilities and all. There must be twenty people on that third floor by now. They've got it – not sealed – but, un, sequestered off, I think they say, and you can't even go in there and see anyone or take them anything or sit by them like you might want to. And he – Doctor Rashid – he says that it doesn't make any difference that I had something like it myself; that doesn't mean that I won't catch it again. And what I had was nothing – like a real bad cold, and headachy flu, that lasted, what, three days or so. It's something they've never seen before, he says, and he thinks it's just going to spread and keep on spreading. I – oh, my God, did you – "

"It's all right, May, I've had it, too. And I've been exposed a few more times and not gotten it again. It looks like it depends on a lot of things; age, the combination of medicines you take, and, well, maybe it's in the genes. What was the call about?"

"Oh. He'd promised to cal before he left the hospital and let me know how Donny was. He said he was breathing better, but he had a temperature of a hundred and two and he was complaining of headaches. He's on call tonight an he'll let me know if there's any change; and I'm not supposed to go over to the hospital unless they call."

"That makes it hard. But it makes sense, I think."

"Yeah, that's for sure. I just hope and pray – O'Toole, do you think you got it from the boys? You spent that whole morning – "

"It's possible, but I really don't think so. I had a run-in with – some other people that same day, and I tend to blame them."

"You look like you might have had a lot of run-ins lately. Hungry?"

"Well – yeah, I guess I am. But that's not why – "

"You just sit right there. I got some eggs and bacon and stuff, just in case Joey was feelin' good enough to eat something tonight; would that be okay?"

"That'd be just fine. I'll keep an eye on Joey, then."

I sipped the Utica Club, dabbed at Joey's face a couple of times and listened to May moving around in the kitchen. I didn't know what Wendell LeCourier was up to that night, and I didn't want to ask just then. But he was passing up one hell of a good thing if he didn't straighten himself out and do something to get back with this strong and beautiful woman.

She was laying the eight, thick-sliced strips of bacon on a flattened brown paper bag as I joined her in the kitchen.

"Why don't we just eat in here, save the trouble?" I suggested.

"That might be good. We can talk, and I can go check on Joey every little while."

There wasn't all that much talk. I sat in the Airstream's standard equipment breakfast-lunch-and-dinner dining booth, and it took me all of eight and a half minutes to wolf down three scrambled eggs, most of the bacon, and a whole wheat English muffin. She nibbled on a muffin and a strip of bacon, and cleaned up the kitchen while I ate. She checked on Joey, and when she came back into the kitchen, she sat down across from me in the yellow booth. I wiped my mouth, leaned on the table, and looked at her clear eyes.

"All right, May. I've got to ask you a couple more favors."

She didn't say anything. "It's my opinion that this disease that we've all had comes from something they're working on up at the Beckmann Institute. I think that one of the first people to have had it was Doctor Wager, who the boys found up there past Nichol's Creek last week. I – "

"O'Toole, Doctor Rashid told me that he thought it might have come from that doctor, too; but he thought that Doctor Wager had picked something up in town, or out in the woods. He never said anything about the work up at the Institute. I mean, they work on animals, and industrial things, I thought. And then, 'course, when Doctor Wager got better so fast and all that, I think Doctor Rashid decided that this was something else. I know he called up there, and spoke to Doc Wager, and he was just fine, he said. I mean, Doc Wager himself said so. He's tried to call again for the last couple of days, but he hasn't been able to get Doc Wager since Monday morning. He wanted to ask him what other medications he took, I guess, something like that."

"May, just listen for a second. I don't believe Wager, and I don't think Rashid has all the facts. I trust him, but I don't think he knows just what he's dealing with. Now. The people up there at the Institute don't like me; they've done their damnedest to get rid of me in the past five days. And I think that the government might be working with them; don't ask me any more about that. They're looking for me, and that's why I came here. I need some rest, and I need it badly. And it has to be someplace where they won't look. Second, I need to make a couple of phone calls. To Washington. I work for Fish and Wildlife, but I do some work for some other people, too, and I have to talk with them before I can make any more moves. I want to get into the Institute. I want to talk with Wager, and with another man who was working on this disease that's gotten to your boys and probably to a lot of other people in several states. The Institute people won't be glad to see me. And the military won't be, either. Yes, they're up there, too. They've got fifteen or twenty soldiers, maybe more by now, and they were installing some sort of decontamination gear about five or six hours ago when I was there. The reason I want to talk with them is that I – we – can't afford the time that a political solution to this mess would take. I think they might have something up there that would help a lot of sick people, and I don't think we should wait until they make up their minds to release it."

"But if they have it, surely – "

"That's the point. The only people who could concoct a cure at this early date would be the very people who concocted the original disease. They know that. Admitting that they have the cure would be an admission that the infecting agent originated at the Institute. That's something I don't think they'll be willing to do. I think my way is the fastest way to get some help to Donny, and to a lot of other people."

"So what do you need?" She wasn't going to ask any more questions.

"I need some rest. I need a phone. And I need to borrow that jeep again; with a full tank of gas. I need a box of .38 caliber ammunition, and I need to break these." I gave her a couple of hundreds.

"Okay, O'Toole. Take a shower. The plumbing's good and the water's hot. Towels are in the cupboard across from the door, there. Get your sleep. I'll be up for a while. The jeep is still full of gas, just like you left it. The pay phone outside the Twin Peaks Motel, up at the top of the hill, will probably be best. They moved the office when they put in the pool, and the phone is around the corner. I use it whenever Dan – he manages the trailer court here – is gone on vacation or outa town. Nobody'll bother you. I'll see what I can do about the ammunition and the smaller bills."

While she was saying this, she was ushering me into the hall, showing me the shower, and retrieving some large-size underwear, a blue, work shirt and some fresh bedding from a closet in the larger bedroom. She pushed me into the bathroom, laden down with the clothes, a couple of fresh towels, a new Good News disposable razor, and an economy-sized can of Old Spice shaving cream.

The beard took a while; the shower was the first time I had thought about what it was like to feel good since I had left Bill and Dolores Chase in New York only a week earlier. I was nearly asleep on my feet when I stepped out into the darkened hallway, wrapped in a towel and carrying the clothing, old and new. She got up from her chair, ushered me into the bedroom, and stuffed me into a full-size brass bed with clean white cotton sheets and an old down comforter. There was an open, screened window above my head. She turned out the light; and she whispered good night. I heard her moving in Joey's room for a minute or so. Then she turned out the living room light. I checked the load on the .38 and put it under the extra pillow. I must have forgotten after a while that she was probably sitting there in the dark with her eyes wide open, thinking about boys and men and doctors and why things happen the way they do.

XXVII

It must have been the cool mountain air wafting in through the open screened window above my head. I usually don't sleep all that well when I'm tired. If I knew May, she'd checked on Joey, washed her face, and had a glass of juice or something light – and quiet – before starting up the Plymouth and crunching up the gravel road. I'd slept through the early moves but heard the car. I got the towel around myself, and made it to the kitchen door just in time to see the dark-blue Horizon pass out of sight over the top of the hill between the trailer park and the Twin Peaks Motel.

Joey was over this particular hump. He was breathing better, he wasn't sweating, and his face wasn't so flushed as the night before. It was twenty after seven on the Baby Ben. Thursday morning. She'd left a note in front of the clock, weighted down with a handful of nickels, dimes and quarters.

"O'T. Don't worry about the neighbors that much, and Dan, the t.c. man, works in the a.m.'s. Use the back door in the boys' room if you want. Back by nine, nine-thirty. May."

She'd brushed off the captain's jacket and my pants, and hung them up by the bedroom door. The other clothes were lying neatly folded on a chair by the foot of the bed. She'd made some coffee and left out some breakfast fixings. I dressed, downed a pint container of orange juice, a glass of milk, two cups of coffee and a burnt muffin. I found the door in the back of the boys' room, buried behind a pile of clothes, books and fishing gear. It opened on the woods. I retrieved the .38 and May's pile of small change, made sure that there was no one around, and slipped out the door.

It was too hot for seven-forty in the morning in the mountains. And too still. The sun had just risen into a clear sky above the three familiar mountaintops to the east, but what I could see through the haze to the west was a hazy gray, darker near the ill-defined horizon. Something about the weather was going to have to give by early afternoon.

I circled through the woods, avoided the gravel road, and worked my way up to the Twin Peaks Motel. The phone booth was attached to the gravel road-end of what looked like the original motel. It was seventy to eighty feet from the office in the A-frame-roofed new wing, which was arranged so that all twenty rooms, ten on each level, opened onto the new pool. Two rooms in the lower level had the curtains drawn behind the large picture windows, and cars were parked just outside. A chambermaid's cart was stationed outside the open door of a third room. I didn't know what the nut was on the Twin Peaks, but they hadn't made it the previous night, that was clear. I backtracked down the road about thirty yards, and walked back up the hill, around the old wing, and up to the phone booth, yawning, and trying to look to anyone watching like the sleepy early-rising guest of someone down in Dan's Trailer Court; which is exactly what I was, come to think of it.

I got the number – for $1.75 in change – from a guy at ATT&T information, and made a credit-card call to Hyannis Hospital. I took a few minutes, but I finally got Doctor Driscoll, the guy who had treated Molly on the same shift the previous morning.

"Jesus, mister, what the hell did you people get yourselves into, anyway? Those men from that ship are half of 'em dead from this infection, and we don't know yet what the hell it is, virus, or meningitis or whatever, and the other half are dyin' from exposure. You know, you've got a lot of questions to answer, mister. The girl. Yeah, but it's a good thing you got her in here when you did, she might not be alive at all. We've treated her for everything from that Bolivian Meningococcal to exposure and malnutrition. She responded to the cephalosporin after about six hours, but she's not out of the woods yet. Her breathing this morning is worse than when I saw her last night, and the headaches have come back. And half the staff over here is coming down with something very similar. Even Doc Cates is home in bed, and he's not a young man, don't forget."

"Well, Doctor Driscoll, I'm sorry to hear that. I can't talk much longer here. I'm doing my best to get a little help on this, but I can't talk about it right now. Give the girl my best when she's awake, and tell her the guy she was with is trying to take care of things and will see her soon." I heard some clicking on the other end; someone was trying to make the tap.

"Goddamnitall, Mister, I don't think you realize just what the police and the Coast Guard and now the F. B. – "I hung up. I'd let it go on too long as it was.

I called the unlisted number in Washington. The machine answered, but when I told it nicely that this was number so and so, checking in, good old Miss Quantrell came on the line.

"Hi, O'Toole. We've been wondering where you were. Taking care of yourself up there in the mountains?"

"Hi, Quantrell. Yeah, I'm hanging in. Can you get the chief on for me? I've got to talk to him about something I think is important."

"Just a second. Are you equipped?"

"Not today." My scramble decoder was in the trunk of the BMW.

"Okay. I can get him after about nine eastern, O'Toole, but not 'til then. He's in the air. But I've got a message from him to you that has been on the hold desk here for the past forty-eight hours."

"What's he got to say?"

"Ah. Let's see. Paraphrase. Info provided you by Seventy-Four and recent developments concerning same require immediate cessation, possibly only postponement your current activities. Imperative you return immediately and stay in contact with Seventy-Four, Quantrell or me until you return. Repeat and add emphasis, imperative you cease – "

I flipped the receiver cradle a couple of times, not breaking the connection completely, but interrupting Quantrell's reading of the message. "Hold it, Quantrell, we've got a bad connection here. Say again all after 'immediate', will you? I think you – " then I did sever the connection, cutting myself of in mid-sentence, hoping it sounded like a plausible mountain-Podunk line malfunction. Well, who was going to know? I hadn't been that great a connection, anyway. I hadn't at that point made up my mind not to call back, but I didn't want the "return immediately" instruction to be my only option. Not just yet. Getting whatever they had up in the Institute that might help Donny LeCourier, Molly and the others wouldn't wait for some group of bureaucrats to cook up their fail-safe denials of U.S. participation in, or even knowledge of, the very existence of these activities at the Beckmann Institute. What was needed was action; and three or four days immersion in Washington pettifoggery wasn't going to produce it for me.

Two blue and white State Police cars pulled up to the Cascade Motor Lodge across the road. It was too early for a coffee break, and these guys, two in each car, were in a hurry. Three of them trotted into the little office next to the entrance to the restaurant. A fourth leaned against his passenger-side door, microphone in hand. I squeaked open the door of the aluminum booth from another time, and walked back toward the gravel road down to the trailer court. I saw May's Horizon slow for the left turn behind me, hesitate, then turn right, and pull to a stop in front of the restaurant, just past the two police cars. I continued on down the road. It took May another fifteen minutes. I found some typing paper and used the time to write down some names, numbers, and instructions for Seventy-four, Quantrell and Gregory. I included a short record of my activities since the previous Friday. I crammed the papers and the Claycombe report into the bedraggled manila envelope, and sealed and reinforced it with a half-roll of May's scotch tape. I wrote a Washington phone number under Wager's original "deliver to M. Wager, M.D., Keene, N.Y." instruction and initialed it.

* * * * * *

"I stopped at the pay phone," she said.

"How is he?"

"Still got the temperature. A hundred-and-two. Can't eat anything. And I guess his head hurts so much, he can't even sleep. A couple in the next room are doin' a lot better than Donny. I guess it has something to do with your immunity and all. It's better when you get older, but not too old, if Mr. And Mrs. Bockus are any example.

"Well, sometimes those antibiotics take a while, you know."

"Yeah, that's what Doctor Rashid said, too."

"What are the troopers up to?"

"Oh, yeah. I saw you walkin' down the hill, lookin' like you owned the place. They're after some guy who gate-crashed up at the Mountaineers' Camp- last night – even beat up one'a the guards, and – oh." It wasn't a very big 'oh'. "Oh. So after you left the Institute . . . "

I nodded.

"Well, I guess you know that those Mountaineers pack a lot of clout around here," she went on. "They've got a description; but it made the guy sound like he was huge. They did say sport jacket, though; maybe you oughta' leave that here."

"Yeah, I will. How'd you do on the hundreds?"

"Oh, right. Here. I told the girl at the truck stop that it was for the Cascade. Five twenties, eight tens; and got the box of .38's at the gun shop by the sports complex. This is the change from the other twenty. Three fifty five."

"Okay, thanks. I saw some fishing stuff back in the boys' room. Do you mind if I – "

"Take whatever you need, O'Toole. But I think maybe you'd better start moving. Two of those troopers were gonna check out the logging road from east 'a the airport on up to Devil's Mountain, but the other two just might get it into their heads to come down here."

I threw the fishing gear into the jeep; a creel, two black fiberglass rods, the reels, a toolbox full of flies and fixing, an old ten-pocket vest and a beat-up, fly-festooned, poplin hat 'that Wendell used to put on every Sunday morning whether he went fishin' or not.' May brought me a couple of foil-wrapped sandwiches, an apple and a plastic pint of Coke, 'to make it all look legit', she said.

I squeezed by the back of the Airstream and pulled myself up into the driver's seat; May stood on the other side, leaning against the framework for the old canvas top.

"Hey, O'Toole?"

"Yeah."

"What is it you're – I mean do you think all this might really do my boy any good?"

""There're two men up there, May. If they're alive, they're Donny's best bet. I'm going to get whatever they've got. Even if it's just information, I think we'll be ahead of the game."

"Anything else I can do?"

"I left a manila envelope and a little cash on the brass bed. If I don't come to collect this stuff, or if you don't hear anything from me within twenty-four hours, use a pay phone, call the number on the envelope, and tell whoever answers that O'Toole left some things with you that they ought to pick up. Keep the money, whatever happens."

"Oh no, I can't – "

"May. Consider it a down payment on this jeep. I'm starting to like it a lot, noises and all. Oh, who's it registered to?"

"Me and Wendell."

"Well, any question, somebody stole it while you were at the hospital, okay?" I turned on the ignition.

"Okay."

I hit the floor starter. May tapped the canvas top for good luck and pushed herself away. I ground the jeep into first, added a little choke, and black-smoked my way out from behind the Airstream.

"O'Toole, you call now, okay?" She trotted alongside, raising her voice above the clatter of the exhaust.

"Don't worry, May. You're the first. You and Doctor Rashid. Thanks for everything."

She waved. I picked up speed, double-clutched into second, and drove on up the gravel. In the big, trailer-towing rear-view mirror mounted to my left, I saw May, standing by the Airstream, brushing the hair out of her eyes with the back of her hand.

There was only one state police car at the Cascade. One guy was leaning against the fender, tearing a hole in the plastic top for his coffee. His partner was standing by the right door, talking into a hand mike. They perfunctorily returned the wave from the hail-fellow-well-met with the funny hat, scrunched down into the seat of the Willys with the New York plates, who came up the road behind the Twin Peaks, turned left, carefully avoided spinning his wheels on the last bit of gravel, and made a noise-abated departure to the east, picked up speed after the first three-tenths of a mile, shifted the .38 caliber revolver in his waistband, and absent mindedly ruffled the edges of the fifty or sixty hundred dollar bills in the pocket of his fishing vest.

XXVIII

It was about nine in the morning. I drove with one hand shielding my eyes against the white laser light of the morning sun pressing through the pitted windshield of the jeep. In two-wheel drive, the noise from the disengaged front axle was reduced to an occasional metallic thump that shook the frame and seemed to make the left front wheel track to the left, into the oncoming traffic. I kept the speed down to about thirty-five until I passed the turnoff to Gilmore Hill Road – Molly's farmhouse and my abandoned BMW were a couple of miles to the north – and started downhill for the last mile and a half into Keene. The noise subsided on the downhill run, and I let the speed build up to forty-five and fifty. The village of Keene was still in the shadow of the eastern mountains. I turned left at Purdy's Elm Tree Inn and headed up Route Nine. Two miles north, I left the two-lane highway, rumbled across the plank-floored bridge over the Ausable, and headed west on the gravel. I passed the cemetery and the LeCourier boys' and my turnoff to the little lake above Nichol's Brook. It was another two-point-nine miles on the odometer to the guard post.

It stood in the middle of a widened stretch of road. Two men – for once bedecked with gleaming silver badges and military band-like insignia on their uniforms, with epaulettes, aide-de-camp shoulder hosiery and business-like side arms – stepped out from either door of the windowed gatehouse and raised their white-gloved hands. As I slowed to a stop, I saw that a few more pine trees had bitten the dust to make room for a motor pool car. It was a Nissan Altima, and it was backed into a garage-sized cut into the forest, on the right and a few feet past the gatehouse. It had a "BI-24" New York vanity plate, and there was some yellow lettering on the driver's door. The car was the same gray-green as the trucks I had seen at the compound the day before. Fifty yards past the parked car, the gravel road began to wind, as it followed the sudden sharp rise in the surrounding terrain up toward the notch between Sentinel and Devil's Mountains. Three, maybe three and a half miles to the Institute. But first I had to get past the gatehouse.

"Howdy, boys, nice morning."

"Yep. No traffic beyond here though, sir." The one who spoke, "McFee," by his black plastic nametag, was about thirty; he had four or five years on Archer, his partner, and he wore two more chevrons below the half-moon "B.I. Security" shoulder patch on his left sleeve. Both were close-cropped, clean-shaven and red-faced, and looked like cream-of-the-crop, top-of-the-class marine recruits on the day of the Presidential Parade.

"No problem," I said. "Think I missed a turnoff. Guy back in Keene told me watch for a loggin' road on the right'd take me on up to this little lake above Clifford Falls where they say the bass're jumpin' into the boats."

"Yes, sir. That'd be back down where you came from about two miles. The first time you see Nichol's Brook on your left, you've gone too far. There's a turnaround right in there; you come on back this way about a hundred'n-fifty yards, it'll be on your right, just past a big ol' split-by-lightnin' pine tree."

"Okay, that sounds easy enough. All right if I make a u-turn around your post? Otherwise I'll have to back down a half-a-mile or – "

"Okay, mister, go ahead," shrugged McFee, obviously preferring to bend the rules rather than put up with the hunky-dory real-estate-salesman manner I was affecting for the occasion. The younger guard had lost interest; he stepped back into the gatehouse.

These are the tricky ones. If McFee hadn't softened enough to okay my u-turn, my part in the story might have been over right then and there. I idled past the gatehouse, threw the troops a helluvaguy-thank you-grin and a General Patton-battalion ho!-lift of the left hand from the wheel. I angled to the right to give myself more turning room, then cut the jeep around to the left just sharply enough so that it wouldn't look like a setup when I missed the one-move u-turn. I nosed the jeep into the trees on the other side, grimaced and lifted my hands for the benefit of Mcfee, who monitored my progress from the gatehouse stoop. I put the jeep into reverse, grinding the gears a little more than was necessary, and purposely stalled the engine. I gave it too much gas on the restart, popped the clutch, and let the jeep leap back across the road, spraying gravel into the trees and headed for the gray-green Altima. I got the jeep stopped in time to avert a five thousand dollar front-end-job on the Nissan, but I still managed to do in a headlight and a square foot of the left front fender.

"Accelerator pedal stuck. Sorry," I yelled back at McFee. He reached into the gatehouse for a clipboard, as I got out to shake my head at the damage. The two of them walked over to the scene of the crime, both looking stern-faced, I thought, but just concealing their amusement at the dude who didn't know his beat-up jeep from a hole in the ground.

McFee started composing a diagrammed reenactment of the complicated moves by the offending vehicle, and Archer kept a weather eye on the gatehouse. I picked up a few pieces of glass from the headlight, and gingerly carried them over toward a "Keep Our Mountains Clean" refuse can installed behind the gatehouse. Then it was easy.

"Okay, boys, just keep your hands exactly where they are and turn around nice and slow." I had pulled the .38 from underneath the fishing vest, I had it trained on them, shoulder high, and I wanted them to see it. They turned; Archer kept his hands on his hips and McFee held onto his clipboard. I aimed at McFee's chest and tried to make myself look nervous.

`"Now, mister, hold on here, there's no need to go off half-cocked – "

"You first, McKee. Left hand, undo belt – faster! – that's better. All right, Archer, Slow-ly – good. McFee, face down on the road, right there. Archer, take your clothes off."

"Nothin' doin', mister. I ain't gonna – "

"Archer. I need a nice uniform and if I have to use one with a hole or two in it, it makes no difference to me. I mean it. Now!" It never ceases to amaze me; I would have shot him, but there was no guarantee that he should have believed it. He grumbled, but slowly stripped down to his underwear.

It took another twenty minutes, and I had to bean McFee with the butt of the .38, but I finally got them trussed up and gagged with their socks, belts and some nylon fishing line. I loaded them into the jeep and backed a few yards into the forest. McFee was out cold, and Archer had lost some of his spunk when he'd lost his clothes. I took the jeep's single ignition key.

Archer's uniform wasn't a bad fit and the keys to the Altima were above the visor. Their nine millimeter pistols would have faster action and be just as accurate as the fat man's .38. I strapped on McFee's belt and pistol, wrapped the other guns in the fishing vest, and laid the bundle in the back seat. There was a dial-less phone in the gatehouse. I picked it up. It took about five seconds.

"Yo."

"This's Archer, down at the gate." I raised my voice, as if the connection were poorer than it was, and partially covered the mouthpiece with my fingers as I spoke. "They brought some stuff up from Washington for the infirmary. You wanna send somebody down?"

"Rog. Wait one." Fifteen seconds passed. "Hey, Gatehouse, hold on, here's the Lieutenant."

"Go ahead," I said.

"Archer?"

"Yeah."

"Listen, I know we're supposed to cooperate with you people and work together on this, but Jesus, my orders are to get this place cleaned up before eleven o'clock Thursday morning, and this being Thursday morning, you can see why we're a little under the gun. I just can't have a chance of any more exposures, and that's it. You'll have to drive that stuff up here yourself."

"Well, I don't care about that myself, it's just that we're supposed to have two of us down here at all times and no matter what."

"I don't care. I can't have any more exposures until they come up with something in that infirmary."

"All right. McFee says I can drive it up. By the way, he says to tell you this phone is getting worse and worse."

"Yeah, I can hear it. We'll try to get somebody on it."

"Okay, see you later."

I waited a few seconds, then pulled the cord out of the junction box. I used the back of one of McFee's accident report forms to post a sign on the approach side of the gatehouse. "Not on duty Thursday. Check with the guard at Institute."

The Nissan was a big change from the forty-year-old jeep, with its big V-6, automatic transmission, leather, a.c., and power everything. I even played the radio as I drove up the hill toward the notch. Country-western-mountain-Nashville-Santa Barbara mish-mash. There was a prolonged and angry burst of static from the speakers all around me, and I saw the lingering flash of the lightning in the graying western sky. It was sunny, still and very warm on this side of the notch, but I could see an occasional shudder in the treetops ahead of me as they were grazed by the vanguard gusts from the approaching storm.

No one challenged me at the top of the notch. The drive down the switchbacked backed gravel road gave me a few moments to look over the cleared compound below me. The six-by-six army truck was still parked alongside the gravel road, just where it led past the main building. The portable radios had been set up on the lowered tailgate, and two un-uniformed soldiers stood at parade rest behind a third, who appeared to be in charge of communications. The Volvo wagon was parked a few feet behind the six-by-six – and the more junior officer from the previous day was leaning against its right front fender, watching what activity there was in front of him.

The Mercedes trucks were still in position in front of the pyramids-within-a-pyramid main lab building. Two giant vacuum-cleaner hoses, six feet in diameter, led from the rear of each truck through what appeared to be newly-built, constrictive enclosures in a four-holed aluminum wall that covered the entire glass entryway. The hoses were braced and founded, and appeared to give entry and exit for decontamination personnel. I guessed that the trucks were portable labs and decon stations for diagnosis and cleanup of men and material from inside the building. As if to confirm my thoughts, a side door on the truck nearest me slid back into what was undoubtedly an airtight recess in the body wall, and two white-suited men, helmets removed, stepped onto a hydraulically driven platform, which lowered them to the driveway. They helped each other out of the cumbersome spacesuits, and both men lit cigarettes. I hoped that their suits might have incorporated some improvements over the models worn by Big and Little Whitey back aboard the *Edinboro Star*.

The service building was deserted, but there were four more large personnel trucks, unmanned at the moment, in the back of the parking lot. Except for a single armed guard in front of the infirmary, there were no other men to be seen. Maybe they were in the lab building, on decon duty; or stationed around the perimeter of the compound, or even beating the bushes to the south in pursuit of me. It didn't make a lot of difference at the moment. The big trick was not going to be how to get in, but how to get out; and, when that time came, I would worry about the number of men around.

I slowed the Altima as the road straightened and leveled out at the bottom of the hill, and coasted past the service building, the parking lot, the transformers and the fuel dump. I saluted the officer leaning on the Volvo, passed the six-by-six parked halfway out into the road, waved at the communicator and eased on down to the infirmary.

After parking near the entrance, I walked around the back of the car, opened the right rear door, and brought out my vest-wrapped bundle – hiding the .38 and the other nine-millimeter pistol – and McFee's clipboard, lifting and carrying them away from me and high, as if the combined package was very fragile, very important, and possibly even infective. Now all I had to worry about was whether the sentry knew Archer, the man whose uniform I wore.

"Sir!" he challenged. Or acknowledged, I wasn't sure which. The heels on his spit-shined black boots snapped together; the M-16 straightened, but remained at his side.

"At ease," I said. "Yeah, we were told up at main gate that there was some kind of a commotion down here. We had to bring this stuff for one of the doctors, anyway, so I thought I'd kill two birds with one stone. What's up?"

"Nothin' sir, not as far as I know. Nobody's come or went since I been on."

"Well, someone called security; musta been someone inside. These guys must be fightin' amongst themselves. We might as well go in and check it out."

"Mister, I don't care what the orders is orders might be, I'm not goin' in there, no matter what. Whatever's got those geniuses flat on their backs, and not even knowin' which end is up they tell me, well, whatever it is, I don't want it. I'm takin' a big enough chance as it is hangin' around this front door for four-outa-twelve. And if I was you I'd leave well enough alone. There's not so much goin' on in there that I heard anything."

"Okay, okay. You're probably right. Just open 'er up, and I'll deliver the stuff, and be out in five or ten minutes."

"Okay, it's your funeral. They told me not to let anyone out, though, so I'll have to check with Lieutenant Hough before you come out."

"Okay, you do that."

"And you'll have to leave your weapon."

"Of course." I gave him the holstered nine-millimeter pistol.

He walked over to the dark green glass entry doors, selected a key from a ring clipped to the back of his holster, turned it in the lock on the center door, and stepped three or four yards upwind. There was a rumble of thunder from the west, and a gust of wind sprayed us with a few drops of rain from the gray mist that was the western sky. I pushed the door open, and walked inside. I heard him turn the key in the lock behind me.

XXIX

In the dim light filtering through the tinted windows from the overcast morning sky, and despite the layer of dust on the unmanned reception desk and the native oak furniture in the waiting rooms, there was an aura of reassurance, stability and seemliness about the infirmary, that changed the estimate I had made of the architect when I had first seen the building from my treetop on the previous day.

The place did have a funny smell. It wasn't noxious or revolting, and something told me that it wasn't dangerous. It was more like warmish milk, about to turn bad, or maybe the mildewed velvet and leather of an old violin case; not awful, mind you, but enough to turn my taste buds around for a while. Enough to remind me of mortality, and of what had been going on at the Beckmann Institute.

The reception desk had been installed along the back wall of the lobby, and a set of open swinging doors to my right revealed a long corridor leading back into the building's interior, its axis angled outward from the perpendicular, of course. A yellow glow spilling through the windowed doorways of two or three rooms along its length was the only light in the corridor. A sign above the open, swinging doors read: "Doctors' Offices – Examination and Consultation." At the other end of the desk, there was another set of doors, and another sign: "Wards One, Two, and Three." The doors were closed, and the one on the right had an "IN" placard above the brass push plate. I mentally flipped a coin, and opted for the wards.

Ward One was the first one on my left, and the odor grew stronger as I approached it. A shaft of bright light shone into the darkened corridor through a nine-by-twelve-inch window in the closed door. I moved to the door and looked inside.

The plastered wall that had separated Ward One from a similarly sized room beyond it had been knocked down to provide a larger work area. That it had been a hurry-up job was evidenced by the unsightly plastic dust coverings that had been stapled and sealed around the jutting remnants of plaster, lathing and insulation that protruded from the perimeter of the former partition. Eight or ten hospital beds had been dismantled and piled against the back wall of the farther room, which I guessed must have been Ward Two.

The three men working in the enlarged room were of a mold; all five-nine or ten, in their late twenties, unshaven behind their white masks, bespectacled and rubber-gloved, white-coated, and looking over-worked. The one to my left was writing on a clipboard-backed yellow pad, as he moved along a five-tiered battery of cages, installed – piled, really – against the front walls of the room. The health of the white rats, chicks, guinea pigs and hamsters in the fifty or sixty enclosures – sequestered from one another by the white Formica, cofferdammed walls and floor and the set-in wire gates – ranged from the fretful normalcy of one caged hamster, banging out the miles on a spinning treadmill, to a semi-comatose group of baby chicks, haphazardly flopped down on the sawdust floors of three cages on the upper left. Four larger, two-by-three-foot cages further to the right housed what I thought were spider monkeys; they seemed listless, but not deathly ill. Beyond the monkey cages, the far wall of the room angled back into the woods, and I could see through the glass of the sealed windows that a steady light rain had begun to fall.

The man with the clipboard towed a four-wheeled cart behind him. After checking his yellow pad against the label of a cage containing two spindly and wasted-looking white rats, he selected a blue-topped hypodermic syringe from the cart and attached a disposable needle to it. He filled the device from a blue-capped bottle of yellowish liquid, removed one of the white rats from its cage, and, holding the weakened creature in his gloved left hand, inserted the needle under its mottled fur. He injected a few c.c.'s, replaced the rat, and prodded its partner with a tongue depressor. He made a notation on the yellow pad, and placed the used implements into the slotted lid of a plastic box marked with a large, red 'X'.

Most of the space in Ward One had been taken up by what looked like three industrial-sized clothes dryers. They were seven or eight feet high, three feet wide, and three or four feet apart. They had been dragged in – I could see the scars on the cushioned tile floor – and bolted down, plumbed, leveled and powered, without regard to uniformity, cosmetic nicety or economy of purpose. They were wrapped in and supported by yards of stainless steel plumbing, and, if the spoked spider wheel closing devices and the numerous gauges sprouting from their bulbous exteriors were a correct indication, their massive circular doors were built to maintain and withstand high temperatures and pressures. I took them to be centrifuges, of course; giant, spinning pressure cookers. And now I knew where the smell had come from. Fermentation. Bacteria.

Two of the machines were operating. There was very little vibration, but I could see spinning drums behind the windowed hatches, and an occasional puff of steam slipped by a poorly installed or aging rubber door seal. The second whitecoat had removed a metal filter plate from the third centrifuge, and was now carefully scraping a thin, pea-soup-colored paste from the plate into an empty beaker.

The third man was holding a pipette over one of a series of Petri dishes on a long worktable mounted on the wall to my right. The dishes were arranged in long, six-deep rows, and contained a liquid that looked something like green egg whites. He released a few drops into one of the dishes, and moved on down the line. When the second man called, the pipette man returned his glass tube to a tall bottle of blue liquid on the bench, and walked over to assist at the centrifuge. Together, they scraped the residue from several other filter plates, checking an electronic stopwatch every so often, as if timing were very important for this particular operation.

My view of the inner walls was limited, but I could see the upper surfaces of what looked like computer terminals, then an extremely complex and expensive photographic enlarger – which I took to be an electron microscope – and, at the end, a large optical microscope, with five different focal length lenses mounted on a swivel a few inches below the binocular eyepiece. Around the corner, near the long bench and the green egg whites, were a specimen staining and slide preparation station and a console with a graph displayed on a large LCD screen. The legend, "Beckmann Immunoassay #7", was printed on an inspection plate across the top face of the console.

The laboratory equipment had been hastily installed, and there may have been an air of disarray, but the room was clean – there was no plaster dust like that covering the furniture and floors in the receiving area. But the men did appear to be under great pressure. They seemed proficient with isolated procedures, and I had a feeling that they would eventually get the job done, whatever it was, but there was a hurried, ad hoc and reactive approach to their method that bordered on the clumsy. They wore the thin green surgeon's rubber gloves and the operating-room masks, but even the rudimentary precautions that had been observed aboard the *Edinboro Star*

– the air lock, the decon procedures, the ultraviolet light bath – were not in evidence in Ward One. Either they were in an extremely big hurry, or what they were doing couldn't harm them. Or – they could cure themselves if it did. I moved on down the corridor.

The next door on my left was for the now-assimilated Ward Two, and any chance of my getting a new point of view on what I had just seen had been eliminated by the placement of two computer terminals in front of the windowed door.

Ward Three was at the end of the corridor. It was smaller than the others, but even the dust and the clear plastic sheet seal over the door failed to disguise the fact that the furniture and appointments were more luxurious than the other wards. Ward Three must have been reserved for VIP's.

But for now, it was serving as a morgue. The plastic sheet distorted the view, but I could see the uncovered bodies of two men, one in a white coat, the other in a gray work uniform with a "Holmes Plumbing and Heating" shoulder patch, laid out on two beds near the door. Both had been of average size, but their arched backs, their distended arms and legs, and the discolored, apoplectic puffiness of their hands and faces made them look larger than life, and as if they were in a persisting agony. Two other beds were occupied by three smaller, covered figures; from a hand that hung down below the sheet line, I could see that at least one of them was a baboon; it was simian, at any rate, and three or four times as big as the spider monkeys back in Ward One. I didn't tamper with the door seal.

Another corridor ran across the rear of the building to join at a sixty-degree angle with the Office and Examination corridor I had seen from the reception area. There was an office where the corridors me, and someone had written the words "Wager – D-in-C – Knock and enter" on a folded sheet of graph paper and taped it at eye level on the half-opened door. I stepped inside.

In the center of the small room, a lighted reading lamp, its articulated support arm clamped to the upper edge of a drafting table, was positioned over three or four printed pages and a yellow legal pad that were strewn across the tilted white surface of the table. There was a high, adjustable-back, swivel chair behind the table, and a Cinzano ashtray by the papers was overflowing with half-smoked Camel Lights. Dark draperies covered the back wall; I could see a faint line of gray light leaking onto the ceiling from the space above the valence. There was another open doorway to my right, which must have led to Wager's examination room. I looked down at the papers. Doctor Wager had been editing a report of his own. I skimmed the first paragraph and half of the next before I was interrupted by the noise.

TOP SECRET   TOP SECRET

28 Sep

From: HIGHMONT
              P/W MW1
              3432/BIMD

To: CLAMBED
              P/W JJH1
              3431/PENOFFSPECPROJ

No Ref: Courier deliv.   No cop: cf. Internal request

Subj: Status Report Requested

BEGIN SCRAM   BEGIN SCRAM   BEGIN SCRAM

Dear General Harrison:

1. Notwithstanding the accident and the setbacks we have
    experienced since last Thursday and Friday, the decontamination
    of the main building has proceeded speedily enough that we
    can still conduct the helicopter-aerosol-dissemination test
    over the animal (simian) compound by the end of this week.
    In view of the schedule that has been imposed on us (and
    on you, I realize), we should go forward with this whether
    Doctor Claycombe recovers or not. I know he would have
    wanted us to. However, I do strongly advise against allowing
    the contingent from the Mountaineers representing our
    NATO and Central American friends to inspect the facility
    on the 29th, even if we were able to clean up the building by
    noon or one o'clock, and notwithstanding the reduction in
    size of the contingent. It would be much better if they could
    see the Institute when operations are normal, when the staff
    is at full strength, and when the undeniable vitality of a first
    class scientific research lab can be appreciated as it should be.

I do request that you immediately advise Beckmann, Junior, of this suggestion, because today is the 29th, and they are currently scheduled to arrive in a few hours.

2. We were lucky that no CX-2 was involved in the accident, I admit freely. And as for the unforeseen complications with the supposedly weakened Bolivian, I take full responsibility, as would Doctor Clatycombe if he were not incapacitated. It won't be the first time that 'the bugs (have been) smarter than the drugs,' I might add in our defense. As to the complicated series of recombinant viruses that my staff and I have been able to perfect in the last week (I am quick to acknowledge that Doctors Claycombe, Lambert, Mack, Woody and I have been working on this for the last year and a half – well, maybe all it took was the accident to make things 'gel'), it seems to work on the animals, and it should also work on any human relatively healthy prior to the onset of the bacterial infection. We have called the three "manmade" viruses WC-3, WC-4 and WC-6. (Yes, yes, WC's 1, 2 and 5 were failures) They act in concert to energize the cell-directed immune system of the victim, to identify the attacking bacterial cells with an earmarked outer coat easily recognizable by the heightened-awareness antibodies, and – and this was the cause of the original failure in theory and practice – to force the bacterial cells to manufacture certain enzymes <u>themselves</u> to render their own drug-resistant plasmids ineffective in all daughter (subsequent) cells. I'll go into more detail in subsequent paragraphs, but suffice it to say – "

It wasn't a groan; it was more like a sigh of relief. It came from the adjoining examination room. I placed my bundle on the desk, withdrew the nine-millimeter pistol, and moved to the door.

XXX

Wager looked twenty years older than he had in the better-days picture I had seen in the farmhouse a week earlier. The face was lined from exhaustion. He had an unhealthy pallor, a four-day beard, and his clothes were stained and wrinkled. He was slumped into and across an armchair that hadn't been made for sleeping, his head on his chest, his legs crossed, and his arms about to come unfolded with each deep, asthmatic breath. He was sound asleep.

The skeletal figure of Doctor peter Claycombe lay on its side athwart a hospital bed, which had been crammed into the back of the little examination room. His left ribs, pelvic bone, knee and ankle left painful sharp outlines in the sheet and light blanket that covered him. His eyes were closed, he was breathing regularly, and his face looked peaceful, almost happy, as if he were having a particularly pleasant dream. It wasn't until he opened his eyes that I knew he was a madman.

They opened as if he had simply popped off for a forty-second catnap a minute earlier. They were wide-set, and the brown pupils remained dilated, even after he focused on me, standing at the door with the pistol held behind the jamb. I let twenty seconds pass before I raised a finger to my lips, mimed "shh", and pointed at the sleeping Wager. I didn't know if he'd bought it. I had my doubts. The eyes made me feel that this was a man who understood too much. Politics, philosophy, motive – all would be so many self-justifying word games to the brain behind the deep brown eyes. I had seen no puzzlement, no alarm and no calculation in them. They did what they were supposed to do: see what there was to see. Then they closed.

I parted the drapes in Wager's office. A shaft of sunlight nearly blinded me for a few seconds. Then, just as I grew accustomed to the light, a fast-moving cloud cut off the sun, and a rain-filled gust of cold-front wind rattled the window and left droplets streaming down the pane.

They were loading what looked like the last of the decontamination gear into the side door of one of the Mercedes trucks. The other was nowhere to be seen. The six-by-six army truck was still parked in front of the main lab, but the communications man had packed away most of his gear. Two soldiers were resodding the lawn where the first truck had bogged down the day before. I turned back to the papers on the desk.

It was all very complicated. Plasmids. Again. Apparently, they were extra, free-floating bits of DNA, not a part of the cells' chromosomes, which existed in all of us. They 'embodied' a resistance to drugs, including many antibiotics. They not only had a propensity for encouraging invading bacteria to conjugate, they quite readily transferred their drug resistance to subsequent bacteria. In other words, resistance to antibiotics was transferable from one bacterium to another like an infectious disease. A relatively harmless bacteria called Escherichia-coli, commonly found in the human digestive tract, itself already made drug-resistant by the presence of these plasmids, could conjugate with the invading Bolivian Meningococcal Meningitis bacteria and leave them drug-resistant as well.

Wager's sentence concluding his paragraph four admitted that he and Claycombe had not foreseen this possibility. "It is not inconceivable, then, that harmless animal bacteria could have transferred drug-resistant plasmids to our pathogenic Bolivian strain, and that that new strain could have caused a virulent and unstoppable epidemic in humans." He added: "Unfortunately for Mr. Holmes, the plumber, and Miss Lavelle, we had not discovered this possibility prior to their expiring." There were another four or five pages on the edge of the desk. The single-spaced, printed copy looked very technical, and heading read: "Preparation of Antidotal Virus Agents, Sep. 25-28."

There was a weak and guttural cry from the other room. I heard movement, then what had to be Wager's voice.

"Sir, it's me, Wager. Did you – thank God, you're awake, sir . . . How are you feeling?"

The answer was an unintelligible rumble, from a throat that had probably been swollen, inundated with phlegm, dried, caked, and unused for the past week. I knew what it was like.

"Sir, don't try to talk for a while. Do you remember the accident? It was on the mix attempt for Lot Thirty-three. Right, well, that was a week ago, sir. Really. We've tried to help you, but, well, you were very close to the edge most of the time, and it wasn't until yesterday that we thought we could risk the first cure virus – yes, we did it, sir – CW Three, Four and Six. One and Two failed, sir. And Five, too. We've closed down the Institute, sir and Woody, Lambert and Mack and I have made the Infirmary – that's where we are now, sir – into a lab, and a temporary morgue, I'm afraid – "

Claycombe said something that might have been "Who?"

"Miss Lavell, and Hopkins, and a man from Lake Placid who helped us install the refrigeration equipment. He volunteered. And he helped us move what we thought was uncontaminated gear out of Blue Lab in the main building. I guess it wasn't. Uncontaminated. Holmes was his name, I think. He failed to respond to our WC-Two virus, and that's when we moved on to Three, and eventually to Four and Six."

" . . . about yourself." Claycombe was limbering up. I gathered that he was not loquacious even in the best of circumstances.

"Well, after the accident – you see, sir, you took most of the force of the vector blast when the mustard gas canister exploded. Harley and two of the techs from C-Group took you right to the infirmary. I – well – I guess I panicked, sir. I woke up a few minutes later. I didn't know then that the CX-Two virus canister hadn't broken and that neither of us had been exposed to anything but the weakened Bolivian spores. I was paranoid, I suppose, but I was afraid that the whole program would be over if you and I were gone – and I knew that Harrison would cover it all up if he could. After all, those were the rules, and we all knew it. But I felt that someone had at least to know the other side of the story. You see, I was sure at the time that you were dead, and that I didn't have long – and I thought – I felt that someone on the scientific end should be made aware of what had happened. So I – I just left, sir. I left. On foot. I had to avoid the guards, so I struck out across country."

"Code Red?"

"Yes, sir. I did that before I left. It was automatic. Two hundred each of gamma globulin and second-generation cephalosporin. Our own number Sixty-Four, similar to Cefobid, as you know. It took a few hours. I passed out at one point. A couple of kids and a park ranger found me and took me to Memorial. And the security men came the next morning. By then the antibiotic had worked. On me, at least. They told me that you were alive, and of course I returned immediately. But for a while, I guess I didn't – I hadn't known exactly what I was doing. The headaches . . . "

"Yes. Yes, I understand. But why – uhh!"

"Just lie still, sir; don't put any more strain on yourself. Take these. And I'm going to get your pressure and get a blood sample. You need more rest, I'm sure, and we have to inject you with the WC-Six – that's where we made our mistake, sir."

"What . . . mistake?"

"E-coli R-plasmids, sir. They transfer their drug resistance . . . to the invading Bolivian, in our case."

"Good God."

"Yes, sir. And transformed our supposedly innocuous, test Bolivian into a lethal and nearly untreatable first-line biological weapon."

"So the viruses in combination act as an antidote to it?" Claycombe rasped.

"Yes, sir. Our WC-Three virus is very similar to the T-cell activator we worked on with Griggs at N.I.H. Then the WC-Four virus alters the coat on the Bolivian bacteria – "

"To make the key fit."

"Exactly, sir. More antibodies can be brought to bear."

I heard the muffled pop-pop-pop of a helicopter through the draped windows.

"Visitors," said Claycombe.

"Yes, sir. I had asked our friend the General to put it off. He told me to write him a letter. There wasn't really enough time. It's a small group from the Mountaineers' Club. V.I.P. tour."

"I see. And the, what did you call it, WC-Six?"

"Yes sir, it inhibits the transfer of drug resistance to daughter cells."

"I see. After that – "

"After that, we think a combination of second or third generation cephalosporin and simple erythromycin should be effective for any subsequent outbreaks. I – I was just lucky, sir. I used Cefobid, but only by chance. It wasn't because I knew what I was doing, I'm afraid. In my case, the transfer of drug resistance was impeded, and the antibiotic had time to work. There are, as always, things we don't understand. Some people are affected more dramatically than others."

"That doesn't surprise me."

Wager inflated the blood pressure cuff and they were silent for a few moments. The pilot had shut down the turbine engine of the helicopter.

"It's – it's back up a bit, sir. One-oh-five over seventy."

"Lowest it's been in twenty-five years."

"I'd like to see it at one-forty over ninety again – then we'll start work on bringing it down without your having to come so close to – well, without causing harm to the patient."

"All right, Doctor Wager. Except for the early hours, which I can understand, you've done well." His voice was stronger now. It was devoid of emotion. I can't say it sounded like a computer-generated voice, but it was close. He used it as though the spoken word was an untrustworthy hindrance; a painfully slow and unreliable concession to a backward civilization.

"Where is the original CX-Two virus?" Claycombe continued.

"It's safe in Blue Lab, sir. I'm told that the decontamination will not affect anything still intact. General Harrison's orders."

"Very well. Now. If we can be fooled by transferred drug resistance, then so can the enemy. If we can prevent that transfer with your WC-Six virus, we have to assume – "

"That they can, too; yes, sir." Wager was excited now; the star pupil, stabbing at the air with his raised hand from the back row. "They could conceivably make an antidote, as we did. But Lambert and I believe we can make the drug resistance irreversible in a new generation of the Bolivian. He and I – with Woody – are working on cloning the genes from the WC-Six now. As soon as we have a genomic library, we'll start whittling it down. We'll splice the genes from the variant we select into the Bolivian, so that attempts by – un, targeted victims, to introduce antidotal viral agents of their own will be useless. We've turned Wards One and Two into a laboratory, and we have enough equipment from Blue Lab to do the job. We should have a few million phage progeny in another hour. Oh – we're quite sure now that a recombined strain of the CX-Two virus, subjected to ambient temps of 300 degrees Fahrenheit for four hours, will act as a vaccine against infection of our own forces by the CX-Two virus in the field weapon. There are still some snags, of course."

As Wager spoke, I gathered up the papers from his desk, folded them twice, and stuffed them into my back pocket.

"All right, good," said Claycombe. "I'll want a report as soon as possible. Now, why the guard?"

"Oh. Well, I guess it's the military mind syndrome, sir. We're here voluntarily, of course, but they apparently wanted to make sure that we didn't change our minds. They, well, they like to be in control of things, I guess .. . but how did you know – "

"I don't mean the military; I mean the Beckmann Security man I saw a few minutes ago."

"Oh, no sir; there's no – "

I stepped into the doorway. "I suppose he's referring to me, Doctor Wager."

Wager was leaning on the back of his armchair, now closer to Claycombe's bed, and he jerked to his feet and turned toward me when I spoke. I raised the nine-millimeter pistol, and pointed it at his midsection.

"You're – you're not Archer. Who – "

"No. I'm not. My name is O'Toole."

"What do you want?"

Wager spoke almost haughtily, as the uniform I wore had automatically relegated me to the status of underling. Claycombe said nothing. I tried to avoid the baleful stare.

"I came to speak with you – both of you. I thought you might have something I needed. I've heard what I needed to hear, and I've read your report to General Harrison."

Wager opened his mouth, but opted against saying anything. I continued.

"I don't want to get involved in politics, Doctor Wager. I'm not interested in blaming anyone for what happened here. I've had the – Bolivian, as you call it – and something about my immune system, my E-coli, and the initial treatment I received from your wife has combined to cure me, at least temporarily – "

"What do you mean, my wife?"

"It's a long story. But right now, thanks to your snowballing arms race, and your – or someone's – security forces, she's lying in a hospital bed in Hyannis, Massachusetts, and it appears that she is not responding well to antibiotic and other therapy. There are others with similar problems. Which brings me to the point. I'll need six doses each of your viruses Three, Four and Six. When I get them I'm going to leave here. Quietly. I'm going to get the dosages to some people who need them badly, your wife Molly, and one of the boys who found you above Nichol's Brook, among others. If you do as I say, I'll return your report and your discussion on the preparation of the viruses to you; they will have been read by no one but me."

"But – " Wager blurted, his face reddening.

"Never mind, doctor." It was Claycombe who spoke. "Whatever your name is, young man, I don't think you realize what's at stake here. We are doing research that could change the course of global confrontation for generations to come, and which might well make nuclear weapons and even this endless war on terrorism obsolete. What you suggest – "

"Be quiet." I said it just as Claycombe would have said it. Calmly, and without nuance or rancor. I walked over to him and pointed the pistol at his right temple. "Doctor Wager, do what I say. If you don't, I promise you that I will fire this pistol at this man's head in exactly ten minutes. If anyone else returns with you, I will fire in any case."

"Can I say something now?" asked Wager.

"Say it fast."

"We're not sure that the virus combination is what cured Doctor Claycombe. We think so. But we need more tests; more controls, and more human subjects. And we're not sure what the effect of the viruses would be on someone who didn't already have the – the Bolivian. If you were to be stopped by the military outside this building, and harmed, and the containers were to be breached, then – "

"I understand, Doctor. Unfortunately, I have no other choice. And I'm out of time. Your ten minutes start now." I was vaguely disgusted with myself for allowing even this much discussion with a man who was planning to continue testing his wonder weapon, in spite of the foul-ups, and the dead and dying people scattered across four New England states.

Maybe it showed. He stared at me for twenty seconds. Then he walked into his office.

"Doctor Wager!" I raised my voice. "One other thing. I intend to select one dose of WC-Six and have you administer it to Doctor Claycombe. Bring what you need." I could hear his pace quicken as he hurried out into the corridor.

XXXI

There were nineteen red, blue and yellow, wax-sealed test tubes in a folding aluminum box, with a protective fabric holster for each of the tubes and a rubber and Velcro seal around the folded container. One of each, separated by two-hour intervals, Wager instructed. The yellow-tips were the WC-6. I picked one; Wager filled a syringe and injected the cloudy liquid into Claycombe's upper arm. Claycombe didn't wince, of course. He lay there, slowly following my movements with his unblinking brown eyes, no doubt deliberating on the particular hybrid potpourri of incurable new-wave African retroviruses he would foist on me when he got out of that hospital bed. It made Wager nervous, too. I had the feeling that he was improvising, waiting for a moment, and just putting one foot in front of the other. But he wanted to be understood, and even liked, it seemed, while he was doing it.

"You have to understand, uh – O'Toole," he explained, "that neither the creation nor the cure of disease is ever, uh, linear. It's a continuing give and take, walk up two, fall back one, kind of thing. The state of the art is such that preparing a cure is just like preparing a disease, and it just depends on who had the first move, you, Mother Nature, the enemy. It's a fascinating, hoist-by-your-own-petard, pull-yourself-up-by-your-own-bootstraps kind of game, that – "

That was when I hit him. Once. Hard. I split his lip at the left side of the mouth. He looked surprised, then hurt that I hadn't liked him, and resigned as he fell to the floor of the examination room. I holstered the nine millimeter, stuffed the aluminum box inside my shirt, and without so much as a look at Claycombe – I had this crawly premonition that he could infect me simply by locking his eyes on mine – I left the room and made my way to the main entrance.

The guard was still on duty. He was watching the activity near the main lab. A Bell-Jet Ranger had landed across the road from the six-by-six army truck. Several safari-jacketed men were apparently being given an introduction to the Institute by the younger officer from the day before. A second helicopter approached from the south as I watched, and the lecturer had to break off as the noise increased. A gusty wind had followed the cold frontal passage, and the approaching helicopter was crabbed to the west and rocking in moderate turbulence.

The third shot from the nine-millimeter pistol shattered the aluminum on my side of the deadbolt. I yanked open the door and shot the cooperative young American soldier in the left leg, as he raised his M-16 and spun around toward the noise. He fell heavily onto his side, doubling up and gripping his leg with his hands and forearms. I took his M-16 and his sidearm, and walked quickly over to the motor pool Altima. I started it up, made a bumpy U-turn on the damp infirmary grass, and quickly accelerated up the gravel road toward the main lab. Then I saw the half-naked man, running down the switchbacked road from the notch, waving one arm and cupping a hand over his mouth. No one else had heard my shooting and no one was about to hear his yelling, I thought, as the second helicopter hovered almost directly above the first, at fifty, then thirty feet, the whine of its two turbines and the popping of its rotors drowning out other sounds.

I guessed it must have been the helicopter pilot who saw Archer running down the hill in his underwear. The pilot told the communicator on the tailgate of the six-by-six, and the next thing I saw was the radioman, jumping from the truck, and wrenching off his earphones in the middle of the road. I thumbed the horn button on the cushioned plastic steering wheel, and held it down as I approached him. He was fast on the draw. He unholstered a sidearm, and, raising it to shoulder level with both hands, he put three shots into my side of the windshield just after I ducked below the wheel. I hit him at about twenty miles per hour. The car swerved into the side of the army truck and came to a stop.

The helicopter had gone back up to fifty feet. I heard more shots, and before I could get the car moving again, the side windows were shot out and I smelled burning oil. I dived out of the driver's-side door and rolled under the truck, favoring the aluminum box inside my shirt and ripping my shoulder on the underside of the right running board for my trouble. I went up the other side, opened the door, and slipped into the seat, head down. The keys were in the ignition and it started easily. I rammed the gearshift lever into second, and lurched forward. I picked up speed, and wrenched the wheel around to follow the circular driveway in front of the main building. I got the six-by-six pointed back uphill, but the recently-laid Florida sod would never be the same.

I dodged Archer at the bottom of the hill, and made it to the second of the four switchbacks up to the notch before I started thinking. They were mobilizing. Five or six men had emerged from the main lab, and were running toward the one remaining truck parked in the service area. The radioman, injured but still game, was trying to restore some order to the jumble of gear that had fallen from the tailgate of my truck as I had plowed up the gravel road. The officer was giving orders to him, yelling into a microphone, and looking up at the second helicopter. They'd hit a couple of my tires. They might have punctured one of the saddle tanks; I smelled diesel fuel. But I could probably have made it up and over the notch on the first attempt. There were enough wheels still intact and the engine sounded all right. Then it would have been a simple matter of getting past McFee, the other guard at the gatehouse, or staying clear of whatever assistance he might have summoned after hoofing it back toward Keene.

So even to this day I'm not sure why I didn't. They probably weren't the worst people in the world down there. Gray-green-garbed recruits, volunteers, and career men, top-of-the-class graduates from fine medical schools, workaday helicopter pilots just happy to build the hours and get the $28,000 a year while doing it, safari-jacketed captains of finance and industry, not sure yet that the fireworks hadn't been a part of the show, all were investing parts of their lives and fortunes in the furtherance of the vanguard Beckmann research, for what some of them probably thought were commendable purposes.

Maybe it had to do with disease. It wasn't terribly important that I didn't fully understand the intricacies of Claycombe's and Wager's spectrum of weaponry. I knew they had (1) a vaccine, (2) some bacteria, (3) an accompanying virus, very deadly, (4) something called antibiotic-resistant plasmids, and (5) even more viruses, supposedly benign for the right people. If worse came to worst, and you got hit with a combo of (2), (3) and mixed-in (4), and say (1) hadn't taken on you, well, you could always shoot up some fresh (5) to get you back to Go. The combination would decimate the bad guys, and keep our own boys free from harm, stumbling along in their eighty-pound, helmeted white suits, wondering how long the seams would hold, and adjusting the backup chemical breathing apparati in their packs, just in case things really got hairy and some enemy didn't like playing by the rules.

Or maybe it was the view of the scene below me as I angled my way up the hill. There were a few lingering clouds off in the east, and the morning sun shone brightly, glistening on the rain-touched compound, heightening the already-bright colors of the buildings, the grass, the trees and the two helicopters. It would have made a great Kodacolor enlargement like they used to have in Grand Central Station. And maybe that was the trouble. It looked a little too much like an annual report cover photo.

Like I said, I didn't know exactly what made me stop the truck. But if pushed, I guess I could come up with one word. Arrogance. Not that it occurred to me at the time.

I stopped, shifted down, and moved the selector lever to the three-axle-drive detent. I fought the truck over a two-foot embankment, up off the road and onto the steep hill above and behind the service building. I set the brake, climbed out of the truck away from the compound, and stashed the box behind a dead log left behind on the stripped hillside.

As I climbed back into the truck, I noticed a nine-millimeter stream of diesel fuel pouring out of the right saddle tank, missing by inches the bottom of the vertical exhaust pipe that rose up along the back of the cab. I released the brake, and plunged down the hill, right foot to the floor, all axles still driving.

The other army truck was just turning uphill onto the gravel road below. The firing had stopped, and the second helicopter was down to twenty feet or so above a spot alongside the first. I think they were trying to keep a good face on the situation for the benefit of their visitors; the pursuing truck or some other authority down the line would stop the maverick and everything would be taken care of. It takes a quick and willing mind to accept the fact that the hunter has become the hunted and the hunted is now you.

They didn't open up again until I shot out from behind the service building. Then it was too late. I passed the transformer at thirty miles an hour, threw the truck into neutral, and rolled out of the right door about forty feet short of the fuel dump. The five-ton army truck freewheeled into the tank about a second and a half later.

At first I thought I had a dud on my hands. The tank leaped out of its cradle and rolled down toward the main lab all right, but it wasn't on fire. Then the fuel tanks on the truck exploded – first the right, then the left. Maybe the stream of diesel had finally hit the exhaust pipe, I never knew.

There was a ruptured connection at one end of the rolling tank, and the fireball from the truck ignited the escaping propane. Momentum carried the pressurized cylinder up the near side of the pyramided main lab; with the forty-foot-long jet of burning propane and burgeoning black smoke, the tank looked like a giant butane lighter, as it pinwheeled its way up the side of the triangle to the common apex above the main entrance. And there it stopped, lodged among the tops of three triangles, with the jet pointed down and in, onto the dark panes of glass above the main entrance.

Then they forgot about me, I guess. A dozen or more soldiers came running out of an emergency exit on my side of the main lab. The second, pursuing army truck, turned around and raced back toward the service building. Meanwhile, the second helicopter had been shaken by the blast from the truck. In correcting for the concussion and what might have been a strong gust of wind, the pilot had clipped the idle main rotor of the Ranger, and cut his own in half. He added power, but the vibration threatened to tear the aircraft apart. I picked myself up off the ground just as the crippled helicopter went in. It didn't appear to be a devastating crash, but the gear had collapsed on the uphill side, and I saw a wisp of smoke and tongue of orange flame from below the engine enclosure as I began zigzagging up the hill.

I retrieved the aluminum case from the cache on the hillside and looked once more at what was fast becoming a serious conflagration below me. The wooden roof of the main lab was smoldering, and the heat was vaporizing the moisture from the light rain into clouds of steam. The second helicopter was ablaze, and two of the Mountaineeers had managed to drag a uniformed passenger from its partially blocked left emergency exit. They were struggling to free another man before the fuel tanks went. The pilot scrambled out from the other side; he fell, and rolled on the ground in an effort to extinguish his burning flight suit. A lime-green Mack fire truck with several soldiers aboard rolled out of the opened doors of the service building and raced down toward the lab.

Then I saw Doctor Peter Claycombe running toward the main lab from the direction of the infirmary, white hospital robe and gray hair flowing behind him, whipping in the wind. Wager was about ten yards behind him. Claycombe ran to the front door furthest from the burning propane and wrenched it open. Wager caught him and tried to pull him away. With a maniacal and superhuman burst of strength, the disease-ravaged Claycombe threw him violently to the flagstone walkway and disappeared into the building. Wager jumped to his feet and ran to the door. He grasped the aluminum handle and immediately jerked back his hand, writhing in pain from the burn. He stared dumbly up at the façade of the entryway as the glass and its supporting framework began to melt. Two soldiers ran to Wager and pulled him away, just before the glass front wall collapsed into a half-molten pool of rubble at the foot of the pyramids.

The interior of the building was now at the mercy of the seemingly relentless propane torch above it; the inside must have been like an oven. Seventy five feet away, the already-browning Jetglo paint on the fire engine began to wrinkle and smoke. The fire truck was drawn back. The firefighters, the Mountaineers, the military, the medics – and I – watched.

The tank, already stressed far beyond its built-in high pressure safety limit, suddenly cracked open along a welded seam pointed at the sky. A wave of liquid gas shot high into the air, and the steadying, twenty-five knot northwest wind rained it back down over the Beckmann Institute Main Laboratory like napalm. The gas caught fire while still aloft, and formed rivers of blue flame as it cascaded down and across the myriad angular surfaces of the prize-winning structure. I felt a whoof! of air pressure a couple of seconds after the tank ruptured and the gas ignited.

A cloud of black smoke formed over the compound, blocking out the sun. The wind carried the cloud to the south, but the smoke was quickly replenished from the raging, propane-fed fire below. There were several smaller explosions inside the building, and, above the steady roar of the larger inferno, I thought I might have heard some oohs and ahs from the helpless onlookers as, unnoticed, I walked through the smoke toward the notch below Devil's Mountain.

XXXII

Even after the sanitizing by the military and the Institute p.r. team, the local paper had everything it needed for its special edition that afternoon; tragedy, heroism, irony, and residuum of hope for the future of mankind.

"Thursday, September 29. SCION OF LOCALLY BASED CONSTRUCTION FIRM FATALLY INJURED IN BIZARRE ACCIDENT AT LOCAL RESEARCH FACILITY. A truck's parking brake failed earlier today at the Beckmann Institute for Molecular Biology outside of Keene, setting off a chain of events that would spell disaster for the three-year-old research facility.

"After the freak mechanical failure, the driverless military six-by-six plunged down the steep hill at the east end of the compound, colliding with a large propane tank mounted near the main laboratory. The tank rolled up the side of the award-winning building, lodged at its top, and was ignited when the fuel tanks on the truck exploded a short distance away. The ensuing fire engulfed the main laboratory, and, for a while, threatened a smaller building nearby that houses the Institute's infirmary. At least six people were killed as the fire swept across the compound, including Steve Beckmann, Jr., whose helicopter happened to have been approaching a pad in front of the building when the propane tank exploded. The aircraft fell some thirty feet to the ground, and the resulting fire left Beckmann with third-degree burns over fifty percent of his body. Despite heroic efforts by members of the staff of the Albany Burn Center, he succumbed earlier this afternoon. Mr. Beckmann was the son . . .

"Also killed was Doctor Peter Claycombe, director of the Institute, whose last-minute dash into the burning building might have saved the lives of several area residents had it only been successful. According to a Doctor Robert Wager, Dr. Claycombe's assistant, the staff had been working on a cure for the lethal, flu-lie disease that has infected dozens of area people in the past ten days, and Dr. Claycombe gave his life in a futile attempt to salvage the records of the staff's recent research on the cure . . . The latest victim of the growing epidemic was Brigadier General john J. Harrison, who contracted the disease sometime yesterday while visiting friends in the Keene area, and died later in the afternoon, all attempted therapies having proved ineffective. Related stories on p. 2.

"Also killed was Mr. Richard Holmes, of 243 Cedar Avenue, Lake Placid, a local plumber, who had been installing a new air conditioning system in the Institute's infirmary, and who was in the main laboratory building when the fire broke out."

I read the Herald as I nursed a cup of coffee near the pay phone at the Alpine Diner, yet another road stop between Lake Placid and its Adirondack Airport. I'd taken the LeCourier jeep – McFee, the other gatehouse man, had been nowhere to be seen – almost all the way into Keene, and then left it parked on the shoulder of Route 9. Pete of Pete's Amoco was sympathetic when I told him that my BMW had broken down.

"Well, I coulda told ya, young fella, them foreign jobs 're just fine 'til you need to get a starter brush or a caliper piston, sumthin' like that. Then you gotta pay through the nose even if you are lucky enough to find the goddam thing, which you probably ain't gonna be, and that's the whole trouble."

"I couldn't agree with you more, Pete. Listen, you got anything I could rent, or borrow, or whatever for a few hours? I've got to go into Lake Placid on some business and I need some wheels."

"Well, I'll tell ya what. If you'd pick a coupla tires for me over there at the Goodyear place in Lake Placid, I'll let ya take the wife's Escort, no charge, we split the gas."

It was a deal. I drove as far as the diner and called Dan at Dan's Trailer Court. There was a two or three-minute wait while he fetched May from the Airstream.

"This's May LeCourier."

"Hi."

"O'Toole, is that you? Are you – where are you?"

"Y'know the Alpine Diner?"

"Yeah."

"I'm there. Bring the papers I left you."

"Ten minutes, okay?"

"Ten's fine – but hurry; I might have something that will help Donny."

Doctor Rashid was a good one. He didn't make it easy, but he wasn't so hidebound by the AMA and the FTC prescription guidelines as to automatically rule out undertaking a course of treatment not yet proven by the three or four years usually required by the establishment. I let him read Wager's treatise on the preparation of the three viruses, and the appended details of his results with Doctor Claycombe – an apparent alleviation of all symptoms. I didn't show him the reports on biological weaponry by Claycombe and Wager. And Rashid didn't ask any questions about why it was that the Institute staff had known so much about the nature of the disease that he was seeking to cure.

As I told Gregory sometime later, it was one of those "you had to be there" situations. A malfunction at the junction. Butterfingered maniacal scientist and devoted aide screw up, exposing population of Eastern seaboard to new strain of Bolivian Meningitis, first stage of binary biological doomsday weapon. Pentagon involved, cover up developing, and same scientists now seriously considering testing of new and improved version of viral – and assuredly lethal – second stage, even before victims of first are quietly lowered into graves by white-masked mourners. The questions formed on Gregory's lips: why didn't you keep us informed, why didn't you trust your own government, what made you think that you wouldn't receive our full and immediate support, etc., etc. But I'll say this for Gregory. He never asked them. It was unusual. Maybe it had something to do with the Claycombe and Wager reports to General Harrison, which Gregory seemed to find very interesting.

Anyway, Rashid had no releases for May to sign, and no time-consuming red-tape cover-himself conditions attached. He told her the facts, she okayed it, and Donny LeCourier was given a succession of benign viral infections that ended up by saving his life.

I kept two series of the three viruses, one for Molly and one for Gregory, and left the rest with Rashid, along with a Xeroxed copy of Wager's research treatise. May drove me to the airport.

"You got it?" I asked.

"I've got it," she said. "I report the jeep as stolen, and wait 'til they find it north of Keene on Route Nine. I drive down Gilmore Road tomorrow to see if your BMW is still there by the Wager place, and what kind of shape it's in. Oh – and I pick up two tires at the Goodyear place in Lake P. and take'em over to Pete's Amoco in Keene in his wife's Escort and split the gas. Jeez. Vehicles."

"Yeah, you're telling me. A lotta moves. I'll call you tomorrow to find out how Donny is."

"I know he's gonna be okay, O'Toole. I could see it already. And – whatever happens, O'Toole, I want you to know – "

"I'll call you in the morning, May."

"You be sure now."

"Sure."

"You comin' back ever?" Matter of fact. Clear gray eyes.

"I've got to pick up that BMW, for better or for worse, and I wouldn't mind having you and your two boys take me fishing just one time."

"Okay, then, I'll be seein' ya."

"Be seeing you."

She drove away from the terminal in her Horizon. I mused on how she would get back to Lake Placid after she dropped the Escort in Keene, but gave it up after a few seconds. May LeCourier would cope, no question about it.

The guy with the turbo Piper Seneca was glad for the charter, and he didn't mind taking the six slightly bedraggled hundreds for the trip to Hyannis.